Praise for Monica O'Rourke:

"What Monica O'Rourke brings to horror and dark (often erotic) fantasy is something the genre really, really needs—a voice that's not just unique but which is also incredibly and beautifully readable. Only a handful of writers, in and out of the genre, can realistically claim to be her peers. The delicious and lustfully served red meat of her stories could turn even the most determined vegetarian (like me) into a carnivore."

—**T.M. Wright**, author of **A Spider on My Tongue**, **The House on Orchid Street**, and **Laughing Man**

"O'Rourke writes with rare confidence and style. Though undoubtedly disturbing, and sometimes brutal, still her work has something quite rare and special—heart."

—**Tim Lebbon**, author of **Dusk, Berserk**, and **Desolation**.

Also by Monica J. O'Rourke

SUFFER THE FLESH

POISONING EROS,
WITH WRATH JAMES WHITE

EXPERIMENTS IN HUMAN NATURE

Monica J. O'Rourke

Two Backed Books | Landover, Maryland

Experiments in Human Nature
Copyright © 2007 by Cthulhu Sex

Stories Copyright by Monica J. O'Rourke
"An Experiment in Human Nature," © 2001, first appeared in *RARE*, Disc-us books
"Asha," © 2006, first appeared in *Red Scream* magazine, issue 0
"Attainable Beauty," © 2002, first appeared on **Gothic.net**
"Dancing into October Country," © 2002, first appeared in *Octoberland*, F&B Press
"Despair," © 2007
"Feeding Desire," with Jack Fisher, © 2004, first appeared in *Ruthie's Club*
"Five Adjectives about My Dad, by Nadine Specter," © 2002, first appeared in *Full Circle Journal*
"Ginger," © 2002, first appeared in *Reckless Abandon*, Catalyst Press
"Huntin' Season," © 2005, first appeared in *Nemonymous* #5
"Jasmine and Garlic," © 2002, first appeared in *The Fear Within*, 3F Publications
"Lachesis" © 2007
"Maternal Instinct," © 2000, first appeared in *Nasty Piece of Work* #14
"Not with a Bang but a Whimper," © 2004, first appeared in *Brutarian* magazine
"Nurturing Type," © 2007, first appeared in *Doorways Magazine*, February
"One Breath" © 2006, first appeared in *Cthulhu Sex Magazine*, issue 24, volume II
"Oral Mohel," © 2004, first appeared on **Desdmona.com**
"Saved" © 2007
"Searching," © 2007
"Sisters," © 2007, first appeared in *Red Scream* magazine
"Someone's Sister," © 1999, first appeared in *Nasty Piece of Work* #13
"The Rest of Larry," © 2003, first appeared in *Nemonymous* #3
"The Three Wishes of Henry Hoggan," © 2006, first appeared on **Deathlings.com**
"Vade in Pacem," © 2005, first appeared in *Surreal* magazine #1

Published by Two Backed Books,
an imprint of Raw Dog Screaming Press
Landover Hills, MD

First Paperback Edition

Edited by Michael Amorel
Book design by Michael Amorel
Cover art: "Balance" by Mike Bohatch, www.EyesOfChaos.com

Printed in the United States of America

ISBN 978-1-933293-47-9

Library of Congress Control Number 2007902215

www.twobackedbooks.com

CONTENTS

For Teri A. Jacobs, for always being there for me.

AN EXPERIMENT IN EXTREME FICTION:
AN INTRODUCTION BY BRIAN KNIGHT

In 2000, I came down with a mild case of insanity. This particular form of insanity is common among authors trying to make a name for themselves in the small press. Brian Keene, Shane Ryan Staley, Stephen Mark Rainey, Nick Mamatas, Victor Heck, and Monica J. O'Rourke have all suffered from this particular brand of insanity at one point or another, so I am at least in good company.

I call it Anthology Fever. The symptoms of Anthology Fever include a desire to be recognized and respected by your peers, the wish to get a foot in the door of a publisher you respect by presenting them with a project filled with names you believe they will respect more than yours, or to expand your reader base by putting your name in front of new readers who will buy the project for the few big names you managed to con into working with you.

The final stages of this insanity often manifest themselves in an exaggerated form of Tourette's syndrome, or the desire to leave the publishing field for good in favor of something more lucrative and less stressful, like stamp collecting. Often this insanity is catching, and incurable.

The result of my first case of Anthology Fever is a book called RARE, published by the now defunct Disc-Us Books. It was a nice little paperback with some pretty damned good stories by people who have mostly quit the business, but there are a few on the TOC who are still writing and publishing; James Newman, Drew Williams, Gord Rollo, Monica J. O'Rourke, and myself.

The Rare Anthology was a simple but great concept (Weston Ochse's idea, I believe). Each story must contain something rare in it. A rare, two-headed chicken (Drew Williams), a rare record, recorded by the devil himself (James Newman), a rare meat (yours truly), and a rare and violent experience (Monica J. O'Rourke), among others.

The stories were then categorized in three sections; Well Done for subtle stories, Rare for extremely violent, bloody, or weird stories, and Medium Rare for those stories somewhere in the middle.

If you are at all familiar with the most notorious of Monica J. O'Rourke's work, then you can guess into which category her story, "An Experiment in Human Nature," fell.

A blind panel of readers, which is to say none of them knew whose story they were reading, voted on the stories they liked, and upon reading Monica's story one of them emailed me, all but bursting with excitement.

"How did you get Jack Ketchum to send you a story?" she begged to know.

It took several emails to convince the reader she had not just read an original Jack Ketchum, and though I couldn't out Monica as the author at that time, I did tell the reader the author of that story was a woman, and relatively unknown.

Monica found the Ketchum comparison flattering.

I found it accurate.

Nevertheless, there is another side, not often seen, to Monica J. O'Rourke. Anyone who reads her knows her prowess with extreme and gut-twisting fiction, but few have read her quieter work. Her story "Five Adjectives about My Dad, by Nadine Specter" is perhaps the best example of her highly effective, but decidedly more subtle work.

Rounded off with lighter, humorous stories like "The Rest of Larry," this collection showcases an author capable of working with great finesse in almost every shade and temperature gradient, a very versatile author, which in itself is a rare thing.

Back to the subject of insanity.

I eventually overcame the insanity known as Anthology Fever, and have managed to not only hang up my editor's hat, but burn it and scatter the ashes into the four winds. It would be misleading to say I came through the experience unscathed, and at least a little unjaded, but I did survive, and one of my greatest memories of the whole, sick experience was that I had an opportunity to work with authors whose work I have come to love.

Like Monica J. O'Rourke.

If you've read her before, I'm afraid this introduction is a bit of a waste of time for you. I am preaching to the fucking choir. There isn't a damn thing I can say about Monica's work that you don't already know for yourself.

However, if Monica's work is new to you, I envy you. There is nothing quite like the thrill of discovering previously unknown talent. I first discovered Monica back in 2000. Now it's your turn.

Enjoy!

Brian Knight

ATTAINABLE BEAUTY

The painting always reminded Molly of a dream, an unattainable goal, a yearning to touch an unreachable nirvana. A feeling that all was hopeless, that she was less than perfection.

Yet she was drawn to *White Camelia*, effectively sucked into its beauty and grace, unable to avoid it just as she was unable to look away from the violent scenes on the evening news.

White Camelia, a study not only in colors and textures but a reflection of the human spirit, the beauty of the human form. Blossoming spreads of dewy, silky petals, the center of the creation as deadly and alluring as the poison perfume of the Venus flytrap.

Daily visits to the Museum of Modern Art during her lunch hour brought solace, but even that was short-lived; the exhibit wouldn't be there forever. The print hung on her bedroom wall as well, and nightly she knelt before it, said her prayers to it, shared her innermost secrets and desires, her sacred cow in a cheap balsa frame.

Crossing Fifth Avenue, she headed to her small one-bedroom in SoHo, the apartment nestled amid a dozen others on her floor in the five-story walk-up.

Nights David stayed over made her prayer ritual impossible. She didn't want him to think her insane. So beneath the sheets, sometimes beneath David, Molly offered silent supplication to the print.

He rolled off and breathed heavily, resting on the pillows. He turned back and smoothed the hair out of her eyes. "That was nice," he said, reaching across her breasts to the night table to retrieve a pack of smokes and the ashtray.

"Yes, nice." She smiled wanly and thought, *Nice for you maybe.*

She could close her eyes and imagine he was somebody else, but even that failed most times. She wouldn't imagine herself with anyone else, couldn't imagine she would be desirable. Such imperfection, Molly was.

"What's on your mind?" he asked, lighting the cigarette.

"What?"

"You're so deep in thought."

"Nothing."

He cupped her breast and lightly stroked it with his thumb, an annoying action he seemed particularly fond of.

"Are you staying over?" she asked.

The room was free of light, the blackout shade pulled past the sill. She preferred it that way. Making love in total darkness, so he couldn't see her imperfect body. Groping clumsily was part of their sex ritual, and they had invented their own style, their own art form.

When he didn't answer her question—he often left after they made love—she assumed he'd shook his head, if he'd answered at all.

The ashtray was between them on the mattress, and he stubbed out the cigarette. He slid away from her. She heard him padding across the floor, and moments later the bathroom light overtook the darkness. She squinted, momentarily blinded. She pulled the covers up to her chin. Touching was permitted but seeing was off-limits.

In the bathroom doorway he stood facing her. Every inch of him was visible, but her eyes trained on the penis dangling between his legs. He scratched his backside and leaned against the doorframe.

"Come take a shower with me."

"What?"

"Come on, Molly. Come out from under there and let me see you."

She pulled the sheets tighter, up to her nose.

"What's your *problem?*" he blurted. "What's wrong with you?"

"You should leave, David."

He padded across the floor again and turned on the overhead light.

Chills danced on her skin despite the covers. Her heart pounded.

"Come out from—"

"No."

"Dammit, Molly. Okay, this is weird. I'm not leaving 'til you get out of that bed."

They'd only met a few weeks ago, so she couldn't even feel surprised by his actions; she hardly knew the guy. There was no way to win here. If she refused, he'd think she was nuts and she'd lose him. If she did as he asked—and he saw what she looked like—she'd lose him anyway. Either way this was doomed. Better to keep her dignity.

The covers were now clutched in a death grip, and her fingers ached.

"Please?"

She shook her head.

He stood beside her at the bed. "Whatever's wrong... it'll be okay. We can't let something like this come between us."

"No, I don't want to. Leave me alone."

Taking the corner of the bedding, he yanked it from her body. The covers flew from her hands and landed in a heap by the door.

She leaned forward into a ball, knees drawn up, arms wrapped around her legs. "Get out," she cried, sobbing into her knees.

On the bed now, he straddled her, pushed her shoulders and forced her back onto the pillow.

She wanted to fight him off but had spent her energy.

"What have you got down there, a dick?" He sat on her knees and forced them flat, pushed away her hands.

She covered her eyes with her forearm and cried, finally relenting.

"My god," he said. "You're beautiful. What's your problem?"

He was Esmeralda to her Quasimodo, his love for her apparently blind, his feelings for her contorting reality. She felt his hands between her legs, caressing her thighs, fingers probing her vagina, stroking the cleft of downy hair between her legs. Fingers played with the labia, spread the lips, found their way inside her.

"I don't understand," he said, breathing hard. "What are you so afraid of?"

But she had no words. If he was that blind, if he couldn't see her apparent disfigurement, then how could she possibly explain it to him? How could she make him understand something he would never accept?

"Just go," she whispered. She knew he'd violated her. He shouldn't be doing this to her, no means no and all that but he'd *accepted* her, wasn't repulsed by her, and somehow she was able to excuse his horrible behavior. Somehow it was okay, he was forgiven. She still wanted him to leave though. Needed time alone to compose herself, to get past this somehow.

"Go?" His fingers rested motionless, still inside her. "I thought we…"

Oral sex had been out of the question—for her anyway. She'd never refused going down on him, but his tongue had never been permitted near that part of her body. Now he seemed preoccupied by it. Maybe that was the problem, she thought: a nihilistic voyeurism. He couldn't help himself, would have to explore her abnormality with a zealous fascination. Like watching circus freaks perform.

"Get out!"

Finally he listened, and was dressed and out the door.

Lying on her side, Molly sobbed, hating the thought she had lost David over this. Even after a few short weeks she had started falling for him. But how would she ever be able to trust him now?

With great trepidation, her hand slid down to her groin, and she explored her most private area, touched the pubis, prodded her labia.

No. He'd been wrong. There was no magical transformation. Either he was blind, or he'd lied to her. Such hideousness could never be confused with beauty.

The following morning she used a sick day at work and headed to the MoMA.

O'Keeffe's art adorned the walls in the wing, and Molly spent a few minutes studying various paintings before returning to *White Camelia*. She didn't want to look like a freak, spending the day staring at one painting. But invariably, that was where she ended up, sitting on a bench a few feet away, studying the texture and color, marveling at the brushstrokes. Female perfection at its finest, the most exquisite example ever dreamed up, ever created in permanent form.

She wondered if she was alone in the world, the only one who was this way... Because other women seemed so confident, happy. With alarm she realized she might be alone in this... that perhaps they were already perfect, beautiful. Perhaps they weren't deformed. She wondered why they had been so lucky... when they had been graced with the change. And why she hadn't...

The man standing beside her, shoulder-length hair, tuft of chin-hair struggling to form a goatee looked like a throwback Beatnik, sans bongo and cuppa java. "Lovely, isn't it? Possibly my favorite O'Keeffe."

The distraction irritated Molly, but she felt ignoring him might be construed as rude, or worse, odd.

"Mine too," she said. "It's incredible."

He pulled at the goatee as if trying to pluck the hairs, a gesture Molly found incredibly pretentious. "Still," he said, "it's not as if there's a wide variety. It's a great piece, considering."

"Considering?"

"Well, yeah. Flowers and steer heads. Flowers blooming *out of* steer heads. A few churches... O'Keeffe as a rule never did much for me."

She started to reply, but the first word tumbled out of her mouth as a wheeze, and her bottom lip began to quiver with anger. His remark was taken personally, as if his words were an attack on her character. If she loved O'Keeffe's work so much, then he must also feel fans such as Molly were as limited as the art. And his views of the prolific Ms. O'Keeffe were so wrong, she couldn't possibly begin to address that.

"I'm sorry, I didn't mean to offend. Can I buy you a cappuccino to make it up to you? There's a café—"

"No," she said, "you may not. We clearly have nothing in common, and you clearly are a moron."

His head snapped back as if he'd been struck. "Hey, that wasn't necessary. A difference of opinion is healthy."

"How can you not love this painting?" she said, hands displayed before her as if pleading. "Or O'Keeffe? How can you have such a narrow-minded view, miss the beauty of her work? How can you not see it... ?"

He stepped closer to *White Camelia*. "It's a flower. A big white flower. And beside it, *Jack-in-the-Pulpit No. II?*—a big black flower. See what I mean? More of the same."

"My god." Molly covered her mouth with her slender fingers. "You really can't *see...*"

He stepped back to view *White Camelia* from another angle. Shook his head. "No, sorry, I see a flower. What do you see?"

"Perfection," she whispered into her hand.

"Pardon?"

"The perfect female form. Delicate blossom representing all that is wonderful about... about... Can't you see it?" She reached toward the painting, caressing the air. "The pattern is so revealing. As if Ms. O'Keeffe knew the secrets and wanted to share them. As if she could see into your soul," she said wistfully, "and created the image she saw. Like God, creating the perfect woman."

Molly turned her attention to the man beside her. "So rare, a visionary such as O'Keeffe, a woman as perceptive as she was gifted. She saw more than just a *flower*. She saw the secrets of the universe, understood women could be as Nature intended. She unlocked the secrets... don't you *see?*"

For several seconds he stared at her, his eyes big, as if filled with a new understanding. For a moment she felt hopeful, believed maybe she'd found a counterpart, a soul mate, someone who fathomed what she was trying to say. Someone not David, hopelessly lost in his own blindness, his own dislike of modern art.

But then he looked away, this nameless Beatnik, and she realized the understanding dawning on his face was his realization she was crazy.

"Nice chatting with you," he said softly, and then disappeared into another room.

She sat again and studied the painting, dismissing him, but the tears fell. Tears of loss, of loneliness, of knowing she was so terribly lost in knowledge no one else could seem to grasp.

Later that evening David called, and she let the answering machine pick up. She curled up on the sofa, the living room cloaked in darkness.

I'm sorry, he'd said. *Can we try again?* he'd asked. *I think I'm falling in love with you.*

Impossible, she thought. He couldn't love her. He didn't know the meaning of that word. He was selfish, and cruel, had made her face the reality of her deformity. She could never love anyone that evil.

Surely he'd been with other women, so he must have seen their transformation. What had he been comparing Molly to when he'd called her beautiful? Some mock adolescent girl, an atrocity, an affront to Nature itself, well past the stage where she should have blossomed into her purity. What was *wrong* with her? Why were all the others so fortunate? Nature could be so cruel, toying with her body that way, holding back its ultimate gift.

Molly had promised to babysit her sister's daughter the following day, and Katherine arrived around noon with eight-year-old Samantha, a quiet, brooding child who seemed to be in early rehearsal for her teen years.

Katherine left to run errands, and Molly offered to take Samantha ice-skating at Rockefeller Plaza.

Samantha shrugged, banged Barbie's and Ken's heads together. "Can I have some hot chocolate?"

"I don't have any in the house. Why don't we take a walk?"

"Never mind." The girl collapsed into herself and sighed dramatically. "Can I watch cartoons?"

"Don't you want to go out?" When Samantha didn't answer, Molly answered, "Be my guest."

With the Power Puff Girls blasting in the background, Molly retreated to the bedroom to escape the noise, to take a break from the joys of babysitting. Children weren't something she was interested in. Not someone else's, and certainly not her own. She wondered how Katherine maintained her sanity day after day. Surely the child's dour mood had to affect her. Samantha was rubbing off on Molly after less than an hour.

Molly lay on the bed with her head by the foot-board and studied every nuance of *White Camelia*, every shredded nerve relaxing.

"Aunt Molly?"

She glanced at the door. Samantha approached her and looked down. "Taking a nap?"

"I was."

Samantha climbed onto the bed and lay beside Molly with her arms folded beneath her head.

"What happened to your cartoons?"

"I got bored by myself."

"I offered to take you skating, to go for a walk, to get hot chocolate. I can't help it if you're bored. You're very lazy."

"Mom says that too." She snuggled into the mattress. "Why are you laying on this end?"

"I'm admiring my favorite painting."

"Oh. It's very pretty."

"You like it?"

"Uh huh. I've never seen a flower like that."

This was the most extensive conversation they'd ever had. The notion that it was about the painting endeared the child to her.

"Doesn't Mommy take you to museums?"

Samantha shrugged. "I went to the Natural History one once. But that was a long time ago."

"Would you like to go with me?"

"Sure. Sometime."

"How about now?"

"I don't feel like it now."

"Okay." Molly looked from the painting to Samantha. Strange how she finally found someone to talk to about this and it turned out to be a child. But an old soul was an old soul, and Molly recognized it. Perhaps the child was more perceptive than anyone had ever given her credit for.

"What do you see when you look at the painting, Samantha?"

The girl glanced at her. "What do you mean?"

"Can you see the deeper meaning? Can you see what it represents? What it's trying to say?"

"Say? Is it going to talk to me?"

As quickly as she found her, Molly was losing her young soul mate. The girl was too young to understand, her perception and understanding of the world too naïve. Molly had to explain it somehow, had to show her. Samantha was on the verge of a great discovery, a deeper knowledge. Perhaps her innocence would be the enabler. What better mind to shape than a young one?

"This is more than just paint on canvas." Molly turned on her side, leaned on her elbow. "This is knowledge, Samantha. Great truth. Great power. If you can understand the secrets, you will own the world. Do you understand?"

"No."

"If all you see is the paint...then you're not understanding it at all."

Large brown eyes opened wider, as if trying to comprehend, trying to figure out what Molly was trying to say. But the confusion was apparent, the lost look etched in her expression revealing her thoughts.

"You don't have to be afraid," Molly whispered. "Tell me. Do you look like that painting?"

"Do I look like it?" Samantha's brow creased, and her eyes rolled up, as if she was searching for the answer beneath her hair.

"Or are you a freak of nature, like me?"

Samantha didn't answer, only stared at Molly with her mouth slightly open.

"The woman who painted *White Camelia* understood. She wanted the world to know. And in doing so, she made me realize there's something wrong with me."

"What is? What's wrong with you?" Samantha voice was almost a squeak.

Molly sat up and leaned over Samantha. "I have to know. Are you normal? Are you beautiful? Or are you a freak?"

Samantha blinked, shrugged.

Molly unzipped Samantha's jeans and yanked them down her hips before the girl could protest. Samantha struggled to sit up but Molly pushed her back down. "Stop that. I'm not going to hurt you."

Sobbing, Samantha shook her head. "What are you doing, Aunt Molly?"

"Shh. Stay still. I just want to see."

Obediently, the child lay there as Molly pulled down her underpants.

"My god," Molly said, staring at the hairless pubis. "I'm sorry, Samantha, I didn't know. I thought I was the only one."

"Can I get up now?"

"No. Stay there." She left Samantha on the bed and rushed into the kitchen.

When she returned, Samantha was struggling to hide beneath the bed but hadn't gotten far; boxes and empty suitcases blocked the way. Molly pulled the girl out and lifted her onto the bed.

"Maybe we can fix this. Maybe it's not too late." She pushed the girl back down and knelt between Samantha's legs, spread the knees apart, revealing the pre-pubescent labia.

White Camelia loomed over her shoulder like a sentinel, and Molly glanced from the painting to the child. In her hand was the chef's knife from the kitchen.

"Aunt Molly? What are you doing?" Samantha wept even harder.

"Stay still, Samantha. Do as you're told. I'm going to make you beautiful."

Again she looked at the painting, although she knew every brush stroke by heart. Now she looked to it for direction, guidance. Perhaps it wasn't too late to save Samantha. Somehow she would save her from the torment Molly had been forced to live with.

She bent Samantha's knees and removed the jeans and underpants from around her ankles, spread the legs further apart.

Samantha sobbed, her fingers clutching and unclutching the bedspread.

Several minutes later, Molly raced to the bathroom and retrieved a stack of towels.

The girl was inconsolable, thrashing on the bed, tears pouring as steadily as the blood.

Molly piled the towels beneath her and pressed a thick bath towel between Samantha's legs.

"I'm so sorry, baby," Molly said, applying pressure to the wound. This wasn't supposed to happen. The flesh was supposed to cooperate, to follow its natural course. So much blood. When she removed the soaked towels shortly after, Samantha's vagina looked the same as it had before.

*   *   *

"Can you tell me what happened?" In the ER, the social worker questioned Molly while the police officer, named Rayburn by the badge on his chest, stood by.

She looked at their faces, but they revealed nothing. The social worker was young, with red-rimmed eyes, as if he'd been on duty an eternity. Rayburn the cop looked like he'd be good at poker.

"She... Samantha... It was an accident."

"What happened?" Mr. Mellick, as his hospital ID revealed, folded his arms and cocked his head, the first indication he suspected something, that his questions weren't casual.

"Please answer the questions," Rayburn said.

"She was playing in the bedroom." Molly tried to swallow but her mouth was arid.

"Where were you?" Rayburn asked. Much older than Mellick, his short hair peppered with gray, he looked too old to be a uniformed cop.

"I was in the bathroom and heard her playing."

"Playing how?" Now the officer had a notebook and pen in his hands. Mellick seemed to blend into the background as Rayburn took over the questioning.

"With her dolls." Molly watched him scribble. "Am I under arrest?"

He looked up. "For what?" After a moment of studying her eyes, he said, "Then what happened?"

"I, I heard her, you know, scream. When I came out, out of the bathroom, she was holding the knife. And covered in blood. She was, I mean. You know. Covered in blood."

"How?"

"*How?*"

"Yes—how did she cut herself so badly?"

"She did it... to herself. You know, an accident."

"You're saying she sliced herself open like that."

"Um, yes."

Rayburn nodded. "Why would she?"

The air in the hall seemed to have thinned out, and Molly was having a hard time dealing with the lack of oxygen. She swallowed, cleared her throat. "I don't know. She was just playing. Kids do all kinds of strange things."

"According to the ER doctor, that knife wound wasn't self-inflicted," Mellick said.

"Was anyone else there at the time?" Rayburn asked.

"Just me." Molly's voice was barely audible. "Has Samantha said anything?"

"She's been sedated," Mellick said. "It required forty-six stitches close the wounds. When she was brought into Emergency, she kept repeating that she was sorry, that it was all a game."

Molly's eyes lit up, a new spark of hope. She'd coached Samantha before the ambulance arrived but had had no faith the child would say what Molly wanted her to. How Samantha had done this to herself. How Aunt Molly had nothing to do with it.

"She told me she wanted to be a flower." A faint smile touched her lips, and she shrugged.

"A what?" Rayburn asked.

"I have a painting on my bedroom wall. O'Keeffe's *White Camelia*. Samantha said she wanted to look just like it, just like the beautiful flower. The perfect..."

"Perfect what?" Rayburn asked.

"Perfect woman, I guess. She believes the flower represents perfect womanhood and…" But she felt she was saying too much and didn't finish the thought.

"That eight-year-old child said that?" Rayburn closed his notebook, but Molly could tell by his expression what he was thinking. He blamed her for everything. He didn't believe a word of what she'd said. She knew it, could feel it.

"She's… advanced for her age. A very smart little girl." The way they stared at her, the puzzled looks on their faces—she knew men could never understand. Now they probably thought she was insane, and possibly Samantha was as well, if they even believed the child had damaged herself.

"That's all for now," Rayburn said. "This investigation is still open, and I'm sure I'll want to speak with you again."

Molly nodded, and held her hands together in front of her stomach to keep them from trembling.

Katherine showed up a few minutes later—Molly had reached her on her cell phone—and demanded to know what had happened.

Molly told her sister the same story she'd told Rayburn and Mellick, but Katherine wasn't buying it.

"What did you do to my baby? What did you do to Samantha?" Rage burned in Katherine's eyes, and she was ushered her in to see her daughter before she could act out on her anger.

*   *   *

Home again in the dark, slowly rocking on the edge of the sofa, seeing the child's blood on her hands even without a source of light. Illuminated, like iridescent paint, spotlighting the damage she'd caused, accusing her of harming the child.

Tearless sobs, wails of anguish, feeling sorry for herself, for not being able to show the world what she knew as universal truth. She'd never meant to hurt Samantha; the excess of blood had shocked her, made her quickly realize she couldn't do this, she didn't know how. O'Keeffe was the only one who knew, and she was dead. No one left in the world to take Molly's hand and guide her along, to show her the way it was supposed to be done.

The phone rang and she listened to the machine intercept the call.

"You sick bitch! What did you do to my baby?" Despite Katherine's yells and sobs, Molly understood the words clearly. "The cops told me what happened. Pick up the phone. God *damn* you, Molly!"

The line went dead. Molly dragged her fingers through her hair and clutched her head. "I'm so sorry, Katherine…" she muttered. Molly knew her sister's hysterics, knew that although this was bad, terribly, terribly hideous, Katherine would eventually get over it. Molly was blood; her sister wouldn't stay angry forever.

And when she saw the end result... maybe Samantha would be more beautiful now. Maybe Molly had done enough to help her. Then Katherine would thank her, and not be angry with her. Katherine must have wondered why Samantha was still abnormal... must have wondered how long it would take for the girl to blossom.

Though she was shocked she hadn't been arrested. The cops had spent forever asking her questions and taking pictures. It seemed as though Samantha hadn't implicated her in the crime. Though crime wasn't the right word. Any harm had been unintentional, had been caused by an eagerness to help. Surely they would see that. Not that she'd volunteered any information. Not yet. She knew she should speak with an attorney first, and she planned to call one in the morning.

The answering machine intercepted another call. "Please pick up," David said. "I want to see you. *Please*, Molly. Don't let it end this way."

"I'm here."

"I'm so glad you answered. Can I come over? I really need to see you. I want to work this out."

She cradled the phone between her neck and shoulder and squeezed her eyes shut. "Come over then," she said quietly. "I'll leave the door unlocked."

He'd be there soon. David's apartment was a ten-minute walk from her place.

The bedroom was just as she'd left it; the bedding was painted with Samantha's blood, and it had dried to a sticky, shiny hardness. It had soaked down to the mattress. The towels lay in a pile like giant blood clots.

Molly combed her hair with her fingers and slipped out of her clothing. She pushed the ruined bedding aside and pulled a clean comforter over herself. To wait for David, *White Camelia* above her head standing vigil, protecting her, guiding her. Almost shining down on her. Molly smiled, knowing no matter what else happened, she would always have *White Camelia*.

Beneath the comforter, her hands roamed her body, gently caressing her stomach and breasts, bringing her to a state of relaxation. Closing her eyes, she wished to dream of *White Camelia*, wished it could have been so easy. Wished for the pain that would be so soothing.

She heard David inside the apartment fifteen minutes later, heard him before he even spoke. Recognized the pattern of his walk, the sounds of stealthy movement through the hallway and living room. All else was silent in her apartment; no TV, no radio, just the soft rhythm of her own breathing.

"Molly?"

"In here," she said, but she doubted he'd heard her.

"Sweetie, what are you doing in bed? It's not even five—" He stopped in the doorway. "Oh my god—Molly?"

Her arms were covered in blood, and the knife dangling from her fingers thumped on the carpet.

She smiled at him. "You can see me now, David. It worked. I'm not afraid anymore." Her voice was weak, drained, as if her life was leaking out of her body.

The comforter was saturated with her blood. He yanked it off her body, dragged it toward her feet.

Hands over his mouth, he staggered back until he hit the wall, unable to find another step.

"Hardly even hurts..." But that was a lie. When she tried to glance down, the pain tore through her body. She could see everything in the mirror she'd placed at the end of the bed. In spite of the crimson splashed over every inch of her from the belly down, she could see the beauty she'd created, the beauty beneath the blood.

Legs spread, revealing the labia she'd cut away and pulled back, flaps of mangled fatty tissue. Her vagina, carved out and spread until it rested on the mattress.

And later, she thought, they would clean her up, and after all traces of blood were removed, her body would heal, become the beauty it was supposed to be. It would retain the shape it was meant to be, the pinks and whites, and downy peaches, an explosion of colors and softness, unfolded in a flowery splendor.

So much better now. So much more natural.

"Come to me," she whispered, bloodied arms spread in a welcoming embrace.

HUNTIN'
SEASON

"Well it ain't exactly pleasant," I remember Miller telling me. Like that would've made a difference.

By this point, the meat had turned a lovely shade of vomit. Kind of yellowy, a bit of brackish brown. Like heaving out the contents of your stomach after a real rowdy Saturday night. Kneeling before the Porcelain God, butt-crack smiling sideways at the world.

I held my nose. "Been in the sun too long, Miller."

Miller nodded. "No shit, Dick Tracy. We'll cut around the bad parts. At last we don't hafta go hunting tonight."

Hell—he was right. Ain't nothing scarier than the hunt—because you're not really the hunter. They come after *you*. They're not scared of nothing.

Given the choice, I'd rather eat green meat.

But the next day, we were out of food again.

Was more spoiled parts than good anyway, and I mean *real* spoiled—not the *sorta* spoiled that's still okay as long as you cook the shit out of it—but so spoiled even the maggots won't touch it. That meat doesn't go far, not when it was feeding me and Miller and Miller's old hunting dog, Shep, who didn't do no hunting no more.

So that morning we grabbed the shotguns and headed into the woods. My hands were shaking already, and we'd barely left the cabin.

"Calm down," the old geezer said, following up his words with a phlegmy old hawk that he deposited all over the grass. He slapped me on the shoulder and shoved me toward the woods. As big as he talks, he always makes sure I go first. Sneaky old bastard.

We don't usually have to go far—we set up traps, and sometimes they're sprung.

The scariest is when they hunt in packs—when they come after *us*. Holy shit, if that happens, you may as well stick your head between your legs and kiss your ass goodbye!

Cracking noises in the bushes. Something moved in there... tiny grunts and groans. Bloodhungry gurgles.

Miller grabbed my arm. "What was that?"

The hell should I know? I wanted to say but my lungs felt like I'd just smoked a whole pack of Camels.

There it was… crawling toward us on its elbows and knees, dragging its belly along the ground, its small ass sticking up in the air. This was a young-un all right—not even walking on its own yet. But sometimes that's how they try to trick you. Sneaky bastards.

I raised my gun and pulled the trigger. The head exploded, its hairless scalp flying through the air and sticking to a tree trunk like a patch of moss.

"Awwww, what'd you go an do that for?" Miller grunted. "You blew his fuckin head off! The brains is my favorite part!"

Miller grabbed the thing and stuffed it into his sack, shaking his head at me like I farted. Them lil' buggers sure could bleed. I make less mess slaughtering pigs.

"We got enough," I said. "Let's get back—I got a bad feeling."

Miller shook his head. "We ain't got enough. 'Sides, this was easy."

I nodded. "Too easy."

Miller laughed. "You're givin' 'em too much credit, boy. Their brains ain't even done forming yet."

But then they came swarming out like locusts, on their elbows, on their bellies, on their feet. They just came and came and came and it never seemed to end. Falling out of trees, staggering or crawling through bushes. Some of 'em dragging that 'bilical cord between their legs. Some of them still dragging parts a their mommas that tore off when they tunneled their way outa the womb. I seen that once. In the woods. Lil bugger came bursting out his momma's twat, chewed her clit right off. Sucked it down without even chewing.

They were coming at us like the Calvary—a fuckin' herd of babies. I started to run, but hell—they just aren't that fast. Even the toddling ones.. well, they just toddle. Some a them may be on their feet, but a two-year-old just ain't built for speed.

They went after Miller first, tiny hands grabbing, little chicklet baby teeth gnawing at his flesh. He tried to run but they had him down in no time flat.

Miller was real old, and he kinda toddled too. And they were coming from everywhere, biting and clawing and scratching, chewing on anything they could wrap their teeth around. He was screaming his head off and trying to get away, but there were too many. One was at his throat, chewing on his Adam's apple like it was its momma's teat. Every time Miller opened his mouth to scream, one a them babies tried to grab hold of his tongue, or stretched its butterball head over his face, glops of baby puke slopping into his mouth. Chunks like cottage cheese but curdled, stinking like a boggy swamp. Miller's mouth filled up with the stuff and he had to swallow it just so he didn't choke.

Wasn't no place to run to yet—they were still dive-bombing from branches or moving in low, biting at my ankles. I was kicking 'em off, punching at 'em. Two a them hooked onto my leg, tiny arms wrapped around my calf, and I tried to shake 'em but they was stuck tight, like bloated ticks on a dead dog. One jumped me from behind and clung to my head like a bad toop. I was banging at it with my hands and he was gnawing away at my scalp, trying to rip out a chunk. His tiny smelly fingers found my nose and dug in, tried to yank it off my face. Then his hands slipped down my face and found my mouth, grabbed hold of my tongue, started yanking away at it. I bit down hard as I could til I heard them cursed fingers snap like kindling, til the little fucker started to screech its fool head off and try to pull its hand out of my mouth. It managed to all right, but not before I kept a few of them digits as a souvenir. I spit 'em out though—I tasted better things in my dead wife's snatch.

I bashed another one in the head with my gun and it still wouldn't let go of my leg. By now her little head was all dented in, baby teeth cracking off. I hit the soft spot on the top of her skull and the gunstock sunk in like a spoon oozing into a bowl of oatmeal. Brains dribbled out the hole and she finally fell off. I kicked my leg out hard several times, and the biting rugrat went hurtling through the air. I never even saw her land.

Far as I know, the little fucker's still flying high, sailing over some trees.

There wasn't time for me to help Miller. The ol' geezer was still trying to get away from the bastards, but he wasn't gonna be getting up again.

And they were coming at me and I was dodging 'em, and finally saw my chance. I grabbed the sack with the headless baby torso and tore off through the bushes.

A few of 'em saw me take off and tried to follow. But hell, I could have strolled off and they still couldn't have caught me.

But then I heard the baby-cry—a kind of gurgling mew like a cat in heat. I sure heard that noise before. It's their war cry. They were telling others up ahead I was coming.

I plowed through another group of them, stomping their little bodies into the ground, jumping up and down on them til their malformed heads popped like grapes. They tried to grab me but I ran like my ass was on fire.

I made it back to the cabin but some others had beat me there. Poor ol' Shep won't be lying 'round the fireplace no more. Now he's lying 'round the porch instead. All around the porch...

I made it inside the cabin.

I got me this here baby corpse to eat, and I guess it'll have to last me a few days. I opened up the sack and dumped it on the counter. Baby shit had smeared all over the bag.

I scraped up as much as I could, wiped it off the dead rugrat's ass, and put it all in a bowl. Licked my fingers—ain't gonna waste none—tastes okay, a little strong. I can tell it's been eating berries. This one had too much roughage in its diet—it was kind of runny, like mustard. Golden brown mustard. And there were ribbons of gore streaked through it. Probably from when I blew its head off. Baby poop is pretty special all right—one of my favorite meals is shit-on-a-shingle. But Miller was right—the best part's the brains. Warm and squishy like Jell-O. Slurp 'em back, suck 'em between your teeth.

Though you ain't lived til you tasted fried baby pecker. Especially one that ain't been drained. Biting into that and getting a little piss surprise. Salty brine against the smooth sweet taste of tiny testes.

And even when the meat turns, it's still good. Rotten baby flesh goes real soft, gets all squishy and spongy. Sometimes it gets a little *too* green... then it's like eating cottage ham... or maggoty Spam.

They're crying again... shrill screams that cut right through your head like a chainsaw. When they're all together, they scream so loud it makes your ears bleed.

They're out there now. Pounding on the walls and scratching at the dirt. I can hear babygrunts, the little bastards fornicating right under my window. Fighting to get inside the cabin... they got themselves a taste for blood. Though the li'l fuckers ain't figured out how to use their thumbs yet so they can't open the door to get inside.

I think I can wait 'em out. Sooner or later, they gotta take a nap.

VADE IN
PACEM

It was almost impossible to see her in the blackness, but the fetor of her unwashed body permeated the bricks. The stench of musky, sweaty hair mingled with feces and unwashed teeth. The smell of hunger oozed from her pores.

Eventually the moaning would stop.

"Die already," he muttered, fists clenched.

Movement inside. Had she heard him?

"Help me." Just the hint of her voice. "Why are you doing this?"

Why? Because Adultery is a sin.

"I hear you," she sobbed. "Save me."

"I *am* saving you." He peeked between the bricks, studied the cracks as if they were fine art.

She found his eye and met it with her own. No tears... her body no longer able to expend water. "Please don't do this. *Please.*"

"This isn't my choice. You cheated. You sinned."

Her ravaged throat tried to imprison her words. "God, please." Hours of screaming had ruined her voice, screams muffled by the surrounding bricks and the insulation of the outer walls.

Dominic had yearned for her silence.

Six hours later the rasping death rattle finally stopped. A blessing.

Using a chisel and mallet, Dominic pried bricks from the woman-sized hole he'd made in the wall. What remained of her slumped into his arms.

Her hands were now deformed, mangled ruins.

The pittance of nourishment he'd given her had been at head level, unattainable through normal means. Days earlier she'd had to dislocate her shoulders and wrists to reach the cracker and ounce of water.

He'd warned her to ration it.

She'd cheated on her husband, she'd told him in tears. What should she do? She would do anything to make it better. Anything.

Arm around her shoulders. So comforting, so paternal. *Come inside my rectory. We'll think of a penance that will wash away your horrible sin. Catherine, let me tell you a story about adultery in the days of the Crusades... about punishment.*

Kneeling now, he folded her arms over her chest, prayed over her. "*Vade in Pacem.*"

Depart in peace.

Mass was to begin at 6:00 p.m. Dominic left the rectory to greet his flock.

FIVE ADJECTIVES ABOUT MY DAD, BY NADINE SPECTER

Assignment: Using five adjectives, write a 350 word essay describing your father. [Eds. Note: Miss Maginty verified that of seventeen First Grade students, thirteen had a surviving father. The other four children were asked to write about their favorite pet.] *Give examples.*

My dad's name is Ken. He is kind, smart, funny, fair, and happy. Those are my five adjectives. An adjective is a word that describes a noun.

My dad is kind. He is good to me and my brother Aaron. Aaron is five years old. I am two years older than Aaron. I am seven. He can be a pest. My dad is kind because he knows privacy is important to me.

(The grass outside Nadine's bedroom window sprouts patches of brown. The blades bow respectful of the wind, reaching in unison toward the ground as if a single blade. Nadine is hypnotized by their rhythm and tries to count them. She loses track after fifty-seven.

Nadine pokes her head out of the bedroom door a short time later. Being punished. Nadine had been bad. Again.

"Dad?" she whines, knowing it annoys him but doing it anyway.

He responds to her plea for clemency with a shout from the sofa downstairs.

She whines louder. He threatens a spanking.

Nadine pouts. "Can I come out of my room now?"

When he doesn't respond she creeps down the stairs and stalks into the living room. Shakes his shoulder. "Can I come out now?" she whispers, not realizing the irony.

His eyes gleam open, blinking back crocodile tears that had formed during his nap. Cold dark pupils glare at her under the dim lighting. "Dammit, you woke me up."

She steps back, but she has no reason to fear him. He has never struck her, no matter how many times he's threatened.

She leans forward and clings to his arm. Smiles charmingly. Disarmingly. Hugs his arms, the hairs tickling her cheek.

"Go back to your room."

"But can't I—"

"Back to your room." More slowly. Teeth clenched.

She doesn't relent, wants to spend time with him. Even time fashioned in anger.

"I'm hungry. Can I just get a snack?"

"I won't tell you again."

Nadine stares at him, willing him to change his mind, trying to control his thoughts. It isn't working. But she practices and waits and stares and hopes he will suddenly say the opposite of what he had moments ago, but he gets angrier for some reason, some stupid reason, and she sees tiny red dots on his cheeks.

After a minute that feels like an hour, Nadine's father slithers around in his seat and shifts one eye toward her. Finally. Not directly at her but it's close.

She smiles and wonders if she has succeeded in changing his mind.

"Get to bed."

"But I—"

"Now! Move! Bed! And don't leave that goddamned room!" Still the words comfort. She feels a connection.

She runs away, crying, wishing Mom had stayed home that weekend, or wishing she'd gone too.

She wishes she could travel back in time and reverse the events from breakfast, the reason for the exile: A glass slipped through her soapy fingers and shattered in the sink. She yelled sorry as she tried to clean up the shards, placing them inside the shattered bottom. She should have been more careful—it was his favorite glass.

He snatched the glass corpse from her hands and examined it. He didn't check her hands for signs of damage, but the glass he cradled. "My crystal scotch glass."

"Sorry," she muttered again, eyes downcast, dismayed by her clumsiness. She often broke glasses and dishes. He accused her of breaking it intentionally and told her to go to her room, to stay there until he says she can come out.

And here she has been ever since, realizing of course the punishment fit the crime, knowing it could have been worse. She sits in her room, waiting since breakfast for a parole than never seems to be granted, knowing her stay of execution might expire before Mom returns from Aunt Kathleen's.

She sits cross-legged on her bed and scoops out a handful of cereal from the box of Cheerios she's stashed.

Mom and Aaron come home around two the following afternoon, and Nadine is allowed out of her room.)

My dad is smart. He tells me I should go to college one day because I'm almost as smart as him. He knows all the capitals of all the states but won't tell me any answers and says I should look them up.

(Nadine's class participated in a spelling bee and Nadine came in third. Mrs. Fisher gave her a Third Place Award Certificate and a ribbon. Nadine spelled *rabbit, maintain, battery* and *justice* correctly. She misspelled *tomorrow* because she forgets if there are two "M"s or two "R"s. Sometimes she spells it tommorrow, but that never looks right.

Everyone congratulated her, even Jeffrey, the boy with the habit of flicking spitballs at her.

Nadine races home, flushed from the heat, sweaty from running. The corners of her Special Award are damp and wrinkled from her moist fingers. She bursts into the house. Her dad's already home.

Out of breath, grinning like a Cheshire cat, Nadine waves her paper in front of her chest, dangles it beneath his nose, rocks excitedly on her heels.

He reaches out and accepts the paper.

"Third place?"

She nods, her smile faltering the tiniest bit, still hopeful that—

"What word did you miss?"

"'Tomorrow.'"

He grunts, and she can't remember why this noise disturbs her so profoundly.

He hands the paper back without saying a word and returns to his newspaper.

She stares, again trying to read his mind… trying to change it, make him attentive, make him like her… make him love her. But still, she hasn't figured out how to do this. So she waits for a response, waits for him to say something. Waits for his congratulations. Waits for a hug that just will never happen.

She swings her arms, and he finally responds.

"That was a stupid word to miss. You should've won.")

My dad is funny. He tells good jokes. He makes me laugh when he tells me jokes. He tickles me and makes me laugh. Sometimes I laugh so hard I pee my pants. That only happened one time. That one time he stopped tickling me after I peed, and after tears started to come out of my eyes. I don't even remember crying, I just remember my eyes being wet. He laughs and laughs and finally stops tickling me when I think I'm going to throw up. He tickles me sometimes when he tucks me in at night.

(And he smiles, wrapped around his daughter's still form, tears drying on her cheeks, her hair a tousled bird's nest piled on top of her head.

Nadine pretends to have fallen asleep, but he knows she hasn't. Nadine knows this because she sneaks a peek and can see the expression on his face. He can tell by her breathing she is still awake, can tell by the darting movements beneath her eyelids. She realizes she has to learn to pretend better.

Nadine's mom tiptoes into the room, wanting to not disturb her sleeping child. Nadine peeps at her mother through slits, still trying to pretend sleep, believing she has fooled her parents but knowing her dad probably knows the truth.

Dad plays along with it for some reason. "Shhh," he whispers, nodding his head toward the door. "Don't come in. I'll follow you out."

Mom smiles at the sight, the beautiful and perfect sight, daughter entwined with daddy, Raphael's *Madonna* fashioned in masculine arms and Barbie pajamas.

Mom leaves. Dad pulls his arms away from Nadine so he can rise from the bed. Nadine's mother has left and has not seen where Nadine's father's hands had been. Her mother probably wouldn't have liked it.

Nadine drifts off to sleep for real after her dad leaves the room. She buries this memory along with every other she doesn't want to acknowledge.)

My dad is fair. My brother Aaron and I fight sometimes, and Dad makes us stop. He yells at us both and says we shouldn't fight. I think my dad is fair because even when he punishes us, he does it fair. Some dads are very strict. My friends say their dads are strict, but my dad says he's not strict, not at all. My dad punishes me, and Aaron too, but I think he's fair when he does it.

(Nadine's friends have come over for a pajama party. Three girls from her class: Rachael, Emily and Sarah. They've decided to camp in the living room because Nadine's mom said they could. Nadine's room is too small to comfortably fit four girls. Besides, Nadine wants to use her sleeping bag like her friends do.

The girls giggle about the boys they like, and they gossip about their classmates. Nothing out of the ordinary for a pajama party, and Nadine is excited she's making new friends, something that doesn't come easy for her.

Dad trudges into the living room with a towel wrapped around his waist. "Shut your mouths and go to sleep," he says. There is no other warning, just a final decree. He disappears down the hall and closes his bedroom door behind him.

Nadine snuggles into her sleeping bag and closes her eyes, prepared to sleep, expecting the other girls to do the same.

Emily turns on the flashlight and shines it down the hall. "Grump," she says with a giggle. Rachael and Sarah titter into their fingers. Nadine pulls the blanket up to her nose. Her heart beats a little faster.

"Grump," Rachael echoes, which cracks up the visiting girls and terrifies Nadine.

"Shh," Nadine says, but the girls giggle even more.

Her parent's bedroom door is flung open. A chunk of light fills a black section of hallway.

Again draped only in a towel, her dad storms the room. "Goddammit," he says. A shocked Emily gasps at the curse word.

"I told you girls to shut up. I mean it!"

Nadine's mom calls him from the bedroom. "Everything okay?"

He stands in the center of a circle of girls. "Not another sound," he warns, and disappears down the hall.

The girls remain quiet for several minutes. Nadine is relieved they have fallen asleep, and the tension in her body, which begins in her toes and works its way up her legs and torso and fingers and arms and neck relinquishes its stranglehold.

But a sudden flashlight beam pierces the darkness. Emily aims it at Nadine's face. "What's wrong with your dad?" Her voice is twangy, nasal. She says the word as *dah-aaaad*. "He's creepy."

"Yeah," Sarah adds. "He scared me."

"Please," Nadine begs. "Be quiet." She squeezes her eyes shut and wills the girls asleep. Tries to control their thoughts, to tell them her father isn't kidding. But they don't get her psychic message.

"Big dopeyhead," Emily says, her voice deepening, her girlish impression of Nadine's father: "Goddammit." Her cheeks puff out and her head drops against her chest. For some reason she believes this makes her look something like Nadine's father.

Rachael and Sarah think this is one of the funniest things they have ever seen and burst out laughing, holding their noses to quiet the laughs, burying their faces in their pillows.

Nadine flips over on her side and pulls the blanket up to her ears. She pretends she is asleep.

This time, when she hears the bedroom door open, and sees the light once again fill the dark corridor, she can pretend to sleep through it all.

The other girls realize he's coming. They drop in supine positions and try to burrow into their sleeping bags, but it's too late.

He sees them.

He stands in the center of the circle of girls.

Emily starts to cry and buries her face in the crook of her arm.

He stands over Nadine. "Let's go."

She looks up at him.

"Why?" she says. "I didn't do anything wrong."

"*Now.*"

"But I was sleeping."

The three other girls stare in silence.

"I said let's go."

Nadine jumps up. She scoops the sleeping bag in her arms and follows him to her bedroom. He stands in the doorframe and waits for her to pass.

"But I didn't do anything," she cries, her voice hitching, tears pouring down her cheeks. He doesn't seem to notice her tears. Or if he does, he doesn't seem to care.

"Stay in your room. Don't come out until I tell you to."

"Can my friends—"

"No." He pulls her door shut and leaves her standing in the dark.

Sobbing, Nadine climbs into bed. She cries until she's weak and exhausted and a short time later she is asleep.

Nadine wakes to the sound of laughter and the smell of coffee. She climbs out of bed and bounds down the stairs. Dad is cooking breakfast, which Nadine's friends appear to be enjoying.

Dad looks up from the waffle iron. He's laughing, probably telling them jokes. She catches his eye and his face hardens. "Why are you out of your room?"

This question barely registers. How can he ask her that? How can she still be punished? Especially when her friends are still here.

"Get back to your room."

She waits for the inevitable laughter, certain this is a joke. A cruel joke, but a joke nonetheless. Any second now he's going to laugh—might even flick waffle batter at her.

"But—" She doesn't finish the sentence because she can tell by the expression on his face that this isn't a joke at all.

She backs away from the table, from the girls staring with dewy doe eyes, forks suspended in midair. Nadine's cheeks burn with embarrassment.

Nadine runs up the stairs and sits in the doorway of her bedroom, listening to the sounds of breakfast. The clinks of forks and knives against plates, the giggles and laughter from the girls, who have no choice but to pretend everything is fine, to continue as if nothing has happened. Girls who have no clue what injustice is but feel strangely grateful for their own parents, who aren't as strict as they had once imagined. Girls who only want to finish eating and hope this pajama party ends sometime soon.

By lunchtime, Nadine is allowed out of her room.

By then, her friends have gone home.)

My dad is happy. He smiles a lot. He's always in a good mood. I'm sad when Dad doesn't smile. I wonder if he's upset with me, if I've done something else wrong. I do a lot of dumb things. I try to be good, so he stays happy.

(It's Saturday, mid-August. Nadine and Aaron get dressed early because Dad says to get out and enjoy the sunshine.

The heat is sweltering, oppressive, the humidity almost a life form. The children play outside for a while but it's just too hot for any real enjoyment. The water in the kiddy pool is hotter than bath water. Splashing around in it isn't fun, it's painful.

The rubber bicycle tires ooze into the tar melting on the 101 degree street. The metal seats on the swing set are untouchable.

The children return to the house and go into the kitchen in search of a cold drink.

Mom has gone shopping. Dad's sitting at the kitchen table reading a newspaper.

Cheeks are red from heat and from the beginnings of sunburn. Nadine and Aaron collapse onto the cool linoleum kitchen floor.

"Why are you back already?"

"It's so hot," Nadine says, waving her hand in front of her face like a fan, her tongue lolling out the side of her mouth like she'd spent a week traversing the Sahara. Her halter-top slides on her slick skin, refusing to stay in place.

"Go back outside," he says, although he allows them a drink of water before they go.

Outside again, and somehow it's hotter. The trees droop, succumbing to the weight of the onerous air, branches sagging with the burden of humidity.

They find the garden hose and turn on the tap. Icy water gushes out, and she runs it on their faces and arms. She wets her brother's head and thinks she sees steam rising from it.

They relax in the shade beneath a birch tree and peel the bark off in strips. She thinks she's pulling off the tree's skin and feels sad yet excited. She wonders if she is hurting it but continues to strip away its bark anyway.

The wind evaporates the moisture on their skin but stops cooling when their flesh is dry, a strange and inconvenient magic.

Mosquitoes buzzing about their ears are not a problem, something tolerable if somewhat annoying. But then the black flies come, and black flies tend to swarm, often in the hundreds, biting and stinging in unrelenting attacks.

They run to the house and manage for the moment to outrun the black flies. Their small porch is screen enclosed and offers asylum from the attack, but there is no room to maneuver.

Nadine grabs the doorknob. It refuses to turn; the door is locked. Perplexed, she knocks. After an interminable wait, their father opens the door but blocks them from entering.

"Stay outside," he tells them.

"But—" Nadine licks her parched lips. Aaron is crying. His cheeks are the color of brick.

"I want a quiet and peaceful house for once. You and your brother stay outside."

"But the bugs—"

"Swat them."

He shuts the door.

And right before he does—she notices he's smiling.)

My dad is a great man. He's kind, smart, funny, fair, and happy. The end.

[Eds. Note: Nadine's grade for this paper was a B-. Miss Maginty thought the adjectives used were weak. She later pointed out that adjectives used by other students in the same class included *compassionate, jocular, intelligent,* and *equitable*. She conceded these students might have had parental guidance when writing their papers. Miss Maginty later confessed another reason for the B- was Nadine's life didn't seem to have the hardship or stress the other children seemed to be experiencing. Miss Maginty thought Nadine was experiencing a rather simple and mundane childhood. She said that might not have been a fair way to grade, but after forty years of teaching, she knew a thing or two about human nature, and graded accordingly.

Nadine has since said she wishes she could choose a different set of adjectives to describe her father.]

JASMINE AND GARLIC

He always started with the breast exam. Eye contact. Eye to chin contact, anyway. They rarely looked directly at him; too humiliating. Her right arm at ninety degrees: stretch the breast. Circular motions, outward in, fingertips then palms. Lightly squeeze the nipple for discharge.

Never sexual, never lingered on a particular part of the breast. Even hot breath conjured a sexual connotation; dangerous. Repeated with left arm, left breast. Pulled paper gown closed, pretended to offer boundaries, privacy. The woman on the table sighed, and he felt her tension dissipate.

"This was real good of you," she said hesitantly. "Seeing me like this. I know you're busy."

"Mmmmm." He didn't look at her but continued to fumble with instruments on the tray above her legs.

"I, I know it's late, but I couldn't get away before now. I missed the clinic hours," she said anxiously.

He stopped what he was doing and looked into her eyes. "It's fine."

Sinking back into the padded table, her muscles unclenched, facial tension oozed and melted into her hair.

"What do you mean you couldn't get away?" he asked, locking eyes with hers. "Are you working now? Have you found a place to live?"

"No," she whispered, eyes downcast. "I'm still on the streets. But I'm trying real hard. I know it ain't good for my baby."

He looked at her stomach, which protruded with the growth of the fetus, its advanced age apparent.

"I don't think you're trying hard enough. Want me to abort the baby?" he asked casually, speaking to her groin.

She flinched, an invisible slap draining the blood from her cheeks. "Nuh-no," she stammered. "I just want you to examine me. I said I was sorry."

Smiled again. "It's at least seven months old," he said. "Maybe eight."

Awkward silence for several seconds. Awkward for her. He absorbed her, inhaled the scent of her dismay and confusion, a jasmine-garlic odor emanating from her pores, sweating out her fear in perfume and remnants of lunch.

"Doctor, um, Windling? I think I should maybe make another appointment I mean—" She cleared her throat but didn't finish the sentence.

Lower lip contorted. "Why? We'll do this right now, Miss—" Miss what? Forgot her name. Cassandra, maybe.

Moving to an overhead cabinet, he retrieved additional instruments shielding them from her sight.

"I should go. This don't feel right." She pulled the halves of her paper gown tighter.

Like a dog picking up the scent of the kill, he stuck his nose up in the air.. jasmine, garlic… wafting in and out of his nostrils… yeast, cheap after-shave from the last guy she probably blew for a few bucks. Odors from deep within her bowels, part of her inner workings. He smelled it all, sucked in its savory richness.

"Just relax," he said, patting her thigh. "We'll do this now. You're already naked."

Her cheeks flushed and she looked confused. "No, I… really. I can just get dressed." Tried to sit up but the tray was in the way, and her swollen belly prevented her from mobility. Besides, she didn't want to be *rude*. These women never wanted to be rude, to make *him* feel uncomfortable.

How considerate they were, these women.

Pushed her back. "No trouble," he said, not unkindly, his beautiful eyes manipulating the situation, manipulating her. How could anyone with such beautiful eyes ever cause anyone harm? Such a handsome face. Good-looking people never harmed anyone.

Almost never.

They played out the act once more: her protesting, him comforting, until she finally conceded, resting against the thick padding of the table, laying her arm across her swollen breasts.

Cheeks flushed, but willing now to continue, having lost the round. "This has been an uncomfortable pregnancy," she said. "A lot of pain, especially during the exams. Can you give me anything for pain?" Her voice was losing its strength, and her hands clenched the robe halves tightly together, fingers bleeding sweat through the tissue paper gown.

He stared out into the hall.

"Doctor?"

Listening… Everyone had gone home, hadn't they? Was someone still working and—?

"Doctor?" More loudly.

He looked at her finally, and again she said, "For the pain? Can you give me anything?"

"Pain," he mumbled, holding his hand up in a *just a second* gesture as he moved toward the door.

Her eyes followed, her head tilting back as she watched him leave the room.

He scanned the reception area. Dark waiting room, only the hallway lights still burned, leading the way through the darkness to the outside world. He double-locked the front door, throwing the deadbolt, the one key the cleaning woman didn't have.

Quickly he returned to his patient, knowing she would leave given the opportunity.

She was trying to push the tray out of the way when he re-entered the exam room. Embarrassed, caught in the act of trying to escape, she lay down again.

He pulled up the metal stirrups, patted them. Smiling, he nodded his head in the universal *slide down* gesture.

Moved along the length of the table, planted her feet in the stirrups.

"You never answered me before," she said meekly. "I'm sorry I'm being such a baby."

"No, you're fine. And I'll give you something in a sec." He pulled her down a bit further. "Let's have a look first."

She flinched when his cold hands touched her inner thighs. Maneuvering the light above his head, he aimed it at her groin. Snapped on a pair of Latex gloves.

Leaning in, he sucked in and exhaled loudly. Her pubic hairs bristled. Vaginal muscles clenched in anticipation of his touch.

Using his thumb and index finger he separated her vaginal lips, shoving the middle finger of his free hand inside her. The muscles tightened around his finger. He jammed another finger inside, moving in deeper, thrusting them in and out of her.

"What are you doing?"

"Time for that shot now," he said, removing his hand.

He retrieved the syringe from the tray. Being finger-fucked by her doctor was likely a new experience for her, and she wouldn't know how to react. He was counting on that, on her confusion.

He lifted her arm and lay it above her head.

"Wha-what are you doing?"

"Quiet. Works better this way." Swabbed the nipple with an alcohol pad. Flicked it with his fingers.

Again she began to question him but he shook his head. "Hold still." Grabbing hold of the breast, he injected the rather large needle into the nipple.

She screamed. "What the fuck you do?"

"Relax," he said. Then, moments later, he smiled, and quietly added, "That was nothing."

"Nothing?" Her cheeks puffed out a few times. "You're a fucking psycho. Let me out of here!"

"I said *relax*."

"No!" Her face was contorted in anger, and her robe fell open in her struggles to sit up. She tried to pull her feet out of the stirrups but her pregnant belly prevented it. "I'm getting the hell out of here, I... I'm—"

But the shot kicked in and her body went limp, and she lay back on the table, her eyes bulging.

"What..." was the last thing she was able to say. Tears streamed into her hair.

"Curare," he said to her. "Numbs the nervous system. Causes paralysis. You said you wanted something for pain, didn't you?"

She didn't respond. *Couldn't.*

"Oh... You wanted something to *stop* the pain? Ah, well." It was cruel to toy with her, but she'd made him work damn hard. So many questions. Such a difficult patient.

"You'll feel everything," he said from between her legs, looking up and peering at her face, his breath hot and fast. Her face, beauty enhanced by terror. Pain would make it exquisite. He knew she wouldn't thank him, even though she should.

He lubricated the speculum with K-Y Jelly and inserted it, pushed it inside her, spread the vaginal walls so he could see inside clearly.

She didn't move. Even her vaginal muscles were limp. But her eyes—he could see the fear in her eyes as they rolled back into the sockets.

He picked up the scalpel next and approached her upper body.

Moved her limp hands out of the way. He separated her robe, exposed her breasts. Unlike the rest of her, the nipples responded to his touch.

Lightly he trailed the scalpel along her breasts, tracing delicate patterns in the skin, trickles of blood dancing on the surface of her flesh. He sliced an *X* into both nipples.

"Now you're mine. Branded."

He repositioned himself between her legs and pushed the speculum deeper, lifted the cervix, took in every bit of her. Blood trickled down her buttocks.

Her eyes blinked in response to pain he couldn't even begin to imagine. Using only his hand, he reached up inside her. He would use the instruments shortly.

The baby kicked, as if squirming to escape him. He removed his hand and looked up again. Her eyes were focused, staring back at him as if pleading one final time for mercy.

He raised the curette and waved it in front of her face. "I won't use most of my traditional tools. Not for this. A vacuum would ruin everything." He studied the instrument, carefully tracing his fingers over the sharp curved hook.

"This will have to do."

He pushed the curette inside her vagina, scraping the lining of the uterus, oosening cells and tissue. Careful not to perforate the delicate skin.

Blood gushed, washing out amniotic fluids and tissue matter. He quickly removed the curette, waiting to catch whatever washed out. The placenta slipped out and he carefully laid it in the table beside her.

The baby poured out next, and he caught it, severing the umbilical cord with the curette. The infant was still alive.

He could see the mother screaming. Her eyes, screaming for the baby, the bloody pulp lying in the doctor's hand. He laid it on the tray.

"Oh *god*," he moaned, bloodied hand pressed against his groin, head thrown back in the throes of orgasm. Trembling, he knelt at the end of the table and shoved his face into her mons. The inhaled flecks of gore and chunks of flesh filled his nostrils; blood washed into his mouth.

Lifted his head, his face bathed in her viscous fluids.

Her groans were barely audible. The curare was wearing off.

The speculum jutted from her like a metallic dildo. How had one woman once described the feeling to him? Had said the exam had been like a never-ending cramp, an unrelenting spasm of pain and nausea.

His eyes rolled, the only white on a face of crimson, baptized in her blood. Oh, how he envied these women, how he longed to feel what they felt. Not that he wanted to be a woman—only wished to understand this pain. To know the joy and agony of childbirth.

"Bay..." she whispered, her teeth gritted, every nerve and muscle in her body frayed and alive and in agony.

Baby.

The air stank of babies. Of newborn flesh and rancid drops of new life. Damn thing was almost dead and it was infecting his air. He hadn't cleared its nasal passages or its airways. He hadn't checked it for abnormalities or for its sex. It wasn't the baby he was interested in.

He lifted the baby from the tray. Starting from the top of its head, he licked the remnants of the placenta and the amniotic fluids and sac, working his way down its prone body, cleaning it of all traces of birth and afterbirth. Inadvertently, he dislodged its air passages and it started breathing tiny gasps of air.

Months premature, it was so little, molded practically to his palm. But it was whole, and appeared undamaged. The abortion had been untraditional; the fetus hadn't been torn apart by a vacuum but had been rejected from the mother's body in one piece. Not usual, but not unheard of. He put the squirming baby back on the tray.

Once more he stuffed his face into her groin, lapping greedily at her, sucking back soft tissue, avoiding the metal of the speculum. He felt rejuvenated. He felt alive. There were incredible healing properties in these vital fetal fluids; nutrients and vitamins and holistic antioxidant properties. People questioned his motives when he tried to obtain placenta, even in

Europe. He'd had to be careful.

He held the placenta in his hands and slowly ate it, savoring the taste and feel in his mouth.

"Please…" she groaned. "*Take it out.*"

He wiped the back of his hand across his gore-soaked mouth. He'd forgotten about the speculum.

The baby mewled, kicking its impossibly tiny limbs. He leaned over it, and it pissed in his face. And just like that he fell in love with it. How instantly endearing; the little boy was all piss and vinegar. Impossibly tiny body, premature yet fully formed. He carried it to the portable incubator across the exam room.

He returned to the baby's mother and pulled the speculum out of her vagina. She trembled as it slid out of her body.

Downstairs in his soundproof basement he maintained an apartment. He carried her down, dropped her onto a pile of rags and scattered newspapers now growing damp with her sweat and seeping body fluids.

Waited for her eyes to focus, to remember what had happened. She would be delirious with fever, insane with pain and fear, and it would be deliciously gorgeous.

Lightly he slapped her face, trying to bring her into focus. Her head rocked from side to side, eyelids fluttering, sweat tricking from her pores, her skin glistening.

"Where am I?" she managed to whisper, licking dried lips with a parched tongue.

"Home," he said, wiping her face with a towel.

"No. Not huh-home. I—I can't… move…" Her head fell back again.

"I know," he said gently.

He slapped duct tape over her mouth. She hyperventilated, and breathed heavily through her nose. She shook her head, tried to loosen or throw off the tape.

She still couldn't put up any sort of real struggle.

He dragged her over to a drainhole in the floor.

"Listen to me," he said, trying to be heard over her muffled screams. He shook her, grabbing her chin and turning her face in his direction. Snot and tears coated her face. Her eyes were bloodshot with broken blood vessels.

He leaned in and spoke into her ear. "Knock it off or I'll kill the baby."

Her head jerked and she stared at him.

"That's right. Your little boy is still alive. If you want him to stay that way you'll do as I say."

Groaned, in reluctant concession.

"I'm going to remove the tape now. If you scream, I'll put the tape back and I'll snap his scrawny little neck."

She nodded, and he ripped the tape off her lips.

"I'll be right back." Moved across the basement to work at the utility sink.

"Can I see him?" she asked, her throat raw, voice scratchy.

"Later." He brought the supplies over. "We have some unfinished business first."

She started crying again. "No more. Please!"

"What did I say? Think I'm kidding? Want me to kill him?"

"No!"

"I'll do this as quickly as possible."

He knelt before her and injected a syringe into her neck. Lay her flat on her back and tilted her head back, as if he were about to administer CPR.

"Good," he said, slightly out of breath, trying to contain his excitement. From this angle he could still see her face... her eyes... distorted with fear and pain, dread plastered on features in a frieze of beauty.

Drool dripped from the corner of his mouth. That was too much, even for him. Looked away, embarrassed, wiped the spittle away with his thumb.

Her raw fear attacked him, crushed his balls, stroked his cock... and again he felt himself losing control. He rubbed his painfully erect penis against her thigh and it discharged. Shuddered from the powerful orgasm.

Scalpel in hand, he leaned over her to perform the trach. He cut a hole beneath the crichoid cartilage, creating a new airway. He inserted a breathing tube in her neck and rinsed away the blood, packing the wound in gauze. This way, after she was healed, he would still be able to communicate with her by covering the tube. Her voice would barely be above a whisper—and she wouldn't be screaming any more.

He worked quickly, as promised, but she felt it all. One of the more unusual side effects of curare. He could tell by her eyes she felt everything.

Later he started an antibiotic drip to ward off infection. He didn't want her getting sick. After all, she was *his*—he wanted to keep her healthy. And she'd given him a son, so it made her a little more special. In a way. Maybe in a few years he'd even let her meet the boy she had birthed. Probably not.

He stroked her filthy hair. Watched her sleep. He leaned against the brick wall where the last one had lain after dying, after seven years of service. Used up. Heartbroken, no longer wanting to live. He could keep their hearts beating and could keep them somewhat healthy, but after they gave up, there wasn't much he could do. What had her name been? He was so bad with names... he'd called her Number Four.

This one—Cassandra was it?—seemed like a fighter. He hoped to be able to keep her for a while.

He felt the placenta working its magic, its healing properties coursing through his system, keeping him healthy. He found the Fountain of Youth, but the problem was in its supply. People still frowned at fetal studies, as archaic as that was. That forced him to provide his own.

He stuck his face into her vagina, inhaling the remnants of the earlier smells; of jasmine and garlic and semen, mingled now with blood and gastric juices. Later he would mix her foods with rosewater and primrose; would cleanse her in patchouli and milk baths, douche her in honey and chamomile. Would keep her healthy, keep the placenta healthy.

In the meantime, his other tools were lined up and ready for use: the bone saw, acetylene torch, scalpel. For now, she needed to rest. In a week or two he would finish.

*   *   *

It had taken several courses of antibiotics to fight the infections that had taken over her body, but weeks later she was finally coming around.

Eyes almost perfect circles, screaming voicelessly at the horror at looking down and seeing her limbless torso. She looked up at him, her blotchy red face twisted in terror, her body trembling in shock.

Raspy, mummified air poured out of her mouth and trach hole.

She'd get used to it, just like the ones before her had. And in a few months she'd supply him with fresh placenta, which he would harvest, ripe with fetal antibodies and antioxidants.

He rolled her onto her back, careful not to disturb the cauterized stumps still not completely healed. Retrieved a tube of K-Y Jelly from his pocket and lubed his fingers and cock. He stuffed the fingers inside her to get her wet then massaged his cock, closing his eyes to imagine someone else—he still hadn't gotten used to seeing this one without her limbs, but that was an easily made adjustment.

He leaned into her torso, pushed his cock inside her.

She lay there quietly, her face stone. Unable to fight him off, unable to scream her horror, she seemed to have accepted her station and waited for him to finish, gasping choked, stale air through the hole in her neck.

He grunted, pulled out. In six months she would supply fresh placenta, rich with vitamins, full of nutrients, the Elixir of life.

Hefted her in his arms—so much lighter without her limbs—and carried her into the adjoining room, hidden behind a wall of particle board and tools.

The walls: adorned with black and white photos of his women in various stages of pregnancy, some with limbs, most without, bloodless, cauterized stumps like birth defects. His hobby, a way to enhance his fetish.

And lying on their makeshift beds on the floor, in varying stages of pregnancy, his five other women stared at him without a glimmer of hope, mouths open and gasping, faces dry because tears now were wasted effort.

THE REST
OF LARRY

At first it felt normal.

He opened his eyes, blinked back grains of sand and flecklets of dried blood, tried to remember how he'd gotten there, in the middle of nowhere. The stars blanketed the sky through peepholes in the treetops, thick foliage exploding overhead.

With grimy fingertips he brushed the dirt off his face, and licked his lips, which lay on his face like bloated leeches.

Then he looked down.

He wasn't so much *person* now as he was torso. A skeletal torso at that, most of the meat having rotted off the bones or been picked clean by scavengers. He'd been chopped in half; that much was obvious. Parts of the blade were still imbedded in a rib bone. From the base of the ribcage down, he was… well, in the immortal words of Gertrude Stein, *there was no there, there.* Nothing but flapping tissue and shredded tatters of shirt.

Larry pawed at the earth and tried to push himself into a seated position. Damned hard to do without legs, he quickly discovered.

Beneath the tattered remains of his shirt, more of the same. A hollow cavity where internal organs had once nestled. He slipped his hand inside and through the cavity and lost his balance, tipping over and banging his head against the pine-needle bed.

"No…" he muttered, shaking his head. "… Impossible." Words that began as whispers steadily increased in volume until he was shrieking. "*Impossible!*"

Regardless, it *was*. Whatever reality had cast its shadow and now occupied Larry's time and space, this was it.

Sobbing, he crossed his forearm over his eyes. He realized that his upper body seemed to be intact; his arms, neck and face, he discovered after a quick prodding, appeared whole.

Deep in the woods. Surrounded by thick trees and thicker greenery, heavy, cloying fragrance that reminded him of Christmas and fresh dirt. Crickets chatting it up by the millions until they sounded like one solid note. Squirrels flinging themselves from tree to tree, birds twittering and dive-bombing. He sucked it all in. The thick, mulchy smells of a peat bog and blankets of moss warming the ground. Great, swell.

Mother Fucking Nature.

Larry dug his fingers into the earth, fingernails taking root in the grass and knotty stumps, and pulled himself along the ground. Occasionally he found himself tangled in some underbrush, jagged edges of rib cage snagging on a briar patch or a tree root, but he persevered, clawing himself free.

Pulled further along the ground, blocking out the chorus that was Nature, trying to recall what in hell had happened to him. From the state of his decomposition, he had obviously been exposed to the elements for a while now.

Snow. He remembered snow. That was the last image floating around in his brain. Damned driveway always filled faster than he could keep up with his shovel. Neighbor kid Chad SomethingOrOther had offered to clear the path for ten bucks. Larry agreed and then paid him five. What did a twelve-year-old semi-retard need with ten bucks anyway?

This was going to take a while. Larry finally recognized the area—Buck Pond, on his own property, about three miles from his house.

He snorted, wiped his runny nose on the back of his hand, and crawled further along. Slow going, but steady. He didn't feel as if he was tiring.

Images flooded his mind now, of trips to the mall, of relaxing on the couch, or sunning himself in a beach chair in the back yard. Molly bringing him a sandwich and beer. Of course—Molly. It was coming back to him now.

He came upon an abandoned campfire pit, sooty clumps of charcoal disintegrating in the breeze. The cairn was cold, dead; no one had used it in a while.

He dragged himself away, toward the house again, the distance slowly closing. A mile finished, then a second, marked by red paint on nearby trees in times past. Two and a half miles traveled now. The tool shed loomed across the field in the backyard, the house spitting distance away. Lights burned in the kitchen window and in a bedroom upstairs. Molly never did listen when he told her to shut off the lights. Not that Larry cared about energy conservation, but the damned electric bills were staggering.

Using the doggie hole at the bottom of the door, he crawled into the house. First his head, then arms, then pulled his torso through.

On his knuckles now, his palms filthy, hands exhausted, he pulled himself into the living room.

Molly, asleep on the couth, short red hair still damp from her recent shower (she was still so predictable, he mused), body wrapped in a terry robe. And beside her—snuggling with Molly!—who the hell was cuddling Larry's wife? Jason Campbell?

"Jesus christ!" Larry yelled, settling back against the baseboard for support so he could angrily fold his arms across his chest.

Molly and Jason woke, startled at Larry's voice, both searching the room for the source of the disturbance.

"Over here," Larry muttered, frowning, pointing at himself.

Molly screamed. So did Jason. In fact, Jason jumped up and ran behind the couch.

"What the hell?" Molly cried. "Oh my god!"

Larry scratched his itchy forehead, and this invariably cost him his balance. He caught his tipping torso by the using his palm flat against the floor.

"What the *fuck*?" Jason said. Sounding more like a yelping puppy than a man.

"Jesus, Larry," Molly groaned. "What are—What did—What—"

"Calm down, sweetheart. One question at a time." Larry dragged himself to the sofa using the surface of his knuckles and leaned against the coffee table. He struggled but lacked the strength to pull himself up.

"Uh, one a you want to give me a hand here?"

Neither moved. Splayed fingers obscured most of Molly's face. "Does... does it hurt?" she asked.

Larry shook his head. "Surprisingly, no."

Jason broke his frozen stance and moved behind Larry, and dug his fingers into Larry's armpits and pulled him onto the sofa. He then moved behind it again and spoke to Molly, but his stage-whispers came through loud and clear.

"You think maybe it's a trick?" Jason asked her.

"No, *genius*, a fucking torso just crawled into the house. Of course it's some kind of trick."

Larry wasn't too keen on the *trick* reference. "Screw you both. And I can hear you *whispering* you know. I lost my legs, not my hearing."

Jason continued as if Larry hadn't spoken. "Someone found the body. Dug it up. Somebody knows."

"Nobody knows," she said, slapping his arm—Larry had turned his head in time to see this and grinned. "Unless you opened your big fat mouth again."

"I didn't tell anyone!"

"Where'd you come from then?" she asked Larry, her voice teetering on the edge of a shriek.

"The woods. Near Buck Pond." Something didn't feel right... other than the obvious. What were those two talking about?

"Where's the rest of him?" she asked, and Larry knew he was being ignored again.

"How the hell should I know?" Jason yelled.

"What are you two talking about back there?" But of course he knew. He'd lost his body, not his mind. He hadn't lost a functioning brain.

Larry craned his head back and pushed his bony spine into the cushions.

Rested his head on the edge of the couch and looked at Molly and Jason upside down. "Just what in hell did you do to me anyway?"

"What should we do about this?" she asked Jason.

"I… we'll put him back. And this time we make sure he stays down."

Larry—who probably should have been terrified, or at least slightly uneasy—rolled his eyes and wobbled his head from side to side. If he still had a heart, it might be pounding madly by now. But he wasn't concerned. Hell death—real death—couldn't be any worse than spending life as a torso.

"Get the axe," she said.

"Get the flashlights," Jason replied.

"Get a fucking life," Larry mumbled.

Five minutes later they returned to a dozing Larry, who opened and blinked his eyes and smacked his dirt-encrusted lips. Jason was brandishing an axe and a shotgun; Molly carried several flashlights.

"Going on a picnic are we?" Larry said.

"Let's go," Jason said.

"Oh, and how do you suppose I'm going to do that? Shall I walk on my hands again? We'll be at the end of the driveway by morning, I should think."

"Goddammit," Jason said, bundling the axe and gun in the crook of one arm and resting the items against his shoulder. He grabbed Larry's wrist and with a jerk of his head indicated Molly should do the same.

She grimaced, then cringed, shook her head.

"Just take his bloody paw for christ's sake," Jason whined. "He's your husband, after all."

"Was," she said.

"Still am, darlin', still am."

"Shut *up*, Larry," she muttered.

They flanked Larry and dragged him across the room by his wrists. Every few feet his jutting tailbone would catch on a wayward nail or an edge of furniture and the procession would suddenly halt, and Molly and Jason would lose their grip on Larry the torso. Repeatedly crashing to the hardwood floor was not Larry's idea of a good time.

"God *damn* you people are idiots!"

"Shut up, you—you—" Jason sputtered, at a loss for the proper word. "You torso!"

"Can't you lift him properly, sweetie?" Molly asked. "He's not that heavy, being mostly head and all."

"My other hand is full, *sweetie*," Jason snapped. "This isn't easy you know." They each grabbed an arm and lifted Larry a bit higher until he almost cleared the floor.

Night had fallen. The damned crickets were louder than ever, an insane chorus of offending notes. So many stars filled the sky there was barely any room left for *black*.

Larry was dragged across the yard and into the field, into the thicket of perfumey pines and evergreens, through choking clouds of ragweed spores and slippery clumps of Spanish moss, over jagged clusters of rocks and bramble bushes. Buck Pond was to the right. Bullfrogs convened beside stagnant, bug-skimmed water.

They trudged through the woods led by flashlight beam but also by the moon and stars fingering their way through the lush foliage. They passed the spot Larry remembered being last, the spot where he had suddenly woken.

They kept going.

"How much further?" Larry asked. He was ignored.

"Over there," Jason said, but Larry was fairly sure Jason wasn't talking to him.

They dropped Larry, and he rolled onto his side and was stopped only after smashing into a rock. Jason and Molly dropped the tools beside Larry.

"This way," Jason yelled, rushing away into the darkness.

Larry propped himself up against the rock and his hand brushed against the axe. Not interested. What could he do with an axe? Not like he could balance himself well enough to use it.

He could make out their figures silhouetted against the trees. They were staring at the ground.

"Hey!" Molly cried, waving her arms overhead as if trying to land a plane. "I see your leg, Larry!"

Silence while they studied the ground some more.

"Looks like an animal got you. Probably dragged you out of the ground. Coyote I'll bet, maybe wolf." Molly seemed fascinated by her thought process.

"Great," Larry muttered, for his own benefit. "I'll probably turn into a torso werewolf."

They were headed back in his direction. He wondered for a moment just how large that hole was.

"Sorry, bud," Jason said, "end of the line. Time for you to go back where—"

Larry shot Jason in the stomach from about four feet away. The recoil would have knocked Larry off his feet, had he had feet. As it was, the gunblast slammed him further into the rock.

"Oomph," Larry grunted, shaking his head. "That fucking hurt."

"My god!" Molly screamed. "What'd you do that for?"

"Three's a crowd, baby. Now be a good girl and push him into that hole, would you?"

"You're insane!"

"Oh, sure, right. I'm insane. You kill me, then try to kill me again in the middle of the goddamned night with your murdering boyfriend along for the ride, but *I'm* the one who's insane!" Spittle flew from his nightcrawler lips.

He could barely see her face because of the tree shrouding her head but knew from her silence she was pouting.

"Go push him in the hole. Cover it up. Maybe *someone* around here will stay dead."

Molly did as he said. He imagined pointing the gun at her might have been the deciding factor.

Now the dilemma. In order to move on his own, he would need both hands free—no gun. In order to make her carry him, or at least drag him home, he'd be in her hands—literally and figuratively. Again, no control of the gun.

He'd have to trust her. Then again, she'd already killed him once.

"Let's go home," she said.

"Home?"

"Sure, Larry," she said wearily. "Jason's dead. Killing you was his idea anyway. I never wanted it to happen."

"So just like that, we go home?"

"It's not like I can go to the cops or anything..." With incredible speed, she snatched the shotgun out of his hands. "See? I could hurt you if I wanted. I just want to go home."

She hefted him in her arms and propped him on her hip, like a mother carrying a child. His tailbone rubbed against her thigh. "Oh, honey..." she crooned, "that feels nice."

They traipsed through the woods and finally reached the house, and they locked the door securely behind them.

Had to be sure to keep out the weirdos.

Molly and Larry remained happily married until her death at age seventy nine. She gave birth to six children and raised a happy, healthy family.

Larry often suspected the children weren't really his.

MATERNAL INSTINCT

She didn't notice him... her three-year-old with the hazelnut eyes, thumb jutting from his mouth, hand wrapped over hand. Dirt crusted on plump, brown cheeks. She didn't care that he lay on the stained, naked mattress, curled into a fetal position as if trying to remember the womb, staring across the room, unblinking, unfazed, in her direction.

She didn't notice him, because the only thing in that claustrophobic studio apartment that mattered was the pipe, to smoke the few vials of crack she'd scored.

She took a hit and her head exploded in pleasure, her already-bulging eyes now seeming to engulf her face, that feeling of ecstasy consuming her, feeding her. She tossed back her head, holding the feeling, knowing it would never be this good again, knowing that each hit would just be weaker and weaker, none as effective as this one.

Hand shaking, she lifted the pipe again to her mouth and using the 33 cent purple lighter ignited the tiny pebbles inside.

"The fuck you starin' at?" She held the pipe stem a few inches from her lips, her shaking hands eager to make another connection. "I said..." But she turned away, ignoring him for the moment, closing her eyes. Part of her knew this was wrong for him, the little boy staring at her from the mattress, knew she should take care of him. The same part of her which knew she had five other kids roaming around the neighborhood somewhere and maybe they were hungry, maybe they were tired or dirty. Some part of her knew her responsibility as a mother, but that same part no longer controlled her. It was overwhelmed by her addiction's need to control. Motherhood didn't stand a chance.

Peering down at her three-year-old, curled like the family pet on the cum- and whisky-stained mattress did nothing for her except remind her he'd be crying for food sooner than later. And it pissed her off. Where was she supposed to find food? Even her tits weren't of any value for the baby—tainted with any drug she could get her hands on. She sold the milk one really desperate night... an old druggie smelling like vomit and urine, hanging from the tit like a bloated parasite, looking for that ephemeral high. Still, it'd worked for him, and she'd made ten bucks.

She took another hit. This one was weaker; the momentum had reached its crescendo and would be more and more disappointing after each toke. It was like sucking the bottom of a glass with a straw, trying to find the phantom wetness.

She felt the boy searching her. It made her uncomfortable, made her feel cheap. Who the fuck was he to be judgmental? She never cursed him when he shit his pants (she didn't curse him for it any more, anyway, not any more!), she rarely got upset when he touched her stash, she rarely yelled and slapped and punched when he walked in on her fucking a john on that same stained mattress (he should have been sleeping anyway—it wasn't her fault). She was a good mom. Her five other kids could swear to that. She squinted, eyes peering up as if trying to get a peek inside her own head. There were five, weren't there? Where were they, anyway? She glanced at her wrist, forgetting again she'd hocked the cheap Timex months earlier. She glanced outside through the filthy, sooty window, the brick façade of the opposite building the only view. The darkness indicated the late hour and she wondered for the moment where her other kids had holed up for the night. There were plenty of places a kid could sleep. The warmth of a burned-out tenement would be safe enough for a night. She was sure her 14-year-old would take care of the eight-year-old. The other three fell somewhere in between. With any luck, she wouldn't have to worry about scrounging up dinner for them. She was too tired to think about having to whore herself for a box of spaghetti. Not this evening, anyway.

She'd had enough of his staring. "Trev... the fuck you lookin'..." She was tired, the words weak, falling from her lips like ash. Her hand slumped to the table and she rested her head on it. Anger built in her, but she was just too tired to react. Her eyes narrowed into slits, nostrils flaring. She slammed her hand on the table's surface. "Stop lookin' at me!"

He was moments away from getting the crap beat out of him. She rose slowly from the table, trying not to topple over. She moved across the tiny room, a room furnished only by mattresses and a table and lamp. The smoldering crack pipe lay turned on its side, forgotten for the moment.

Her jaw was set in anger, teeth clenched and grinding slightly. She raised her hand to slap him but he didn't flinch. So instead, she reached out and stroked his hair, and his thumb fell from his mouth, and her little boy rolled onto his back from sheer momentum.

She realized finally just how cold he was, how rigid his small body.

How his unblinking eyes were now focused on the ceiling.

She moved slowly away, knowing she'd have to eventually deal with him, but for now she returned to the numbing bliss burning away at the table.

GINGER

When Jeremy opened his eyes, he was lying on a cot. Ginger was on the floor beside him.

His mind flashed back on the last events he could remember: dinner at the Roadhouse, drinks at The Pit. Then he remembered the conversation with Louis, that the last thing he'd done was fall asleep for some reason. But even now he was relaxed. There was no reason to be concerned, not with Louis. If anything, Louis might be playing some bizarre, moronic joke, but there was never a reason to worry.

Except…

Sat up, rubbed his tired eyes. The cot was inside a large metal box, surrounded by bars. He stood up and moved in a circle to get his bearings. His head throbbed in his temples, his mouth was pasty.

He was inside a cage, in Louis' basement.

"Louis!" he yelled. He wrapped his fingers around the bars and rattled the cage. "This isn't funny! Goddammit!"

Ginger followed Jeremy around the cage, her ears pricked, her tongue bobbing in and out of her mouth like she was amused by the situation. She was enjoying this; somehow it was a game to her. Chasing after her master was more fun than chasing wild rabbits in the field.

"Louis!" he screamed. Kicked the cot, upended one side, and it crashed back down on the concrete floor.

The retriever scuttled away, tried to stay out of the line of fire. She ran behind him, tail tucked between her legs, waited for him to finish his tantrum.

He turned around and saw her cowering. "Sorry, girl," he said, kneeling. She rushed up and licked his cheek. He wrapped his arm around her neck and pulled her to his side. The beating of her heart against his stomach felt soothing.

At the top of the stairs the basement door creaked open. Louis descended, his shadow crossing the din and filling the room.

"What the *fuck* is going on?" Jeremy yelled. "Goddammit, Louis, what the fuck are you thinking?"

"Calm down, Jere. No need to get all psycho on me."

"Oh, fuck you! Let me out of here!" He rattled the bars. "Open this fucking door!"

"Calm down or I'll leave. I mean it."

Red-faced, sweat trickling into his collar, Jeremy released the bars and let his hands drop to his sides.

"Sit down. Okay?" Louis pulled up a folding chair and drew it to the bars. He sat across from Jeremy.

Jeremy sat as well, trying to regain his composure.

"I'm going to let you out. *Of course* I am. But I thought this would be a great way for us to finally settle our argument."

Jeremy shook his head. "You're nuts. Just let me out."

"Hear me out, okay?" He didn't wait for an answer. It wasn't as if Jeremy had much of a choice anyway. Louis leaned forward and rested his forearms on his knees.

"How many years have we been having the same stupid argument? Ten? Twelve? How many more years will this go on? I don't want to go to my grave wondering about the answer."

"Jesus H Christ on a fucking stick, you have *got* to be shitting me." Jeremy lifted his Yankees cap and planted it on his head again. "Just let me out of here! You're pissing me off."

"Here's the condition—the challenge. I'll let you out. After you kill that dog of yours."

"Fuck you," Jeremy spat. "I been telling you for years that'll never happen."

"That's what I'm saying, Jere. That's where we disagree."

"I'm telling you, it'll *never* happen. Never."

Louis stood up and walked to the cage and pressed his face between the bars. Clicked his tongue. "I say you're wrong. I say you'll kill the mutt to save yourself. And if you don't, you'll be in there a *very* long time. Your choice man. And so begins the challenge."

"*So begins the challenge*? Who the hell are you, King Arthur?" He approached Louis at the bars. "Open this goddamn door!"

Unfazed, Louis crossed his arms. "You're just mad because you know I'm right."

"You're insane."

"Say it. Tell me you know I'm right."

"Fucking nuts."

"I always win, Jere. You should know that by now."

"I have a life out there! People will look for me. You know it."

Louis shrugged. "I'll even help them search for you. It'll be fun."

Then Louis turned away and headed back toward the stairs. "Where are you going?" Jeremy cried.

"Upstairs."

"No, wait. Wait! Don't go."

"I'll be back later." He started climbing the steps.

"Don't go, Louis! You have to let me out. Joke's over, okay?"

But Louis was gone.

Jeremy moaned. He kicked the cot, knocking it onto its side. The dog jumped out of the way to avoid being hit. She dropped to the floor and planted her muzzle on her paws.

Exhausted, he sat beside her on the floor and stretched out his legs, laying his head on her side. He moved with the rhythm of her rising and falling ribcage. Tired from his fit.

When he woke, the room was dark. The light in the room earlier had been from the sunlight streaming in from the overhead basement windows. A network of spider webs covered the windows like silken stained glass.

"Louis," he called out, hoping he'd returned, or at least could hear him.

He stood, stretched the stiffness out of his spine. Stared at the basement door, as if this could somehow magically summon Louis. His watch was impossible to read in the sparse light.

The door creaked open and light flooded the room. Louis descended the stairs. "How do you feel?" Louis asked, an amiable smile on his lips.

"Let me out of here."

"Are you hungry?"

"Let me out!"

"Look, Jere... you're not getting out, not until you kill that hairy bitch, so you might as well save your strength for something better."

Louis handed a canteen through the bars and then pushed a rectangular bowl filled with water through the very small opening near the bottom of the cage. Jeremy had tested it earlier. It was way too small for him to fit through.

Louis looked around. "You've made a mess. Better clean it up or you'll have no place to sleep. Lights out in ten minutes."

"Lights out? What?"

Louis didn't stick around for conversation and headed upstairs.

Jeremy upturned the cot and replaced the pillow and blanket, then collapsed on top of it. The basement was warm, stuffy, filled with choking dust and mildewed boxes. It was a refuge for insects and leftover childhood toys. A Flexible Flyer was propped in the far corner. Frisbees and Slinkys and Tonka trucks spilled out of an assortment of boxes. The basement was unfinished, not meant for human living. Or human storage.

Within ten minutes, the light was turned off.

*   *   *

"Wakey, wakey."

Jeremy lifted his head from the pillow. From the corner of his eye he spotted Louis near the cage door.

"You win," Jeremy muttered, sitting up. "Whatever it is we're supposedly arguing about, I give up. As usual you were right, I was wrong. You win."

"Wonderful! But it's not that simple."

"Look, I said I give up. You win. This is over. Over! I don't want to play anymore. Just open the door and let me out."

Louis crossed his arms and sighed.

"*What*." Jeremy scowled, turning away.

"There's only one way you're getting out of there."

"Fuck you!" he screamed, turned his back on Louis. Focused his attention on Ginger, stroked her ears, tried to ignore Louis.

"Here's breakfast," Louis finally said, almost a whisper.

Jeremy turned. Louis was sliding a pan of kibble through the narrow space at the bottom of the cage. Just enough room for the pan of dog food.

"What's that?"

"Breakfast for your mutt."

"What about me?"

Louis smirked. "A little more incentive for you. You can eat when you get out."

Ginger waited for Jeremy to let go before she trotted across the floor.

"Wait—did you put anything in her food?"

"Of course not. That wasn't part of the agreement."

"Agreement? I never agreed to any of this."

"You know what I mean."

Louis pulled up a chair and sat across from the dog and watched her eat. "Smells pretty good, don't you think?"

Jeremy scowled. "Why don't you stop this? Let me out of here."

Louis stood up and returned the chair to the corner of the room, out of Jeremy's reach. He closed up the bag of dog food and left it on the workbench, also far from Jeremy.

Before leaving, he tossed a fresh canteen onto Jeremy's cot.

"Stupid prick," Jeremy muttered, watching Louis disappear up the stairs. The dog food *did* smell good… Jeremy hadn't eaten since an early dinner the night before. He glanced at his watch. His last meal had been fifteen hours ago.

No wonder he was so hungry. An annoying gurgle and slight hunger pangs quickly turned to nausea. He really wanted to eat.

Ginger had left a few nuggets of food in her bowl, but Jeremy turned away in disgust.

He wasn't *that* hungry. Wasn't about to eat dog food.

Bored, hungry, nauseous, he stretched out on the cot. There weren't many options. Louis hadn't even given him a book or a magazine or a radio. Nothing to keep him company but the sound of his dog's warm panting breath, or of water rushing through the network of pipes that hung suspended throughout the basement. Soothing though. Before long, he was asleep. There wasn't a lot to do besides nap.

When he woke, his dog was missing.

"Ginger!" he cried, panicked, not knowing what Louis might do to her. When he tried to stand, he discovered he was handcuffed to the bars.

"Louis! LOUIS!"

The basement door opened and the dog ran down the steps.

"Take it easy, Jere. I took the mutt for a walk. I don't want her shitting on the floor in there."

Jeremy rattled the cuffs. "And *this?*"

"Keep you inside. Can't take chances when I open up the door, right?" He turned the key and the door sprung open. Ginger trotted inside and jumped up on the cot.

"I have to go."

"Number one or number two?"

Jeremy stared incredulously. "*What?*"

Louis laughed. "Piss or shit, asshole?"

"Ah, fuck."

"That's not an option."

"Just give me a roll of toilet paper, you stupid prick."

Louis placed a bucket and a roll of toilet paper inside the cage. "Leave it by the door when you finish."

"Hey—can I have something to read? It's boring down here."

Louis stared, a blank look in his eyes.

"Well?"

"I'm thinking..." He looked from Jeremy to the dog and back again. "I guess it doesn't matter. You're not going anywhere. It's not like it'll speed things up if you're bored."

"Yeah, gee, thanks."

Louis rolled his eyes. From the corner of the room he pulled a corded bundle of newspaper and magazines and dragged them into the cage.

"I left you fresh canteens. And your dog has water too."

"What's for breakfast? Or is this brunch?"

Louis smirked. "Old rat dog here eats in a few minutes. I left her canned food upstairs. I'm having scrambled eggs, with crisp bacon, I think. Oh wait, make that sausage."

"Screw you."

He slammed the cage door shut and tested it to make sure it was locked. Then he went to the side of the cage and uncuffed Jeremy. "Enjoy your magazines."

Then he was gone.

Jeremy's hunger had dissipated and was now a constant, dull ache. Thoughts of food of every kind popped in and out of his head like some smorgasbord chorus line. At times he was sure he smelled something cooking, even before Louis had left, even during the night when it was doubtful he was cooking anything. Now he smelled that salty, greasy odor of bacon frying, that dry, crisp smell of bread toasting. Real or imagined, those aromas were torture, and they were wonderful.

He turned to his reading material. Page after page of food ads assaulted him. "Bullshit... I can't be this hungry yet."

Louis returned with Ginger's food.

Jeremy could smell the canned dog food—rich and salty and beefy. Probably had gravy in it. A surplus of spit pooled in his mouth.

Louis dumped kibble into the bowl and mixed it with wet food.

Ginger lifted her head and licked her lips; her ears shot straight up. Jeremy licked his lips and wiped the corner of his mouth.

"This is for Ginger," Louis said to the dog, in a singsong way, as if playing with a child.

Louis looked from the bowl, to Jeremy, back to the bowl. "Oh don't. You don't want to eat *dog food*."

Jeremy exhaled through his nose, his lips shut tight. "Of course not," he said. "But I'm starving! Bring me some food, goddamn you."

"You know the deal."

"What deal?" he screamed. "There is no *deal*! This is just you being a sick motherfucker! I swear to god, I'm going to kill you."

"Whatever." He put the bowl on the floor. "Step back."

"Drop dead!"

"If you don't stand back, your dog doesn't get to eat either."

Louis pushed the flat dish through the hole beneath the bars. The dog ate quickly and was done within a couple of minutes.

"Good fleabag," Louis said in a playful voice, rubbing her head.

He put a floor lamp near Jeremy, on the outside of the bars. "I'm turning off the overhead light. Turn this off when you want."

Again, gone.

His stomach was gurgling again, set off by the smell of the dog food. But he wasn't ravenous. Not yet. He guessed people had gone a lot longer than he had without eating. People fasted all the time, for days, even weeks. He could do this. He could hold out.

Kill his dog? That was beyond insane. Why would anyone even suggest such a thing? Especially Louis—Louis knew how much Jeremy adored that dog, how Ginger had been with him for over eight years. This was a demented bet Louis had proposed, a nasty, sadistic thing to even bring up.

There was just no way he could harm Ginger. He could never be that hungry. Never.

The first day Jeremy had been trapped inside the cage had been a Saturday. Late Saturday night, to be precise. The only way he could mark the passage of time was by watching the light streaming in through the windows, or the lack of it, watching the patterns change on the ceiling-high glass panes. Louis mentioned at every meal what Jeremy was missing: breakfast on Wednesday was blueberry pancakes dripping with Vermont maple syrup, fresh squeezed orange juice. Dinner Thursday was barbecued spareribs and corn on the cob.

By then, Jeremy was deliriously hungry and swore he could not only smell the food but could now taste it. He had a peculiar craving for peanut butter and touched his tongue to the roof of his mouth, imagining the sensation.

"What's today?" Jeremy's face itched from the new beard growth. His breath was foul, noxious, his teeth slimy.

"Wednesday."

"Wednesday? I've only been in here…" He counted. "Four days?"

"No, Jere. Today's the 17th. You've been in there for eleven days."

Louis opened the bag of dog food and poured some into the dish. Ginger knew the routine and sat patiently, waited to be served. Jeremy also knew the routine and stood on the other side of the cage, gripping the bars.

Jeremy sniffled, his nose jumping, not even aware he was doing it. The dog food smelled so fucking incredibly delicious. He had to have some.

"Don't move," Louis said, as if anticipating Jeremy's desire, as if reading his mind. "I mean it. Stay where you are."

Jeremy growled. "I need—"

"No! Take one step and she doesn't eat either."

Jeremy wrapped his arms across his stomach, doubled over as if in sudden pain. Clutched his sides, his ribs poking his forearms. He'd been on the thin side to begin with, and now his frame was nearly skeletal. No stores of body fat to rely on. His skin stretched across his frame like the skin of a snaredrum.

His stomach squirmed against his wrist.

The dog finally finished eating her goddamn bowl of food.

He was beginning to hate that dog.

She never saved him any food. All she ever did any more was eat, shit and sleep, eat, shit and sleep. He was sick of it.

He turned away, hating himself for feeling that way. Ginger jumped up on the cot and pushed her muzzle into his hip. He leaned over and stroked her head, and kissed the top of her nose. He could smell the food on her breath. She licked his face, his lips, and he tasted the remnants of food on her breath, on her tongue.

He stuck his tongue into her mouth, probed her teeth, searched for remnants of dog food. She tried to pull away but he gripped on her neck. His tongue explored her mouth, and her tongue darted everywhere, trying to push his out, to lick her own lips. She began to panic, struggled more, planted her paws firmly into the mattress and pushed herself away.

He let her go.

She broke away, yelping, and she jumped to the floor and crawled beneath the cot.

"Just what the fuck was that?" Louis said.

Jeremy scowled and turned away, stretched out on the cot. There was a dull throbbing in his head, an unrelenting pain that sometimes subsided to a small ache but never fully disappeared. A layer of plaque coated his teeth. His skin felt tight, ready to crack, pulled over his gaunt features. A fine layer of peach fuzzy hair cropped up everywhere on his body.

By day sixteen, Jeremy no longer felt hunger, not in a way he had once been used to. He didn't obsess over food any more, and the images in the magazines no longer tortured him.

Until the aroma of the dog food attacked him through the bars of his cage and raped his nostrils. Then his body remembered what it was missing and craved whatever it was smelling. Just the *thought* of a morsel caused uncontrollable salivating.

And every day, that dog got fatter, eating like a ravenous little glutton, her belly protruding, practically dragging along the floor when she waddled around the cage. Stared at him with her pig eyes, annoyed him with puffy dog cheeks. Fat dog with so much meat on her bones.

But that wasn't part of the deal. He didn't have to eat her. Only kill her. That had been the argument, after all. Louis had insisted Jeremy would sacrifice the dog to save his own life, and Jeremy had insisted Louis was crazy. That dog was Jeremy's life. She was like his child.

But at this point, he would have gladly sacrificed his child, if he had any.

He watched her trot around the cage and wondered how he could do it. Not whether or not he *could* do it, but what he would use to do it. She was just a dog. He kept saying that, his mantra, over and over, she meant nothing to him, she was just a stupid dog.

So how would he do it? Break her neck? Did he have the strength for that? The string that had been used to bundle the magazines and newspapers was still in the corner of the cage. He could use it to hang her. It should be strong enough. Or he could smother her with his pillow or drown her in her bowl of water or—

Christ! What was he thinking?

He leaned forward and sobbed into his cupped palms. He loved his dog. It would be like killing a daughter. There was just no way he could do it. He was going to die in this cage.

By day nineteen, Jeremy no longer acknowledged Louis when he came down to the basement.

This didn't appear to faze Louis.

"Come 'n get it!" He banged the food dish on the bars. "Come on, Ginger. Yummy yum!"

His exaggerated tone, his incessant teasing no longer bothered Jeremy. Like every other bit of stimulus, it rested quietly in the back of his brain, perhaps to be retrieved later, but not worth the energy or expenditure of calories.

Ginger ran over and wolfed her food, bits of kibble and chunks of gooshy canned food flying. Jeremy didn't bother watching any more. He didn't bother trying to steal the food away from her; Louis always stood vigil over it. So he folded his forearm over his eyes and tried to sleep, ignoring the overpowering smell of the food.

"How's it going in there?" Louis pulled up his chair; Jeremy could hear it scraping across the concrete. "Are you ready to kill her?"

He asked Jeremy this every single day, often more than once a day.

Today, he ignored the question. He was retreating inside his head... where there was no hunger... it was warm and safe. Comforting. Slipping away would be bliss...

"Well shit," Louis mumbled, moving to the other side of the cell, approaching Jeremy from the outside. "This can't be good. Come on, Jere. Don't shut down on me. Come on, man." He reached through the bars and touched Jeremy's shoulder.

"Here—I have something. Hang on."

Jeremy moved his arm and watched. Louis fished through his pocket and pulled out half a Snickers bar. He unwrapped it and ripped off a chunk and carefully pushed it into Jeremy's mouth.

Jeremy gasped, made a gurgling sound. It was akin to giving a man dying of thirst a drink of water—the rejuvenation was remarkable.

Jeremy inhaled the piece of candy, groaning as if in orgasm. He first looked over his shoulder, then turned full body, snatching the candy out of Louis' hand.

Louis let him keep it.

Jeremy devoured the small remaining piece of the candy bar, licking his fingers repeatedly, running his tongue over his teeth and lips. He stuffed the wrapper in his mouth and chewed it until it was a wet paper ball on his tongue.

"Please!" he screamed. "I need food! God PLEASE!"

Louis grabbed Jeremy's wrist and cuffed him to the bar.

He ignored Jeremy's rants and pleas and took the dog upstairs with him.

"*I hate you, motherfucker!*" Jeremy banged his head into the bars, cursing Louis for reawakening his hunger, re-igniting his taste buds.

Jeremy was back to square one. Emaciated, weak, and hungry beyond belief.

Shortly after, Louis returned with Ginger, and after he locked her in the cage he uncuffed Jeremy.

"How can you live with yourself?" Jeremy asked.

Louis shrugged.

"Isn't anyone looking for me?"

"Sure, lots of people. They think you took off with that bartender whatshername. The one over at Dempsey's."

"Why would they think that?"

"Maybe because that's what I told them." Louis laughed. "Don't worry about it. In a few years, we'll have a good laugh over this."

"You're completely out of your mind."

Louis cocked his head. "Runs in my family."

"No kidding."

"See you later, Jere."

"No, wait! Why don't you stay? You never stay. I just want to talk."

"Talk to your dog."

"Louis! Come on. It gets so fucking boring down here."

He ascended the stairs, ignoring Jeremy's pleas.

Jeremy stared at Ginger through hollow, shrunken eyes.

The dog stared back at him from across the cage.

As if she knew what he had been thinking. He shuddered, suddenly cold, suddenly nauseous.

Wonderful. The nausea was back.

"C'mere, girl."

She stayed where she was.

His new beard felt itchy, uncomfortable. He scratched his cheeks until he felt the skin beneath his nails, until the tips of his fingers grew pink with the blood he had drawn.

Shoved his fingers inside his mouth. Chewed the bits of skin. Licked the drops of blood.

Suddenly he smiled.

"C'mere, Ginger." He walked toward her, slowly, gently called her name.

She backed up an inch or two and then hit the bars with her hind legs, her tail shooting through the bars.

"I'm not gonna hurt you, you dumb old dog," he cooed, and he leaned over and grabbed her around the neck, pulling her into his arms. He lifted her off the ground, her feet dangling, kicking, trying to find the floor.

"Come on, Ginger," he grunted. "You know I won't hurt you. But I have an idea."

The strength in his arms was minimal, but he used what he had left to lift her, and to play with her, try to toss her in the air. He chased her around the cage, playfighting and boxing and running.

The dog scrambled, unsure at first how to react. They played a game of tug-of-war with a sock, and he pulled her from one end of the cell to the other, egging her on, exciting her, making her crazy and bark and jump up and down.

"Go on, girl! That's it! Come on!"

Ginger panted, her tail a frenzied whip.

Jeremy chased her some more, encouraged her to run and jump, to overexert herself.

He couldn't take it any more. Exhausted, he dropped to the cot. The dog seemed fine. He clutched his stomach, tried to catch his breath.

Ginger lay on her side, panting, licking her lips. She stood up to approach him and gagged, her mouth opening wide. She licked her lips several times, as if trying to swallow some phantom object in her mouth.

She suddenly leaned forward and threw up on the floor, spewing rapidly eaten dog food that had not yet been digested. Kibble chunks sat in a gravy of bile detritus, steaming on the floor merely inches from Jeremy's bed.

Jeremy fell to the floor, landing on his hands and knees beside the pile of vomit.

And he reached into it and began devouring the kibble. The wet food was harder to handle because it had already started to digest and was rather liquidated, was already enmeshed with gastric juices. So he dipped the nuggets into it and sopped it up like it gravy.

The kibble hadn't yet softened, crunched in his mouth.

He'd forgotten what food tasted like—the candy earlier had gone down his throat as a reaction to the stimulus of being fed, but he couldn't remember its flavor. Couldn't even remember if he'd chewed it, or swallowed it whole.

The dog vomit, however, surpassed even the most delicious prime rib he'd ever eaten. He wondered, as he sifted through the puddle on the floor, why dog vomit wasn't a viable commodity, and vowed that when he was finally released, he was going to market it.

"No!" Louis descended the stairs two at a time. "Stop it! Stop eating that, goddammit!"

He pulled the hose from the corner of the room and turned the valve, and sprayed the water over Jeremy's feast, washing it away.

"Fuck you!" Jeremy screeched, reaching for the vomit as it floated away. "That was mine. I want it back!"

"Jesus..." Louis dropped the hose and approached the cage. "You're a mess."

Jeremy started to cry and pressed his head against the bars. "Please," he sobbed. "Please stop this."

"Don't you see?" Louis said quietly, urgently. "I *can't*. We have to finish this."

"No..." His voice was small, filled with tears and desperation. "It's over. It has to be over."

"It's almost over, Jeremy. You know what you have to do."

"But *why*? Why do I have to do this?"

"You know why."

"For a stupid bet? I can't!" He sobbed into his arm.

"It's more than that. And it's the only way out of there."

Jeremy called Ginger over and she went to him, jumping up beside him on the cot. He pulled her into his arms and rocked her like she was a baby, kissed the top of her head. Her fur was downy against his palm.

She licked his chin and nuzzled his ear, poked her head into the crook of his arm.

"I love you, Ginger," he whispered. "Please forgive me, please."

He had never felt so much pain before, the thick, palpable ache in his heart, feeling heavy and unnatural in his chest.

But he knew Louis was serious. Knew he would never let him out of the cage.

No time to think. No chance to change his mind, to consider the most humane way to do this. He couldn't second-guess himself.

He wrapped Ginger tightly in his blanket to restrict her movement. One last time he hugged her, feeling her heart pounding excitedly through the blanket. And one last time, he kissed her.

Ginger seemed to sense something was wrong; felt nervous and stiff, but she didn't resist. She had no real reason not to trust Jeremy. Had never had a reason before.

Laying her on the bed, he pressed his body against hers, pinning her down. Now she started to panic, not liking this at all. She jerked her head around and stared into Jeremy's eyes, as if pleading. A small yelp came out of her mouth.

He pressed the pillow over her face and shoved her head into the mattress.

She struggled frantically, tried to escape, thrashed beneath him, but her movements were limited.

Less than a minute later, she went limp.

Jeremy wailed, and tears poured down his cheeks. He bundled her in his arms and rocked her, pulled her against his chest.

Louis had watched. "It's better this way. And you know it."

"Go to hell."

"You were way too attached to her."

"*So?* So what?" he screamed.

"You *know* what. It's just better."

After a while, Jeremy placed the dog on the bed. Her small black tongue protruded from the corner of her mouth. He pushed it back in.

He looked up at Louis. "You're not going to let me out of here."

"Of course I am. That was the deal."

Jeremy looked confused, even after Louis unlocked the cage door, even after he pulled it open.

"What are you doing?"

Louis shrugged.

Jeremy blinked several times, scratched his head. "You know I'm going to kill you."

Louis shrugged again. "Maybe. Whatever."

"What's *wrong* with you?"

"You still don't get it, do you?" He stepped back so Jeremy could exit.

"Get what?" Jeremy said, his legs shaky. He clutched the bars for support. "This was a two-parter. One was the obvious challenge. I knew if you were faced with your own demise, you would do anything to survive. And you did. You killed the one thing you loved most in the world.

"But on the other hand, you had an unnatural love for that dog. You were way too close, and that bond had to be broken. It was freaky."

"No it wasn't," he said weakly, sinking to his knees. "Not... not—"

"It was the only thing Mom left you before she killed herself. It was your tie to her. So of course you clung to it."

"You're just jealous," he said, panting, gasping for air.

Louis sat beside him on the floor. "Goddamn right I was jealous. Psycho bitch finally offs herself and you get the one thing she owned. Fuck you, and fuck her."

"You're as crazy as she was."

Louis grabbed Jeremy by the waist and lifted him off the floor. "You're a mess. Come on." They headed toward the stairs.

SISTERS

Sunlight from the high barred windows sliced the darkness. The girls shielded their eyes and pressed closer together, as if trying to melt into one another, into the stone walls marred by fingernails ripped from small bloody fingers. They huddled like trapped rats in the corner of their cellar prison.

Then the footfalls, like mallets pounding their coffin nails. They were beyond shrieking, had reached a state of denial and refused to believe any of this was happening. And as twins—identical in every way but for a slight difference in height—their reactions were identical. As though they shared not only appearance and personality, but soul as well.

The man stood before them, long fingers gripping the cell door, his face pressed between the bars. They turned their heads slightly and he smiled, sticking out his tongue and wagging it at them.

"Hello, my pretty girls."

They faced the wall, eyes squeezed shut. Holding hands, drawing strength from each other. But even that was useless. Even that gesture had become meaningless. But still they tried, still young enough to feel a kind of invulnerability. Understanding the concept of death but not truly believing it could happen to them.

Despite what they'd seen.

Death was something like car accidents and cancer—something that happened to other people. To old people. Death didn't happen when you were twelve.

The man sighed. Noisy, kind of silly, his lips flapping like a horse whinny. He pulled three oranges out of his pockets and juggled them, not very well, dropping one, retrieving it, trying again. He laughed, threw his arms up in the air.

The girls didn't find it funny.

"Come over here," he said, his voice quiet, gentle. Not the scary voice.

They were afraid to go to him. He always brought something different with him, some kind of twisted surprise, and each time was worse than the last.

"Come here." Scary voice this time. The girls looked at each other, waiting for the other to answer. They always ended up doing what he wanted, but if they waited too long to obey there would be punishment.

They nodded, almost imperceptibly, just enough so the other would recognize it. They released their grip on each other and crept toward the man.

"Good. Wanna see what I brought you today?"

They shook their heads.

"Aww, come on."

A cardboard box rested on the floor by his feet. The girls glanced down without meaning to, not at all wanting to know what he'd brought.

The man drew his hand down over his goatee. "Before I open it... I want to tell you something. I got this feeling, like you're not taking me serious and all. Maybe you think I'm not gonna do what I say. Right? Like you think I'm lying or faking or something."

No, he was wrong. They believed him.

"See, if you disobey me..." He leaned over, opening the box flaps. "All I can say is—" He shrugged.

They leaned forward to peer inside. At first they saw nothing but darkness. But he lifted it, offered it more closely.

The girls jerked back. One gasped, the other moaned.

"God, no..." The older girl—taller than her twin by two inches, just as she'd been born first, by two minutes—hid her head in the crook of her arm. "Don't!"

He smiled as he lay the box on the floor again. "Have fun, girls. And remember what I said. I don't want to have to warn you again."

Then he was gone.

"Why'd he leave it?" the younger girl cried.

"Because he's a pig. A horrible, smelly, rotten pig. *That's* why."

The girls sat on the floor and stared at the box.

"I think I can reach it," the younger girl said, wiping tears from her cheeks with the back of her hand. "Maybe I can push it away or something."

"Don't go near it." She pulled her sister away from the bars. "Please. Just.. don't."

"But why'd he have to leave it *open*?" she whispered, and buried her face against her sister's shoulder.

Slowly they wandered away from the bars, huddled again in their usual corner.

The sun that dribbled through the window slats had faded to a pinkish gray and had moved away from the cellar. The girls knew it would soon be nighttime.

The man would come back soon with dinner. They waited anxiously, because no matter how terrible the food, it was their only meal. Sometimes the man didn't come when the sun faded to black and the dark shadows filled the room. Sometimes it seemed like hours before he came back. And as much as they dreaded seeing him, the cellar was scary. Scritching noises sometimes, the whistling of air through cracks in the walls, darkness that was thick with despair. When he came back, he brought light.

He returned later, carrying a tray. He pushed the box aside with his foot and balanced the tray in one hand as he unlocked the cell door with the other. He set the tray down on a small table inside their cell. Burgers and fries from McDonald's. He folded his arms across his chest and watched them eat.

He didn't move except to blink, and one time to scratch his arm with the fingers tucked beneath it. "Finished?" They nodded while stuffing the last of the fries into their mouths. "Terrific. What do you wanna do tonight then?"

They didn't answer.

"Oh hey, almost forgot—let me show you something. You're gonna get a kick out of this." He pulled a folded-up sheet of paper out of his back pocket. He grabbed a roll of duct tape from a workbench in the corner of the basement and taped the paper to the wall beside their cell.

The paper was a *MISSING* flyer, the word *REWARD* written in large letters. Right below a photo of the girls. He slammed his fist on the bottom of the paper for emphasis.

"Cool, huh?" He laughed, shook his head. "I've been helping with the search. I'm even in charge of my own group! Sad the search isn't going too well."

The girls stared at the flyer. They began to sob.

"Hey, don't cry! Watch this. I'll cheer you up." No juggling this time. Instead, he started to tap dance.

They stared up at him. What the hell was he thinking?

"Stop!" the younger girl cried. "Why are you doing this to us? *Why?*"

The dancing stopped. He scratched his head, dipped in half until his face was pressed against the bars. He rested a moment, catching his breath. "Okay. Maybe it's the song. Let's see." He cleared his throat. "I'll be home for Christmas… You can plan on me…"

They cried harder. It was nearly *Christmas?* Stolen from their home on Halloween, the one time of the year they loved. Making their costumes took months, they were so elaborate. Now Christmas? They should be home with their family. Christmas was a time for miracles. Where was *their* miracle?

"*Fine,*" he said. "Be that way. You girls don't appreciate a goddamn thing." He crossed his arms over his chest and tapped his foot against the concrete. "Anyway, we're gonna play a game we haven't done yet."

"A what?" the older girl whispered after an unbearable minute of silence. "Nuh… No game."

"It's just a question and answer game, silly. It's easy. You'll see."

He popped the latch on the bottom of the crate and approached the older girl. Her hands flew up to ward him off, but he pushed them down.

"You know what happens if you fight me." She cried out at the pain he inflicted on her arm, twisting the wrist, bruising it. Then he showed her the inside of the crate, showed her it was empty.

She sobbed and let him place the crate on her head. The heavy weight rested on her shoulders and she sagged beneath it. A horrible feeling of claustrophobia overwhelmed her and she pawed at the box.

"Settle down!" and she heard the muffled sound of his voice, guessed at the words he yelled at her. She knew enough to calm down, before he got angry.

She couldn't see, couldn't hear. Could barely breathe. As if she were no longer alive, cut off from her senses, from the contained world she knew. The box smelled like cut wood and throw-up. She fought the need to scream, to fight, knowing she couldn't escape and would have to wait until he was finished with whatever he was planning to do. Her arms crossed protectively over her chest and she tried to draw in deep breaths.

The younger twin sat frozen, tongue resting on her bottom lip. She could feel her heart pounding in her chest, in her neck, even in her thumbs. It thudded in her ears, rushing like a river in a tunnel. Hollow, empty, echoing.

"Your sister can't hear us," he said. "So this is how the game begins. I need you to make a decision."

She nodded but didn't know why. She wasn't agreeing to anything and could barely register what he was saying. A decision. She was going to have to make a decision. Without her sister she felt useless and so very alone. She couldn't make a decision on her own.

"Here's the deal," he said, moving closer, lifting his hand as if to reach for hers but settling it back in his lap. "I'm going to let one of you go. But just one. The other has to die. I want you to decide."

"What?" the girl asked, finally finding her voice. "Nuh-no... what?"

"Your sister doesn't need to know. If you decide *she* dies, she'll never know it was your choice. Cross my heart."

"What?"

The man rubbed his hands vigorously on his knees. "Look. This is why it's a *game*. You get to play, to see what you'll do. It'll be fun."

"No! I hate you!"

"Calm down," he cooed. "Maybe I should have let your sister decide. Tell me, what would her choice be? Who do you think *she* would pick?"

The girl was startled by this question and stared at the wooden crate that housed her sister's head. What did it matter what her sister would have picked? This was a sick game, with no way to win. This was no *game* at all.

"If you want my opinion," he said, leaning in close again, trailing his fingertips down the length of her arm, "I think she'd want to live. I mean really, what kind of martyr would you have to be to sacrifice yourself? Even for a sister. I know you love her and all, but survival is an amazing thing. Don't you want to live? Do you understand what I'm saying? One of you gets to leave, but the other will end up dead. Rotting, stinking, dead in the ground. No more playing in the yard or playing with your dolls or trying on Mom's makeup or eating batter out of the bowl. Nothing. No more life. Do you *get* that?"

The girl felt dizzy and pressed her hand to her temple. The room was spinning, the walls rotating, bricks racing so quickly they became a reddish-brown swirl.

He slapped her across the cheek and her head snapped back. The spinning stopped.

"Don't pass out on me now." He smiled. "You have until tomorrow to decide. Tomorrow night when I bring your dinner. It will be the last meal for one of you. Understand?"

"No," she sobbed, jerking as if to move away but his hand was on her shoulder. "I don't want to!"

"You don't have a choice." He unlocked the fasteners on the crate and pulled it from the other girl's shoulders.

She gasped a lungful of air, finally released from her confinement, her cheeks splotchy. She looked at her twin, at the tears pouring down the girl's cheeks, her eyes swollen and tinged red. She took her sister's hands and glanced back at the man as he left the cell.

"What'd he say? What happened?"

How could she tell her twin one of them was going to die tomorrow? Even worse—which one was it going to be?

"Why are you crying? Did he hurt you?"

She shook her head, this younger twin, the one who had always felt protected, the one whose sister always took care of her. "He, he told me I have to make a choice." She lowered her eyes, refused to meet her sister's eyes. Blue like hers, blue like robin's eggs.

"What choice?" Older sister clenched the girl's hands so hard it hurt. What. What choice."

"He said. He…"

"*What.*"

Younger girl smeared tears across her face with her forearm. "One of us dies tomorrow, he said. He said… I have to pick who."

Robin's egg blue eyes opened wide, almost too wide, more like ostrich eggs now, and her lower lip trembled. "Why?"

"Nuh uh. Why'd he do *any* of this?"

They wrapped their arms around one another, and both knew they would never let go.

"Maybe he'll let us go," the younger girl said. There was always hope, that feeling of immortality only children understand. The possibility they could get out of this alive.

The older girl was more pragmatic. "Maybe," she said, not really believing it. "I guess."

They didn't want to discuss it further. They slept huddled, arms and legs intertwined, head grooved into shoulder, heartbeats matching, pulses almost rhythmically timed.

Sleep away the world—this was their intention. Sleep forever, undisturbed in a world free of monsters and freaks, a world unmarred by decisions that would make grown men shriek in terror. Sleep forever if they could, and feel no more pain.

At least they felt no pain. At least there was that. The children who had been there before them—freakish children with strange, twisted little bodies bumpy growths on their faces or torsos missing limbs. Children who screamed in the night, who begged for help, called for their mommies and daddies Sounds of torture and pain, of beatings, smells of burning flesh. Then seeing the dead, damaged bodies being carried away, removed from the basement.

The man returned the following evening as promised and called out to the girls. They tried to ignore him, tried to remain asleep but he was persistent He called to them over and over and finally entered the cell and shook them awake.

"Stop pretending," he said, sounding annoyed. "I know you're awake."

They looked up at him.

"So what have you decided?"

There was no initial response other than the quickening heartbeats, the steady pounding fear, palms that grew sweaty.

"We don't want to die," the older girl said.

"That's not what I wanted to hear. I was really hoping you'd be big girls about this, you know? I wanted to leave the choice up to you. So? Pick."

He waited for a response that never came.

"Fine then. You know, you could have made this easy. What's *wrong* with you?" He glanced at one girl and back again. "Jesus! All right… one more chance. Who lives and who dies?"

The girls were pressed together so tight it was as if they were one. They squeezed their eyes shut and tucked their heads down, foreheads touching.

"*Fine*," he said, and grabbed the twisted mess of limbs and dragged the girls across the floor until they reached the bars of the cell.

He wrestled one arm free and pulled it away from the bodies, handcuffed the wrist and secured it to the bar.

The girls were screaming, sobbing, fighting the handcuff, fighting the man as he wrestled them for another limb. He took hold of the other twin's arm and pulled the girls almost apart, handcuffing the arm to the bar.

The girls were no longer entwined but held their uncuffed hands together.

The man stood over them, dripping sweat, doubled over and breathing hard, trying to catch his breath. He swiped his palm over his goatee several times and shook his head. Then he stood tall, stretching his back.

A moment later he retrieved the rope he'd dropped beside the cell door, and bound their feet. He pulled the tied feet further apart, until their legs were bent behind them, and tied the ends of the rope to the bars.

The girls never let go of. They lay on their sides, in opposite U shapes, facing one another, their skin pale, their breath raspy.

A look of resignation had come over them, a feeling of serenity, somehow of acceptance. Still there had to be hope. Had to be a chance. Maybe this was a sick joke. Maybe he wouldn't do this.

"You'll have to decide fast," he said. "There won't be much time to save one of you. Minutes before you bleed to death."

He powered up the handheld jigsaw and hovered over the girls for a second before bringing it down on them.

He carved through the flesh that joined them stomach to stomach, cut through tissue and fat and blood vessels, sliced around the shared organ, and separated the conjoined twins.

He uncuffed the girls and waited to see who would win the fight over the shared organ.

The girls looked down, more terrified by their separation than by the large amounts of blood draining from their bodies, or by the slab of organ meat lying on the floor between them.

He waited for the fight. The twins, barely moving now, eyelids fluttering, bodies rapidly paling from the blood gushing onto the floor, lifted the severed flesh and offered it to one another.

"Choose, god*dammit*! Or you both die!"

Through glassy eyes the older girl watched her little sister die. But she felt nothing now. No pain from the deadly wound, no pain from the loss of the girl. She was moments away from being with her again. This she knew.

There would be no more suffering. This would finally end. "Can't... live... without her," the older sister said.

So hard to form the words... they slipped out of her mouth, almost uncontrolled, words mixed with thick bubbling red-tinged saliva. "Don't... wanna."

THE THREE WISHES OF HENRY HOGGAN

Who hasn't heard some foreboding tale about a dark, desolate cemetery? Who in his right mind would want to be anywhere near a cemetery in the middle of the night? Unless he's there trying to resurrect a dead relative.

As luck would have it—luck being a rather arbitrary thing—there Henry was, at around the stroke of midnight, wobbling drunkenly past the cast-iron gates of the Saint and Sinner Cemetery.

Henry closed his eyes, partly from imbibing too many Kamikazes at his favorite little pub, and partly from the dread of wandering alone outside a graveyard.

But he forgot two things:

He forgot he shouldn't be wandering around cemeteries.

And he forgot, right before making contact with the low-hanging branch, to open his eyes.

There's an old superstition about being near a graveyard at the stroke of midnight during a full moon on Elvis Presley's birthday, when the moon is in the seventh house and Jupiter aligns with Mars. Maybe the Elvis part isn't true. One can never be sure about these things.

When Henry bopped his bean, he landed heavily on the ground outside the cemetery. But his hand hit the fence, slid through the cast-iron slats and landed with a thud beside a grave.

Unfortunately for Henry, this was on cemetery soil. And perhaps coincidentally this happened just at the stroke of midnight.

After Henry opened his eyes, he sat up and rubbed the new bump on his forehead. He clambered to his feet, shook his head, and took a quick look around. He was about to journey on when he felt a sudden cold stirring in his groin at the same time his spine did the Saint Vitas dance. Something cold—something papery—clamped down on his wrist.

He closed his eyes, prepared to keep them that way until the sun rose or until the foreign object was removed from his wrist. Neither seemed likely to happen anytime in the near future, but Henry still refused to open his eyes.

Then, a chuckle—the sound a gentle breeze, a dance on the air.

Henry felt the Kamikazes—that most dreaded of bar drinks—trying to return from the direction they originally went. "Wha-wha-wha?" His best impression of Lou Costello meeting Dracula for the first time. *What the hell was in those drinks?* he tried to say.

The voice of the stranger was as tranquil as his hesitant laughter. "At your service, sir," he said with a bow, which Henry, whose eyes were still squeezed shut, didn't see. "What are your three wishes?"

He tried to peek at Henry's face. "Are you all right? Won't you please open your eyes?"

"No." But then Henry obliged, perhaps out of courtesy (although probably not), perhaps out of newfound bravery (even less probable), or perhaps out of some sort of ghastly curiosity (most probable, knowing Henry).

He wished he hadn't opened his eyes. His skin, particularly beneath the bone-white moonlight, took on the even less healthy tone of underbelly of dead fish. "Is this a joke?" he cried.

This ghastly stranger couldn't be standing there... rather, hovering several feet from the ground, talking nonchalantly, as if these were perfectly normal circumstances. The stranger's flesh wavered, as if composed of swirling cumulus clouds.

Henry assumed he was probably just way too drunk. Or not drunk enough. Why oh *why* had he drank so much? Especially tonight of all nights?

"Please, I mean you no harm. My only desire is to fulfill your wishes." The ghost inhaled, his brow raised. He spoke softly, yet there was a strain to his voice. As if he were trying to contain his impatience. "Let me show you. Come inside."

Without the use of hands, Henry was somehow lifted off the ground, over the fence, and into the cemetery. He glanced down. "How'd you do that?" Henry shook his head, scratched his temple, scanned the area for cables or wires. Grown men just don't float over six foot wrought-iron fences.

"What's your name, sir?"

"What?" He stared at the ghost. "Uh, Henry Hoggan."

"Splendid name."

Henry cocked his head and raised his brow. He resembled Nipper, the dog immortalized, destined to listen eternally to the Victrola and His Master's Voice.

"Splendid? Did you just say splendid?"

"My apologies! I've been dead a long time. I suspect my language isn't as modern as to what you may be accustomed. Eh... Groovy? Right on? Is that better?"

Henry shook his head. "Never mind."

The ghost frowned, bowed his head. "I suppose I didn't realize how long it's been... I suppose I haven't been paying attention."

Henry dropped to the ground and leaned against a headstone flanked with weeds and dead carnations. "Not to worry, really. I'm sure you'll catch up. Besides, those phrases have a way of coming back to haunt—oh, sorry."

The ghost sat on the ground facing Henry. "Please." His tone was urgent. "We're wasting time. Soon the sun will be up. Then it will be too late for your wishes."

Henry nodded. "Sure. My wishes." He snorted. "I have questions for you, buddy. First, what the hell is this wish nonsense you keep spouting off about? And second, why do you care whether or not I get my wishes? Whoever heard of a ghost granting wishes?"

The ghost raised his arms overhead and Henry cowered, expecting the sudden rattling of chains and inhuman howls, a la Jacob Marley.

Instead, the ghost stretched, long-decayed joints popping. "Well, it's not common, I'll give you that. But it does happen, when the conditions are right. You set foot on cemetery soil at the stroke of midnight."

"No I didn't."

"Yes, you did."

"No I didn't," Henry said, getting back to his feet.

"Your arm did."

"So what?"

"That's just it. According to lore, you're entitled to three wishes."

"And you believe in legends?"

"You're talking to a ghost and you ask me about legends? When you bumped your head, your hand touched graveyard soil."

"So now I get three wishes."

"Yes."

Glancing up, Henry said, "Suppose I go along with this? Let's pretend you're for real. What do I need to do?" Henry didn't wait for an answer. "Wait, wait, I know. Click my heels together and say, 'There's no place like home, there's no place like home!'"

The ghost shrugged. "If that's your pleasure."

"You'll supply the ruby slippers?"

The ghost looked confused.

"Never mind."

"Well then. For my first wish I want... hey, wait a sec. You're not gonna give me the 'Monkey's Paw' treatment, are you?"

"The what?"

"You know. I wish for something and get it, but only through some horrible circumstance that will screw up my life forever."

The ghost smiled patiently. "No, Henry. How inventive. But no. Nothing like that."

Satisfied, Henry said, "I want to be filthy rich. A multimillionaire."

"That's fine. But you have to wish it. You have to say, 'I wish I—'"

"Oh, bullshit!" Henry laughed. "You couldn't give me five bucks if cartwheeled from here to Bolivia, never mind make me rich."

"But—"

"Oh, and changing the subject, here's a friendly tip, pal. You really need to clean up your act. Your clothes are a mess. You don't make much of a first impression. It's no wonder I nearly crapped my pants."

"I was buried in these. Dirt does this to trousers, you know."

"Ahhh, don't get your panties in a bunch. Just trying to help out. And it's not that I don't believe your wish story, but... hell. No, I guess I don't believe your wish story."

Henry sighed. "You never did tell me your name, ghost-boy. Let's start with that."

He straightened his filth-encrusted black tie and tucked his soot-stained ruffled shirt into his zipperless black trousers. The ghost bowed grandly, arms extended in a wide gesture. "My name is Ashley."

"Ashley? Really? Sorry, man."

"I happen to be quite proud of my name. I'll thank you not to slight it."

"Touchy! Sorry, Ash."

"Ashley."

"Whatever. Been dead a long time, huh?"

"Yes, I think so." Ashley sat on a headstone.

"How long?"

"When are we?"

"Twenty first century."

"What? I died in nineteen-ought-three."

"No kidding? You're really well preserved."

"You're just saying that."

"No, really. Well, I have nothing to compare you to, but all things considered..."

"Really? I suppose I just aged well. Are you ready to wish now?"

"Sure! Let's get this done. Do I get the money now?"

Ashley stroked his chin. "I believe so. I'll try."

"Let's do this right. Down on your knees, pal."

"Pardon me?"

"Hell, if I'm going to do this right, and have to be master or ruler or whatever to your ghoul-slave thing, then you have to play your part, too."

"Play my part?" He rolled his eyes but quickly genuflected before Henry.

"No way, buddy. Kneel. Knees in the dirt."

Ashley groaned. "You're rather enjoying this, aren't you?"

"Yup."

Ashley fell to both knees.

"Good. Now say, 'Your wish is my command oh lord and master.'"

"I'm not exactly enjoying this. In fact, the only reason I'm doing this at all is because it's required of me."

"Just shut up and do it."

"Your wish is my command oh lord and master."

"Excellent. Okay. I wish I was a filthy rich multimillionaire." He glanced around. Nothing. No sign of a change, no sign of money. "Satisfied, you freak? I told you—"

A suitcase materialized at Henry's feet.

Henry opened it and stared at the stacks of money inside. "Well now," he said, grinning. "I'm out of here!"

"What?" Ashley cried.

"I'm satisfied. I don't need anything else. Keep the other two wishes. In fact, you use them. A gift."

"It doesn't work that way." Ashley squeaked, swallowing hard. "You don't want to do that."

"Why not?"

"You've earned three wishes, Henry. You can have anything you want, anything at all."

"I'm happy enough." He tried to walk away but Ashley blocked his path. "Out of my way, Ash."

"You can have anything you want. Mansions, castles. You could be the most powerful man on the planet.

"I'm rich, Ashley. I can buy anything I want."

"World peace? End hunger? I could make you president or a theater star like E.H. Sothern. Or a movie actor, like Lionel Blythe."

"Who? Never mind. Okay, ghost. Make me look like Brad Pitt."

"Who?"

"You've got to be kidding. Oh, boy, this isn't going to be easy. Let's see…"

"Hurry, Henry, choose someone because soon it will be sunrise."

"What are you, a vampire? Besides, it's only—" He glanced at his watch. "Four forty. We have two hours, at least."

"Less than that. Besides, at the pace you're going…"

"Just give me a minute."

Ashley wouldn't have minded a minute, but the trouble was, Henry used ninety of them trying to pick a face Ashley had heard of, which proved rather difficult, since Ashley had never actually seen a movie. So Henry described, as best as he could, Alec Baldwin's gorgeous features.

"We don't have much time before sunrise—"

"Down on your knees then and—"

Ashley fell to his knees. "Yourwishismycommandohlordandmaster!"

"Well then. I wish I looked like Alec Baldwin."

Henry checked his face in the shiny reflective surface of the back of his watch. Alec Baldwin (or as close a facsimile as Ashley could conjure) stood where Henry had just moments before.

"Your third wish then? There's less than fifteen minutes left before the sun's reappearance."

"Well goodness gracious, I don't know what else to wish for…"

"You could change the world, Henry. You could own the world! Do you hear me? Henry? Henry? You could—"

"I still don't understand what you're so excited about. What do you care if I get all my wishes or not?"

"I told you before. It's a rule.

"Okay, then, world peace." Henry hesitated. "Nah, I really don't care about world peace. I know! Women. All shapes and sizes, all wanting me."

Ashley collapsed to his knees. "Yourwishismycommandohlordandmaster!"

"I wish to be the most desirable man in the world."

"Finally!" Ashley threw his arms up in the air and jumped up and down. "After all this time! I'm giddy!"

"Maybe you should calm down, boy."

Ashley laughed, throwing his head back. "I'm free! You miserable toad, I'm finally free. If anyone deserves this cruel twist of fate, it's you, Henry Hoggan! You horrid, wretched man."

Henry smiled humorlessly. "I'd have to say I agree with you, Ash. I *am* a bastard. You see, Ash, I found this old book a while ago, sitting up in my grandma's attic. I was looking for antiques. She wouldn't miss anything anyway, the nasty, senile crow.

"Anyway, this book was full of bizarre stories. Folklore, old wives' tales, junk like that. I normally don't believe in that crap, but I figured what the hell, been having some bad luck with a couple of loan sharks lately. But I didn't expect any of this to be true, not in a million years."

"What are you saying?"

"I tried a spell a few weeks ago. Some simple little thing involving a coworker and a rash. I'll spare you the details. I thought maybe the success was just a coincidence. Stuff like that doesn't really work, right? But I tried another little spell, then another, and they kept working. So I figured I'd try my luck here."

"But you used all three wishes! You lose, Henry."

"Not really. I made wish number three at six-forty. Well past the six-thirty-two sunrise." Henry burst out laughing.

Ashley collapsed to the ground, trembling. "That's not fair." He lowered his head. "I couldn't have been tricked; I have an internal clock of sorts. I have never been wrong about a sunrise."

"Tricked you with a different spell." Henry grinned. "That book is amazing. Hey, shit happens. Well, Ash. It's been real."

"Real what?"

Henry laughed and glanced around one last time, grabbed his million-dollar suitcase and headed cheerfully out of the Saint and Sinner Cemetery.

Moments after stepping outside the gate, the suitcase disappeared from his hands. He felt his face transform back from Alec Baldwin to Henry Hoggan. "What the hell just happened?" he screamed.

Ashley leaned against a headstone that read:

Here lies Morgan Brackman
1795-1840
Told you I weren't feeling good

"Well, Henry, dear man, you didn't read far enough. Looks like you forgot the Spell of Ephemeral Reversals."

"The what?"

"Anything produced by a ghost stays that way. Unless you invoke the proper spell to offset it, of course. Looks like you forgot that part."

"I didn't see that spell!"

Ashley crossed his arms and smirked. "Could have been written in Latin."

"No!" Henry shrieked, searching the ground for the missing suitcase.

"Oh, and Henry?" Ashley twiddled his fingers at him. "*Carpe noctem, vade in pacem*," and muttered a few more things in Latin. "You've opened up the gates tonight, Henry old boy. Anything goes. Including me!"

Suddenly Henry was inside the cemetery, and Alec Baldwin stood outside the gates.

"Bye, Henry, it's been real." Alec/Ashley disappeared into the night, glancing back once and fully enjoying the look of shock on Henry Hoggan's face.

NOT WITH A BANG BUT A WHIMPER

This is the way the world ends
This is the way the world ends
This is the way the world ends
Not with a bang but a whimper.
                    —from *The Hollow Men* by T.S. Eliot

"That they're kids—that's the worst of it. They can't understand what's happening to them, can't be held responsible. So that really is the worst of it—when you see a kid and you have to put it down."

Harley sipped his beer—bottle only, no tap—no telling what might be floating in the tap line these days. He threw back his head like he was about to bust a gut laughing but came back up with a poker face. His Stetson was tilted to one side, but that was unintentional. It just flopped that way.

"They's all Rotters, though," the bartender said as she wiped a shotglass with a bar rag. "No use feelin' sorry for 'em, Harley."

He shrugged, and looked somewhat disgusted. "It's that sort of thinking's what keeps me sane. But it still ain't easy, them so young. You can't help but feel sorry for 'em. Rotters or not." He took a sip from his bottle. "You never had kids. Did you." He thought about his own son, now dead. And he thought maybe the boy's death had turned out to be a good thing, considering. Not that he really meant it, not really, not at all, but he was grateful his boy didn't have to go through this. He chastised himself for allowing the thought to pass through his brain.

It was the bartender's turn to shrug. "No, no kids." She changed the subject back. "They ain't human no more, Harley."

He paid his tab and left a generous tip and walked out into the sunlight. Sometimes it was easy to forget he'd been drinking so early, and daylight could be a surprise. Like going to a movie matinee—some things were just better suited for night.

The list jutted from his hip pocket and he pulled it out for the hundredth time that day. Mostly descriptions and possible locations. Names were included but weren't useful in his hunt—they no longer responded to their names. He hunted, for those parents who wanted their kids back, no matter what condition they might be in. No matter what condition Harley would inflict on them. *This is what he'd been reduced to*, he'd think bitterly. *Goddamn truant officer with a pistol.*

He didn't bother with a motorcycle—which most people assumed he drove—hell, Harley was his birth name, not his vehicle of choice—and climbed into his Ford pickup and headed toward the sticks. Tim Gorman had last been spotted in the Highland Woods area.

He shouldered his backpack, locked the truck and headed into the overgrown forest known as The Highlands. Long pants and heavy work boots protected him from the elements, particularly rattlers. He hiked about half a mile in, marking his trail by spray-painting small red Xs on tree trunks, when he picked up the boy's trail.

He assumed it was the boy's. Evidence a young man had been here, particularly this young man—tatters of his Megadeth T-shirt were draped over shrubs, caught in brambles and prickers. He'd surely be hiding. One thing the Rotters shared was an uncanny sixth sense, an understanding they were in danger. Even with their now-limited brain function they knew to hide. Until maddening hunger drew them back out into the open.

"Come on, kiddo," he said quietly, treading carefully over branches and mulch, drying patches of mud squelching beneath his boots.

He stopped only long enough to wipe his sweaty forehead with a bandana. Harley's search for the Gorman kid had taken the better part of the morning. Finally he spotted the boy—and Harley thought of the term loosely, because Timmy was almost a man, big and cumbersome in life, now just ogreish in death. Timmy was chewing on something. Something thick, dark; something long and fat like a branch but decidedly hairier and with features branches just don't possess.

Timmy was feasting on a human arm, ripping out chunks of flesh with his rotted teeth, pus dribbling from his facial lesions and soaking his meal. Not that he seemed to mind.

"Awww, god." Harley groaned, wiping the spittle out of the corner of his mouth. Bile clawed up his esophagus and into the back of his throat and he swallowed twice, three times to keep his breakfast down.

There was no hope for this one. Too far gone, too many days had passed and Timmy was a full-blown Rotter now. Carefully Harley aimed, shooting off the top of Timmy's skull. Enough of his face was still intact so the family would at least have the comfort of receiving the body in recognizable condition. Unfortunately, head trauma was the only really effective way of dispatching a Rotter, and as long as Harley removed a good part of the gray matter, he knew the job was complete.

Harley tagged the body and added the name to his report. When he returned to his truck he called Dispatch, who would then notify the Recovery Crew. Hopefully they'd get there before animals or the elements—or some other Rotter—got to the boy first. Normally the crew was timely, but lately business had exploded and they could barely keep up.

Two left on the list for the day. Twin girls. He studied their pictures.

As he drove, he wondered about the survival of the human race. Whatever this was, this disease, this infection that had doomed the children was dooming humanity. Newborn Rotters, chewing and clawing their way out of their mothers' wombs, or children changing into these flesh-consuming creatures... going to bed perfectly normal, parents breathing a collective sigh of relief and falling to their knees in supplication suddenly finding themselves fighting for their lives against their ravenous monstrosities in the middle of the night. No one knew what had caused the disease. Or how to cure it, despite children being studied, examined—autopsied. It was no longer safe to try to keep them alive. They had become too much of a threat.

Harley's job as a police officer and his proficiency with his firearm made him the perfect candidate for this detail. A job he despised. Calls from frantic parents had disturbed him at all hours of the day and night at home. Threats. Pleas. He'd heard it all. Warnings that if he killed their baby they would hunt him down and—

But this was all part of the job. So he'd had his phone number changed and unlisted and the calls stopped.

The kids (he could never bring himself to think of them as Rotters) tended to take to the woods. They avoided the towns. Maybe it was something instinctive, maybe somehow they felt safe. *Safe.*

Molly and Melissa, age six. Born three minutes apart. Changed into Rotters only that morning, and had last been seen heading into the woods behind their house. Woods that covered hundreds of miles. One thing about Rotters, though—they didn't move too quickly. They could attack at rapid-fire speed once the illness had advanced, but they tended to travel slowly, as if lost, as if unable to decide where they wanted to go. And the younger ones, the ones who had not yet developed social or coping skills, the ones who had been clumsy in life and were just getting used to their own bodies were even slower.

It took Harley about an hour to pick up their trail. The air was thick in that part of the woods, swampy, almost soupy; hordes of mosquitoes and black flies assaulted him as he made his way through the dense foliage.

A short while later he spotted them in a clearing, huddled together as they rested beneath a weeping willow.

"There you are, girls," he whispered, catching his breath, closing in on them. He left his pistol holstered as he crept quietly through the bushes and approached them from the side.

One of the girls lifted her head, looked in his direction but didn't seem to have spotted him. The girls appeared almost normal; the telltale vacuous expression wasn't usually evident until several days after the change began. But the other signs were there—the oozing sores, the distorted, runny facial features—as if the kids had been dead for days and were walking the earth again. And the animal-like demeanor—snarls and grunts and mindless predacious instinct—made it obvious these kids were no longer human beings.

Their first impulse at this early stage was to run. In a few days they would turn predator, savage. But for now they fled. The first Rotter twin finally spotted Harley in the brush and took off into the trees, her startled twin remaining behind to watch the other run.

Before the girl could react and chase after her sister, Harley pounced, knocking her on her back. She snarled at him—language was the first thing to go, it seemed—and tried to bite, to claw at his face. The abnormal strength that would inevitably come was also not quite there yet, so her struggles were manageable.

He hog-tied her hands and feet behind her back and muzzled her before chasing after her twin.

The second girl hadn't gotten far and was attempting to burrow her way into a rabbit hole. Harley grabbed her ankles and pulled her out of the ground and tied and muzzled her the way he had her sister.

"I ain't gonna hurt you, kid," he said, lifting her up and returning to the spot he'd left the other girl. He then picked up the second girl as well—both children struggling furiously beneath each arm—and carried them back to his truck, carefully laying them in the covered flatbed.

"Harley, come in."

Harley returned to the cab and picked up the radio. "Go ahead."

"Where you been, Harley? Been trying to reach you for an hour."

"Huntin'," he said. "What's up, Homer?"

"Just wanted your twenty, Harley. Making sure everything's good."

"Everything's fine, Homer. I'm in the woods behind junction three. You sure my location's all you wanted?"

Static hovered in the air for several seconds before Homer finally replied. "The Captain would like to see you as soon as possible. We need you to come in."

"Why? What's wrong?"

Static again. Harley stared at the radio in his hand.

"Just come in, Harley." Something strange about Homer—his usual hard edge had softened.

Harley nodded at the radio. He'd report in. Right after he took care of the twins in the flatbed.

His house wasn't far from junction three. Sarah's car was gone. Odd. One of them was always home; it was what they'd worked out. What they'd agreed to.

Harley unlocked the front door and poked his head inside. "Sarah?" No reply. He left the door open and went back to the truck to retrieve the twins, hoisted them beneath each arm and carried them into the house.

When he opened the basement door, the pungent odor of decay burned his nostrils. He'd never get used to that smell, like sulfur and rotting fish, like gangrenous flesh baking in the midday sun.

He took a deep breath of hallway air before plunging into the fetid stench that waited for him a few steps away. In the basement, he carefully laid Molly and Melissa on the dirt floor and prepared their spots.

This was getting worse, much worse. There was no denying this was a progressive disease.

In the far corner of the room, the little boy once known as Jason Wheeler was developing into something unrecognizable. What had been pockets of pus sores were now runny leaks, consuming his limbs in ebola fashion, distorting his face into a mass of spongy tissue. His nose was missing, the cartilage having dissolved into his cheeks. Black holes filled his mouth, nubs that had once been teeth gnashing and snapping at Harley. That little boy, all of eight years old, was now a misshapen mess, a caricature of his former self.

Around the room: the same. The children he had brought home to take care of and feed and love, the ones he could not bring himself to destroy, were evolving around him. Quickly developing into terrifying things without rational thought, becoming creatures intent on killing and eating and nothing else.

He prayed daily a cure would be found, that if he held onto these children they might be saved. And Sarah had agreed to this since the beginning, several months earlier, was worried about the poor children that the rest of the world seemed to have given up on.

Even though what they were doing was against the law.

Even at risk to their own safety.

He wondered where Sarah was, why she had left the house unattended when they had agreed they never would, that it was a dangerous risk. And he suddenly wondered why Homer had sounded so uncomfortable on the radio.

"Oh, shit…" Quickly he chained Molly and Melissa to their new spots in the basement, working carefully, then untied and removed the muzzles from the terrified girls.

Around the room, the other Rotters reached for Harley, and for each other, tried to claw and chew their way out of their restraints. He knew they would settle down after he left. They always did.

"Sorry, kids," he said, ascending the steps. "I'll feed you when I get back."

He returned to his truck. "On my way in," he said into the radio. "Homer? You there?"

"Yeah, Harley, 'course I am. See you soon."

He wondered why he hadn't asked Homer about Sarah. He thought maybe he didn't want to know; that if there was bad news he wouldn't have wanted to hear it over a dispatch radio. Not that Homer would have told him. Not over a blasted radio. Like last time there'd been bad news, it hadn't been delivered over a radio, it had been delivered by three officers who were like brothers to Harley and who could catch him if he fell hysterically to the floor. But that hadn't happened; Harley had retained control. And then he threw himself into his work to keep his mind away from the horrible accident. Keeping himself busy around the clock prevented him from having to think about his own life.

The warm summer air blasting his face as he drove didn't help with the queasiness in his stomach. Half an hour later he arrived at the police station. Despite driving with the siren and doing sixty along the back roads, he was too far out of town to make it there any quicker. When he pulled up in front of the station, he spotted Sarah's car.

The relief he felt when he raced inside and saw his wife sitting on the bench was enough to make him break down and sob like a baby.

Sarah stood up and threw herself into his arms.

"Oh thank god," he cried, holding her tight. "I thought something happened to you."

She shook her head and started to cry.

"What is it, baby? What's wrong? What are you doing here?"

"Patrick," she said, wiping the tears away with the back of her hand. "It's Patrick."

"Patrick? What?" He blinked rapidly. His heart pounded in his ears. "What about Patrick?"

Sobbing now, unable to speak, she just shook her head and clutched his shirt.

Captain Mellner came up behind Harley and laid his hand on Harley's shoulder. "We need to talk."

"No," Harley said, emphatically shaking his head. "Patrick's dead. There's nothing to talk about."

Mellner took Harley's elbow and led him into his office. He shut the door. "Sit down, please."

Harley sat, unsure his rubbery legs would have supported him much longer. Little specks of white light danced before his eyes. He'd never felt faint before, not even when Patrick had died in the car accident, not even when he'd had to identify his little boy's dead body. Not even at the funeral while viewing his four-year-old boy in his tiny blue suit. Not even then. Control. That was what it had been about. If Harley had lost control—if Harley had been forced to think about these events, which were impossible for a parent to think about—he would have lost his mind.

But now, somehow he knew what Mellner was about to say, and now the specks bobbed and flashed before his eyes like the Aurora Borealis.

"It's not just the living children who are developing this disease. It seems to be reanimating... the... uh, the deceased." Mellner sat on the edge of his desk and leaned forward as if prepared to catch Harley before he tumbled out of his chair and on to the floor.

"The caretaker at the cemetery called earlier—" (*Digger, wasn't that his ridiculous name? Are all caretakers named Digger?*) "—and Patrick's grave had been dug up. His and several other children's."

"Grave robbers," Harley muttered. "Some sick fuck—"

"No. He saw Patrick heading out the gates."

"Oh, no," Harley cried, burying his knuckles in his eyes. "This can't be. Please tell me this isn't happening!"

Mellner wasn't exactly the comforting sort and gingerly patted Harley's shoulder. "We called Sarah in. We wanted you both here. In case Patrick..."

In case Patrick comes home.

Harley looked up sharply, his hands dropping into his lap. "I gotta get home."

"No, Harley. I'll send a car to your house."

Oh, christ.

"No, Captain. I have to go home."

"Harley, I'm telling you, you're not going anywhere. You know as well as I do what the S.O.P. is for this. Parents are not allowed anywhere near their children."

Harley swallowed. "Then let me go with the officers. I won't go alone."

"No, Harley, you—"

"Captain, *please.* If it was Aaron, wouldn't you insist on going?"

The captain winced at the mention of his son's name. So far, Aaron hadn't caught the disease.

"All right. I'll send Tompkins. Ride with him."

Harley returned to the hall and Sarah looked up at the sound of his footsteps connecting with the tiles. *Sarah.* He'd forgotten about her.

"What's going on?" she asked, clutching Harley's arm, digging her nails into the flesh.

"It's okay, baby. I'm going with Tompkins back to the house."

"Oh, Harley," she said breathlessly. "*The house?* Oh, no..."

"It'll be okay. I'll think of something."

"I'll go with you."

"No, baby, you can't. This is a police matter now. Why don't you go on over to your mother's house? Don't drive, Sarah. One of the guys will take you there."

"Call me, Harley," she cried, eyes wide with terror. "The minute anything happens, you call me."

"You know it, baby." He kissed her softly and caressed her cheek, trying to comfort her but knowing he wasn't successful.

Tompkins' attempts at pleasantries and sympathy were appreciated but ignored. Harley knew the procedure, knew what Tompkins was attempting and he didn't want any part of it. The forty-five minute drive back to his house—Tompkins driving the speed limit, the moron—was interminable.

"This bucket go above forty-five?" Harley snapped, breaking his silence.

"Sorry, Harley. We'll be there soon." And Tompkins broke into another soliloquy about how sorry he was, how he'd want to *die* if anything like this should ever happen to little Ginny.

Harley thumped his head against the glass and tried to ignore the man's voice.

Finally they reached the house. They sat in the car in the driveway and stared at the front door for almost a minute.

"Might as well go inside," Tompkins said.

"No, let's wait here. We'll see him if he comes."

"Not if he comes around back, Harley. Besides, it's too hot to wait in the car."

Tompkins got out, his boots crunching on the gravel. Reluctantly, Harley followed, and stood beside the car.

"We can't go in," he said. "The place is a mess. Sarah would have a fit."

Tompkins looked over at Harley, shielding the sun with his palm. "What's going on here, Harley?"

"What?"

"You're acting strange."

"Think about what's happened to me today, and then think about what the fuck you just said."

"No, man, it's more than that. I don't mean to sound like a heartless bastard 'cause I do know what's happened to you today. But Harley, man, you're acting like you're hiding something. And you know the law, okay? You know you can't do what I'm pretty sure you did. But there's still time to fix this. I don't have to tell anyone I found him inside the house. Okay, man?"

The blazing sun wasn't helping matters. Harley felt clammy and chilled at the same time, and his bowels clamped up the same instant his testicles crawled inside his body. "Tompkins," he croaked, "you don't understand. It's not like that. Patrick's not inside. I just found out about it in Mellner's office."

Tompkins started walking toward the house.

Something was stumbling toward them from the woods beside the house. Something small, very small, something human-shaped but not quite human, something pitching and reeling and trying desperately to climb over deadwood and saplings.

"Holy sweet mother," Tompkins said, undoing the snap on his holster and releasing his sidearm.

Harley came up behind him and pressed his gun into the back of Tompkins' head. "I swear, you have no idea how sorry I am. But I can't let you do this. I can't."

"Don't, Harley," Tompkins pleaded. "Don't do this. You know what this means, man."

Harley smashed his gun into the back of Tompkins' head. Tompkins crashed to the ground like a bag of wet cement.

Patrick had reached the edge of the woods, about five yards away now.

The child had been in the ground for several weeks and the decay was evident, even from this distance. Harley shook his head, ignoring the stench that assaulted him from ten feet away. Much of the flesh was missing from his son's face, seemed to have melted away. Part from the car wreck, part from rotting in the ground, part, probably, from being a Rotter. A sob tore out of Harley's throat as the boy approached.

Tiny fingers clasping and unclasping, vacant eyes staring at Harley although Harley imagined the child didn't know what he was seeing. The shredded remains of his tiny blue suit, hanging from and falling off the child's body. Dark hair matted with dirt, alive with whatever maggoty insects had burrowed their way during his climb through the soil from his casket, and nested in with his baby's body.

This was his boy. His child. His flesh and blood, the light of his life.

Patrick had come home.

He subdued the boy easily—his police training had taught him the proper method. Despite the child's attempts to bite, to tear the flesh from his face, Harley had him under control. He carried Patrick into the basement and chained him in a corner of the room. Harley slumped onto the bottom step of the short stairwell and cried. How would he ever be able to make this right? How was he ever going to explain this to anyone?

"Jesus, Harley..." Tompkins stood at the top of the stairs, the gun that was aimed at Harley's head slowly slipping in the cop's fingers until the muzzle was aimed at the floor. His eyes weren't on Harley, they were taking in everything else in the basement.

A few steps separated Harley and Tompkins, and Harley grabbed the officer's leg, pulling him down the steps. Tompkins, his shock catching him completely off-guard, went flying headfirst into the center of the room.

He landed between several Rotter children who wasted no time advancing on Tompkins. The Rotters had moved quickly, tore out chunks of flesh, ripped off the top of the man's scalp and dug out handfuls of brain. Within seconds the man was dead; he'd barely had time to start screaming.

"Oh, god," Harley moaned, his breath hitching, his empty stomach dry heaving. This wasn't supposed to happen. He never wanted anyone to get hurt. He was only trying to save the kids—this wasn't supposed to happen! Slowly he turned and walked up the steps, not wanting to see what the children were doing to the poor man.

Harley stumbled into the kitchen and leaned against the fridge, bent in half, breathing deeply. The light specks had returned and he fought to keep from passing out.

He picked up the phone, dialed his mother-in-law's number and asked for Sarah. When she came to the phone, Harley was crying.

"You okay, Harley? What happened?"

"Come home, Sarah."

"Is—is he there?"

"Yes," he said, fighting tears so he could speak. "Yes he is. Come home, Sarah. I need you. I don't know what to do." His fingers clawed at the smooth surface of the wall phone.

"I'm on my way, Harley. We'll figure this out."

"Please hurry, Sarah," he moaned, and slumped down the length of the wall and squatted on his haunches, the phone dangling from his fingers. He tilted his head forward and sobbed into his hands.

From the basement, the little boy's cries sounded like he was calling for his daddy.

ORAL
MOHEL

"Well of course it hurts. What do you expect?"

"Then—?"

"Look." Alex wrapped his bearpaws around the formerly frosted mug, the large glass almost disappearing. "Really goddamned stupid, if you ask me. Once you hit puberty, you got all kinds of feelings and nerve endings in your dick. This is why they circumcise infants. But if you want to be a martyr…"

Jack sank against the bar, wishing he was drinking something stronger than beer.

"She ask you to do this?"

Jack sipped. "No. But she won't marry me unless I do. She'll only marry a Jew."

Alex shrugged. "She mean that much to you?"

Jack stared at his beer for the longest time, not sure how to answer. He loved Sarah. Yes. He loved her. That was true—but. But *this*? How far was he willing to go for her? So what? they'd have a fucking Christmas tree, right? Maybe a Santa and a Baby Jesus near the mantle. No biggie, right? Was this a crime? She couldn't marry a non-Jew?

But she couldn't. She'd made that clear, Orthodox family, very religious, very strict. Her father's approval meant everything to her.

Stupid bitch.

"You planning to answer?" Alex asked. "Or do I already have your answer?"

"I love her. I adore her. The sun rises and sets on her head, man. But this is my *dick* we're talking about."

Alex scribbled something on a napkin. "Call this number. My cousin Herschel, strict Orthodox. He knows this *mohel*, says this guy's the best, hardly any pain at all."

Jack palmed the napkin and tucked it into his pants pocket. The tension that had held him in a deadlock seemed to dissipate, vanished with Alex's magic words. Maybe there was hope. God—there had to be hope. His dick throbbed with sympathy pain, the phantom pain of the possibility.

*   *   *

Sarah, for a Jewish chick, gave good head. Not as good as the Catholic girls, but the Jewish girls tended to be looser. Six of one and all that shit.

"I'm going to do it," he said, his fingers entwined in her hair, forcing her mouth farther onto his cock. She struggled a bit but was used to it. He felt her throat relax, her gag reflex adjust. All it had taken was a few pukefests on his cock before she'd finally gotten the hang of it. Well worth some regurgitated burritos to train someone to have almost no gag reflex.

"Mmmph?" she muttered, her eyes jerking upward, trying to find his. He arched his back, his head rolling on his shoulders, avoiding her eyes.

"Convert," he gasped. "I'm going... to..." He grunted before he could finish the sentence.

Moments later, when her mouth was again free, she squealed. "Oh, baby!" He could tell she was pleased—she'd swallowed.

"You sure?" she asked, scaling his torso, laying her head beneath his armpit. He cupped her breast and rolled the nipple between his fingers.

"Yeah. I decided tonight. I'm doing this thing."

"You realize what's at stake here, right? I mean, I mean, well, what we talked about, you know, about—"

God she was giving him a headache. "Yes," he snapped. "I know what this means. Snip snip, chop chop, or whatever the fuck this boil does."

"Mohel, sweetie."

"Mohel, right."

"It's not that bad."

Jack glanced down at her snatch. "Oh really? How would you know?"

*   *   *

Sarah and her lack of sweet sextalk pissed him off. Her and her talk of pain-free dick cutting. All dickless women held this bizarre belief guys are kidding, or overstating the sensitivity in this precious area. So that pissed him off too. Her new haircut pissed him off, using jarred pasta sauce in her lasagna pissed him off, clipping her toenails in bed pissed him off.

Funny how none of these things bothered him before mention of a circumcision.

*   *   *

His family took the news of his conversion better than he expected. Aunt Millie, with a penchant for ending every sentence with the term of endearment "you sonofabitch," a woman who resembled Uncle Sal more and more with each passing day, threatened to go to the Pope to prevent her Johnny from ruining his life. And she'd do it, too—Pope Benedict XVI was, according to her, a distant relative. Jack was sure she really believed this.

Momma handled the news better. She quietly and without much fuss threatened suicide.

"They cut off your willy, you sonofabitch," Aunt Millie proclaimed, sopping up sauce with half a loaf of Italian bread. Jack made a mental note to get the recipe for Sarah.

"It's not that bad," he said, hunched over his plate. It was three in the afternoon and he was being forcefed mounds of pasta fazul and stuffed shells. Did they consider this lunch or dinner? This had never been made clear, not even when he was a kid. Judging from their ever-growing size, he figured they considered this a snack.

"Holy Mary Mother of God," his mother said, making a sign of the cross. She threw her arms up toward the ceiling and glanced at the stucco. "What did I do wrong? How did I fail you? Please give me a sign, I'll do anything to make this right!"

"You and Meryl Streep, Ma," Jack said. "Tied for the award. Listen, Ma. I need a favor. Can you loan me two hundred bucks?"

To Millie his mother said, "Set up the candles. I'll say a dozen novenas. Go downstairs to that Madame Golenka, the shyster gypsy fraud with the good candles and get me the biggest one she got."

"Ma? Did you hear me?" He didn't have the heart to tell her the money was for the mohel.

"Quiet, Johnny. I'm saving your soul."

"Christ, Ma, can you loan me—"

"Watch your language, you sonofabitch. Don't take the Lord's name!"

"Oy."

*   *   *

Jack finally gathered enough nerve to call the mohel. Yeah, Sarah pissed him off. Every little thing she did grated his nerves like they were a hunk of parmigiano reggiano, but he knew this was just an excuse. *Knew* it, which made the guilt that much worse.

"Can I talk to the mohel?" How strange that sounded. *Mohel.*

"Speaking." Someone female had answered.

"No. The mohel. The guy that does the, um." He lowered his voice. "You know. Circumcisions."

She chucked. "Yes, speaking. I'm the mohel."

He detected a hint of southern accent, a slight lilt to her voice. She didn't sound particularly Jewish. "But—you're a woman."

"How charmingly perceptive of you." Her lisp was slight, but he caught it. Images of this mohel flashed in his brain, the delicate skin that surrounded that southern belle charm. He saw her with a mint julep in one hand and a scalpel in the other. That pretty much killed the fantasy.

"I wasn't expecting a woman. I'm not sure I'm comfortable with this."

"I understand." *Ah undahstayun*. "But I have to say, you'll never find another mohel like me. Mohalet, actually. That's what lady mohels are called. But I digress. I've done this hundreds of times, and I'm the best there is. Precise. Quick. Almost painless."

"Almost?"

"Let's be real," she said with a slight laugh, her voice a comforting sigh. "There's bound to be a *little* pain. After all, we're dealing with a man's most sensitive area. The head of the cock is just chock full of wonderful nerves. I can respect that, and I take great care when I'm working on this most splendid area."

"I see." His dick throbbed again, pushed against his jeans, only this time he didn't think it was sympathy pain. Her voice was hypnotic, comforting. She was a hell of a salesman.

"What's your name, sir?"

"John Steppolini. Jack."

"May ah ask why you're being circumcised now?"

"I'm converting."

"Ah see."

"Are you sure you're Jewish?"

She laughed. "Of course."

"You sound… southern."

"Ah am. Raised in Georgia. Moved to New York six years ago. What's the matter, Jack? You never heard of southern Jews?"

"Guess not." A few seconds of awkward silence passed. "So. *Mohel*. Or *mohalet*. When can you do this thing? I'd like to get it over with."

"Next Tuesday."

That soon? Christ. Sweat tricked down his neck. Five days left to savor his precious foreskin.

Sarah was such a stupid bitch.

*   *   *

"You have to get that tattoo removed."

"What are you, nuts? I've had it since I was fourteen."

Sarah trailed her fingers over the tat, traced the outline of the name.

"No reason to be jealous," he said. "Maria and I were kids."

"It's not that. Jews can't have tattoos. I'm not spending an eternity in Paradise without you. If you don't get rid of it, I can't even spend an eternity rotting in the ground with you."

"Jesus, Sarah. I'm giving up a shitload for this marriage. What am I getting out of it?"

"Me."

He pushed her head down on his cock and wouldn't let her up for air. He told her about the ceremony next Tuesday.

After she swallowed she said, "Tuesday? How am I supposed to organize this by Tuesday?"

"Organize what?"

"The bris. You know. The *party*."

"Party?"

"This is a big deal, Jackie. All your friends and relatives—"

"Whoa—no fucking way. A roomful of people watching me get my dick slashed? Are you nuts?"

"It's not that bad."

He laughed. "You know what performance anxiety is? You know what happens to a dick when people are *looking* at it? Especially people with sharp instruments?" He shook his head, grabbed her shoulders, stared her square in the eye. "It *hides*. Retreats like a goddamn turtle."

"The mohel will know how to... you know. Handle it."

"Oh. Very cute."

Sarah smiled, then cupped his balls while her tongue flicked his nipple. "Who's this mohel, anyway?"

"Alex gave me the phone number, said she was the best."

"She?"

"Some mohalet."

"A woman? What made you decide to use a woman?"

"She's supposed to be the best. Very little pain."

"So what's her name? Maybe I've heard of her."

"Yeah right. Like you'd know her. Hadassah."

Sarah laughed. "You're kidding."

"No—why? You *do* know her?"

"So she's back in town."

"So you *know* her."

"Huh. I'd heard she was gone."

"Would you *answer* me? You know her or what?"

"No, not really. I've never met her." But Sarah grinned, shook her head.

"What? *What*? What's funny?"

"Oh, nothing. You sure you want to use her?"

"Well... yeah. I guess."

"You know what people call her?"

"Now how the fuck would I know what people call her?"

"She's called the Oral Mohel."

Visions of this woman in action popped into his head. "Uh." He licked his lips. "Huh. What does that mean?"

"What do you *think* it means?"

*   *   *

Repeated phone messages went unreturned. Jack tried everything to reach Mohalet Hadassah, without success.

Tuesday arrived and Jack, near hysterics, told Sarah he wasn't going through with it. "Especially not with her. Not like that. Not how she does it."

"It'll be fine. She's done this dozens of times."

"Hundreds, actually."

"See? Her method is just a little… unorthodox."

"Would you stop with the bad puns already?"

"Calm down, sweetheart. You'll only make it worse. You don't want your little turtle retreating."

Calling his dick a little turtle wasn't helping matters any. "I'm not doing this. When Mohalet what's-her-name shows up, get rid of her."

"No, Jackie." Sarah put out a bowl of bean dip. "Alexander will be here soon."

"What? Why? *Why?*"

"We need a witness."

"A witness for what? My bloodbath?"

"You're being silly."

When Alex arrived, he slapped Jack on his back. "*Mazel Tov*! Welcome to the fold." He leaned in when Sarah was out of earshot and nudged Jack's ribs with his elbow. "So you called the Oral after all. Nice move. Very nice."

"Yeah, well…"

"I wish I had mine to do over again. From what I hear, you're in for a real good time, Jack."

"Yeah?"

"She spends a long time down there. Really loosens you up. If you know what I mean."

The doorbell rang and Jack's skin suddenly retreated from his body. He didn't care how long this woman was planning to spend on his cock, the end result was going to be the same. And he found it unnerving the woman who was going to be performing this ceremony had a title that rhymed with toilet.

Oral Mohalet Hadassah arrived with all the grace of a hurricane and without the finesse. Andrew probably left less destruction in his wake. At least Andrew didn't steal your precious foreskin, rip it from your body like some Jewish ghoul.

"Hello, Jack," she said, taking his limp wrist and crushing it between her palms. "No need to be nervous."

"Welcome, Mohalet Hadassah," Sarah said. "We're thrilled to have you here. Your reputation precedes you."

"How kind." Mohalet Hadassah smiled, tight-lipped. Jack admitted the woman was attractive, but there was also something unsettling about her.

Something not particularly feminine. It could have been her height, her baseball-mitt hands, her enormous feet.

"You look disturbed," Mohalet Hadassah said.

"It's nothing." Jack pulled his hand away.

"Tell me. What is it?" Her lisp was ever so slight. Finally she smiled, and what she revealed seemed more mouth, more gaping hole, than teeth.

Jack shook his head. He wanted to blurt *You look like a drag queen.*

"Let's get started then. So, Jack. What sort of cut would you like?"

"What sort of cut?" Visions of meat slabs popped into his head. "Something quick and painless."

She laughed. "My personal favorite is the 'beauty' cut. Low and tight, though it causes the greatest loss of erogenous tissue."

"Jesus! I'm opposed to doing *any*thing that causes loss of erogenous tissue. What else you got?"

"I'll do a 'loose' circumcision. Okay?"

Jack's lips were numb. Sweat dripped from his armpits. "This is such a bad idea."

"Not at all," Mohalet Hadassah said, laying a rather large hand on Jack's shoulder.

Jack was sorely tempted to squeeze her tits, see if they were real. He really didn't want some shemale messing with his cock.

"I brought along a Circumstraint," Mohalet Hadassah said, looking at Alex. "Do you think we'll need it?"

"Wow. They make those for adults?" Alex asked.

"Not really. This one's, um, homemade."

"What the hell's a Circumstraint?" Jack asked.

"A device used during circumcisions. Normally used to hold down, you know, struggling babies," the mohalet said.

"Oh god." Jack collapsed on the sofa. "This is a bad idea. Very bad. Very very bad."

Mohalet Hadassah straddled him, pressed her crotch against his, ground into him. He was relieved there wasn't a dick pressing into him but was slightly alarmed when he started to get hard.

"Trust me," she whispered into his ear, nibbling the lobe.

Jack looked up at Sarah, who didn't appear particularly bothered by what Mohalet Hadassah was doing.

"We won't need the Circumstraint," she said as she climbed off Jack and retrieved her handbag. "Let's get started."

Jack wiped his face with his palm a few times and swallowed back rising bile. *God* Sarah owed him bigtime for this. She thought a blowjob was a big deal? Wait. He had wonderful plans in mind: whips, wax, whatever he wanted. And he was going to lay the guilt on her big time. He was becoming *Jewish* after all.

"Most men are circumcised at birth, Jewish or not," Alex said. "How come you weren't?"

Jack shrugged. "My mother—" He swallowed, waited for the nausea to pass. "She didn't believe in it. None of my brothers were circumcised either."

The mohalet led Jack to the carpet and pushed him onto the blanket she'd spread out. "Just relax," she said.

Relax? Sure. His cock had retreated faster than if it'd been doused with icewater. She was going to have a hell of a time coaxing it out again.

She undid his jeans and pulled them down his hips and off his body.

"I need complete silence," she told them all. "Save the questions for the end. I go into a sort of trance, and I can't be interrupted."

Everyone nodded.

"I mean it. *Do you understand?*"

"Yes," they said.

Jack nodded. "Let's get this done."

The only item the mohalet retrieved from her bag was a bottle of lotion.

"No knife?" Alex asked.

"I don't need a knife." Mohalet Hadassah knelt between Jack's splayed legs.

"Is it true what they say about you, Mohalet?" Sarah asked.

"No more questions," the mohalet said. She placed her hands on Jack's knees and slowly trailed them up his thighs.

Jack's stomach clenched and his balls withered.

"You have to relax," Mohalet Hadassah said.

"Relax? Are you kidding?"

She hooked her fingers into the waistband of his boxers and slowly tugged them off. His shriveled little cock tried to flee the scene of the crime. "Do they have to be here?" he asked, cringing, looking from Sarah to Alex.

"Yes they do. Witnesses. No more talking," she snapped. "Do you understand? Not one more word."

Jack nodded, closed his eyes to avoid having to see Alex and Sarah. And the mohalet.

Relax. Okay, sure, relax. Ready and—now! That didn't work. He couldn't yell at it, force it to relax. It was wholly unnatural to be so unkind to his cock.

He opened his eyes. Mohalet Hadassah squirted lotion onto her palms and rubbed them briskly together. She took his desiccated cock between her fingers, slowly petting the almost nonexistent shaft. She lowered her head and flicked her tongue on his balls, licked him from his ballsack and up the shaft, settling on his glans.

He didn't realize until he exhaled he'd been holding his breath. Okay, this felt good... and if Sarah didn't seem to mind, why should he? Just another blowjob, right? What did it matter whose head was bobbing on his cock? If he closed his eyes again, he could even pretend it was Sarah. Except Sarah never gave head as good as this. This mohalet chick had just started and already blew Sarah out of the water.

Mohalet Hadassah's breath was hot, her tongue probing, finding all the right spots. His cock responded eagerly. Her lotioned hands squeezed and pulled on the shaft. The tip of her tongue coaxed back the foreskin, exposed the glans. As she took him into her throat, he felt a groove in her mouth, on her bottom teeth. His dick slid neatly into this groove, surrounded by just a hint of the sharpened teeth, tugging oh-so-gently on random pubic hairs.

It felt dangerous in there, surrounded by those carved teeth, but so goddamned erotic. Just the slightest nibbles... a light burning sensation around the head of his cock as it slid in and out of her throat, her mouth.

Fluid dribbled from his cock. Blood probably. Too soon to cum. Very little pain, but what pain there was had mixed with a feeling of ecstasy.

The best fucking blowjob he'd ever had. He didn't want it to end. He'd allow her to shred the skin off his balls if it meant not letting this end.

He wondered if he'd be able to see her again, after this was over. He imagined himself in a threesome with Mohalet Hadassah and Sarah, and his cock got even harder. He didn't think it was possible for it to have gotten any harder than it already was. His fingers clutched the blanket and he threw back his head, jerked his hips, desperate to fuck her mouth.

Mohalet Hadassah deep-throated him, sliding the base of his dick along those teeth, dangerously close to his balls. He doubted his sack would fit in her mouth but she seemed to be able to work magic.

She pulled away from his pulsing, throbbing dick, and when the air hit it, he knew he'd been cut. His eyes flew open and he gasped. A puddle of blood spilled from between her full lips, but before he could say anything she went down on him again.

Her mouth was focused on the head of his cock, tongue flicking and licking the underside, fingers kneading his balls. She then began moving her head in a slow arc, his dick making contact with every inch of her amazing mouth. She went deep again, pulled him into her throat, bobbed up and down on the shaft.

"Oh, god," Jack groaned, unable to help himself, caught up in the frenzy of her actions.

"Shhh!" Alex hissed.

But Jack liked to talk during sex. Liked to moan and yell, liked to express himself. Besides—what the fuck did she care? His words were compliments, expressions of joy and lust. She should be flattered.

"Fucking amazing!" He gasped, catching his breath, stars exploding before his eyes. Reached for the mohalet's mass of blonde hair.

"No! Don't talk," Alex said through gritted teeth, his face draining of color. Don't talk while she's working!"

Mohalet Hadassah jerked her head sharply, clearly startled by their voices. Her face filled with rage as she looked at Alex. Blood suddenly gushed down her chin. Something hung suspended from her mouth. Something Jack tried to ignore.

"Oh, god," Jack said, right before he began to scream.

AN EXPERIMENT IN
HUMAN NATURE

Ernest brushed the hair from his forehead with his fingertips and leaned against the wall, clumsily setting his glass upon the mantle.

Young men playing dress-up, designer knockoffs, daddy wannabes, enjoying Ernest's parents' good food and good smokes and good scotch, crashing in the Tudor home somehow misplaced even among the Hampton elite. Animal heads suspended from the walls gazed at them with their dead eyes. A billiards table sat unused in the corner.

"Okay," Ernest said. "I promised you something interesting. Right? Now we see if you two have the jewels to go through with it."

Caleb uncrossed his spider legs and leaned forward. He set his cigar in the oversized freestanding ashtray (the smoke was choking him anyway) and rose to his full height. Stretching his arms overhead, his fingertips fell inches short of the eight-foot ceiling.

"This should be good," he said, cracking a smile.

Ernest smirked. "It wasn't easy, but I think it's worth it. Or will be, in the end. It's brilliant."

Ian, almost invisible in the corner of the room, said, "What'd you do?" His blue eyes were intense as he squinted at the two other boys. Curly auburn hair and a baby face, he was the youngest of the trio at nineteen, but only by two years.

Ernest closed the double doors. "Keep it down. Some of the staff may still be wandering around. They might hear us."

"So what's the big secret?" Caleb asked.

Ernest cleared his throat and narrowed his eyes. "We swore no matter what, we'd stick by each other. Right?" He strummed his fingers on the edge of the table.

"Yeah, so? What's got you so freaked?" Caleb sounded as if he disagreed, but he nodded. "So yeah. What's your point?"

Ernest blinked, his long lashes almost dusting the tops of his high cheeks. "A study in human nature," he said. "An experiment in perseverance. You guys think you have the stomach for such an experiment? One that'll be messy? I guarantee, it's going to end… badly."

Caleb said, "Messy? What's that mean?"

"It—"

"And end badly? What the hell's *that* mean?"

"Calm down, Caleb," Ernest snapped. "I'm trying to fucking explain here, so shut up and listen." He paused only for a second before continuing. "We'll be running some experiments. Okay? Just some tests. And I got us a guinea pig."

"What kind of experiments?" Ian said.

Caleb cocked his head. "What kind of guinea pig? Why do I get the feeling it's not warm and furry."

Ernest smirked. "Oh, it's warm and furry all right…" He sat on the arm of the sofa. "Do you remember what we learned in Professor Klein's class a few months back? About the strength of the human mind, the ability for a body to persevere, to survive at any cost? What I remember most were the slides of the concentration camp survivors from the Holocaust, and the Japanese POWs. Do you remember all of that?"

He paused a moment but wasn't really waiting for their reply. "I've thought about that. A lot. Wondering… wondering what someone might do if…"

The air in the room felt heavy to Ian, as if it was coated in cotton. He pursed his lips, the color of his cheeks now matching his hair. "If what?" he murmured.

Ernest ignored him for the moment. "Thing is, there's no turning back now."

Caleb sighed and said, "Will you please get to the point? What did you do?"

Ernest stared at Caleb as if deciding how to proceed, whether or not to let Caleb in on the secret. "It's already begun. I need to know what to expect from you guys. Because let me tell you, if I go down, we all go down. One for all, and all that stupid Musketeers bullshit, okay?"

He sat back in the chair and rubbed his palm across his mouth. "Here's the thing. I found a… a test subject. I'd like to see how much it will take to.. for him to break."

"Break?" Caleb asked. "You're joking, right?"

"Oh god," Ian said through fingers splayed across his mouth. He leaned forward in his chair, and his face brightened as he finally realized what Ernest was talking about. "You're talking about torture. Breaking some guy's will. Right? Am I right? Holy shit, Ernest! Who'd you pick?"

"Nolan Pierson."

"Who?" Caleb asked, but Ian knew the guy. Nolan was in their Psych class, and was in Latin and Chemistry with Ian and Ernest. Nolan was rather forgettable, with butchered black hair and oversized Buddy Holly glasses. The scholarship kid. His father was a janitor in the Harper Building on the west side of the campus. Every school has at least one Nolan—the kid whose Sears suit was never quite up to par, whose Payless shoes always fell apart a few months into the semester. The kid who wanted to fit in but just couldn't afford to, his clothes and his efforts always being second rate.

Nolan was a throwaway human being.

"Him?" Caleb said. "I know who you mean. He won't last—the guy's a loser. He's on *scholarship* for god's sake." He whispered the last part, as if naming a dreaded disease, as though naming it might inflict it on him.

"I think you're wrong," Ernest said. "And there begins our experiment. Who better than some poor kid who's had to struggle all his life to get what he wants? A guy who tries to fit in but never manages to. If he didn't have strength of character, I think he would have blown his brains out by now, *n'est-ce pas*? This guy has what we're looking for."

"You're awfully empathetic," Caleb remarked, his eyes at half mast. He snorted. "Like you really give a shit what this janitor's kid's been through."

Ernest opened his mouth but Ian cut him off. "What are you going to do to him?"

"Me? Not me—we. What are *we* going to do to him."

"Sure. Right. Then what?"

"Some tests." Ernest turned toward Caleb. "And to answer your question, dickhead—"

"I didn't ask any fucking question. All I said was you're full of shit. You talk about him being poor and struggling and all that but you don't care."

"Like you do?"

Caleb shrugged. "Never said I did. In fact, I don't. But you. You're full of shit."

Ernest smiled. "Oh yeah? I already have him in the house. Doesn't matter if I feel sorry for him or not. All I wanna do is some experiments. Like I said, this has already begun. I invited him over and slipped some shit into his soda."

"Well, I guess it's started then," Caleb said. "I'm with you. I'm in."

"Just like that?" Ernest said.

"I trust you, man," Caleb said. "We're like brothers. And I think this sounds fucking exciting."

They stared at Ian. He chewed on his bottom lip. "I'm in. You know I'm in."

A smile crept up on Ernest's face. He stood up and began to work the room, head drooping, fingertips dancing on air as if playing an invisible piano. His words took on a singsong quality and he began to list his good fortune. "We've got the house to ourselves... Am I right? Huh? Right? The staff should be *gone* by now. My folks're in the *city* for the weekend." He threw his arms up over his head in a triumphant V formation. "So there's, like, no one left to, um, *hear* anything." He giggled, slapped his hands together. "And... Poor little Nolan's tucked away in a safe place. Soundproof."

He straightened up, sobering in attitude if not blood level, and led them across the room. He reached behind the bookcase. "You ever see them old movies with the gothic mansions that have these hidden passageways and shit?" He pushed a panel concealed behind a copy of de Sade's *The 120 Days of Sodom*. A door disguised to look like part of the paneling creaked open. A light, musky air assaulted their nostrils.

Ernest ushered them inside and shut the door. They each held a flashlight, and Ernest led them down a hallway where the only sounds heard were their footfalls and the steady plinking of a leaky pipe.

They passed through several doors. On the last door, Ernest reached up and punched in a series of numbers on a keypad, locking it behind them. "Can never be too careful. We don't need company."

Ian brushed cobweb remnants out of his eyes as they approached a small room. He smelled something burning.

Ernest told them, "I don't think my parents know about that secret panel upstairs, or even about this place. Jesus, I hope not anyway. But I just discovered it myself a few months ago."

Light overtook the blackness. In the center of the room was a large, thick butcher-block table.

Tied to the table, naked and spread-eagle, was a young man with black hair. He was blindfolded, and his glasses had been placed on a tray beside his head. He was gagged, but that seemed unnecessary since he appeared to be unconscious. The slow rise and fall of his thin chest indicated he was still alive.

That burning smell...

Ian looked at the corner of the room. A large pot had been set up and something inside was simmering on a platform above Sterno canisters. "What is that?" he asked.

"Metal," Ernest said. "A combination of metals, actually. Some old figurines, melted down. Lead and tin mostly. Silica. A bunch of stuff. Carefully mixed and tested."

"Tested on what?" Caleb asked.

Ernest looked up. "Strays. Mostly."

"What, uh, what's the metal for?" Ian asked.

Ernest snapped opened a container of smelling salts and ran it beneath Nolan's nose. "You'll see."

Nolan's head jerked from side to side. He strained against his bindings.

On a tray table beside the butcher block was an assortment of instruments. Ernest stood beside it and picked up a notebook and pen. He tried to hand them to Ian, who refused and backed up a step.

"You have to keep notes, Ian."

"Why me?"

"Because Caleb is stronger. I may need his help with… you know. Other stuff."

"No way. I don't want my handwriting in any journal."

"You idiot," Ernest said. "We're all in this. Someone has to keep notes, and I can't fucking do it. I'm going to be too goddamned *busy* to write, asshole. Besides—" He pointed at the camera mounted in the corner. "—I'm recording all of this. So fuck you and your handwriting. There's a permanent record."

Nolan screamed a series of desperate and incoherent sounds into his gag.

Ian snatched the notebook and pen out of Ernest's hand.

Caleb moved across the room and studied the tray of instruments. "Ernest, you are one seriously disturbed fuck."

Ernest handed him clamps. "Start with the nipples. Just don't cut them off."

"Me?" Caleb's face contorted. "Hey, isn't that kind of queer? I don't want to…"

Ernest sighed, rubbing his eyes with his index fingers. "Look—this is an experiment. It's medical, not sexual. If you get a hard-on while messing with his nipples, that's your hang-up. Otherwise, just goddamn do it. It's part of the experiment."

Caleb moved to the other side of the table. Frowning, he ran his palms over Nolan's breasts until the nipples stood erect. Using the clamps, he grabbed hold, Nolan writhing beneath him.

"I still don't see what nipple clamps have to do with anything," Caleb muttered.

Ernest ignored him and turned to Ian. He said, "You ready? Before you write anything, I need you to help prep the subject. I want you to get a feel for this stuff."

Ian stepped forward and Ernest handed him the next instrument.

"What the hell do I do with—"

"We're all pre-med," Ernest said. "Figure it out."

Ian knew what he was supposed to do with the tool, but—

"Can you handle it?" Caleb asked. "Need help?"

"You couldn't deal with a nipple clamp, but this you're okay with?" Ernest said.

"Fuck off."

Ian swallowed back a mouthful of spit. "I… yes, but, I don't know how… I mean, I'm not sure."

"Just stick it up his ass," Ernest said.

"You got issues, man," Caleb said.

"I know where it goes," Ian said. "I just don't see what this has to do with your experiment."

"We start small, Ian. Clamps, a few tubes. Understand?" Ernest said. "Part of the experiment is a study in resilience, big and small. I have lots more planned. Trust me."

"How will we know what he's feeling? Isn't that part of the experiment? Isn't that what you want me to write down?" Ian wasn't sure if he wanted to know, or if he was stalling. He stared at the instrument in his hands. It seemed to have become very heavy.

"How the hell do you think he's feeling?" Ernest smiled. "Never mind. We'll ask him in a minute."

"Oh." Ian lubricated the end of the tube with Vaseline and tried to push it into Nolan's anus. "I can't do this," he said. "It's. He won't cooperate."

Ernest said to Caleb, "Make him cooperate."

Caleb nodded and took the length of metal tubing, which resembled a thin toilet paper roll, from Ian. He pressed it against Nolan, pushing and twisting until it found its way inside his writhing body, tearing the soft, delicate tissue at the opening of his anus. Blood tricked down his ass onto the table.

Nolan screamed into his gag, and he bucked his legs, but Caleb pushed the tubing in farther.

"It's in," Caleb said. "It's secure." To Ian he said, "Just think of him as a cadaver. Easier that way."

"Good job," Ernest said. He leaned over Nolan's face. "I'm going to remove your gag now. I want to ask you a few questions."

Nolan's head bobbed like a float on a lake. Ernest removed the gag and Nolan screamed and begged for help.

"Please!" he cried, lifting his head off the table. "It hurts! Take it out!"

Ernest stared at Nolan, a wry smile plastered on his face.

"You fucking psycho!" Nolan screamed.

Ernest stuffed the gag back in his mouth and clicked his tongue. "No use. He's just gonna be an asshole. How predictable. Anyway, the interesting part's coming up. I'll do it myself but may need some help."

He took a long thin metal tube from the utensil tray. It resembled a wire, but it was hollow, like the world's most narrow beaker.

Moving to the end of the table, he took hold of Nolan's penis, which failed to respond. "Grab it," he said to Caleb.

"No way! Nipples were bad enough. I'm not touching his dick."

"Look, dipshit, you're pre-med. You think you're never going to have to touch a dick? I didn't ask you to suck it, just to hold it. I told you, there's nothing sexual about any of this."

"You like bringing pre-med up a lot," Caleb said. "Seems more like an excuse for you to play with this guy's dick." Looking away, he grabbed Nolan's penis. It lay unresponsive in his hand.

"I need you both to hold him as still as you can. Ian, pin down his chest."

Ernest grabbed Nolan's penis and tried to push the metal rod into the urethra. Nolan screamed into his gag, his head thrown back, the veins in his neck straining beneath the skin. His body was coated in a fine layer of sweat, and the smell in the room was a mingling of metal, blood and musk.

"Shit," Ernest said, "hold him!" The rod kept slipping. Fitting it into the narrow urethra was more difficult than he had anticipated. "Get him hard," he snapped at Caleb.

"You fuckin' kidding me?" he yelled.

Finally, it slid inside. He dropped Nolan's penis and stood back, panting. Turned to the camera and said, "Goddamn. Okay. All tubes are in place."

Ian moved to the edge of the table. There was a small amount of blood on Nolan's crotch. It terrified Ian… yet somehow it was exhilarating.

"Ready to begin," Ernest said, grinning. He looked at Caleb and said, Pick an orifice, any orifice."

Caleb ran his hands through his hair and shook his head. "You're seriously disturbed, man."

He tossed Caleb a pair of heavy-duty work gloves. "We'll start with the ass. That tube gets hot, so make sure you wear those. Hold the rod tight. Make sure it stays up his ass."

Caleb nodded.

"It cools pretty fast," Ernest said. "I considered putting him in water, but that would have been a real pain in the ass. Can you imagine if we'd had to start dragging bottles of water down here? That sink is useless." Ernest dipped the metal spoon into the simmering molten metal and stirred.

"We should be able to get enough into the tube if we work fast, before he starts flopping around too much. Otherwise it's just going to spill all over his legs." He filled the ladle and held it up, steam rising, the smell of the metal stronger now. "We don't want to get this on us. It's over 200 degrees, so be careful. And work fast. Got it?"

Caleb nodded, getting a better grip on the thick tube protruding from Nolan's ass. Ian stood off to the side, watching them with a transfixed expression of revulsion and horror.

"When I'm done, pull the tube out fast. Then cover up his asshole with the tape and stuff." Ernest poured the contents of the ladle into the tube. Seconds later the liquid reached its intended destination and Nolan went berserk, flailing against the ropes, his agonized screams muffled against his gag. Moments later, he was still.

"He dead already?" Caleb blurted, pulling the metal rod out of Nolan's ass, covering it with bandages and tape to keep the liquid from leaking out.

Using the stethoscope from the instrument tray, Ernest listened for a heartbeat. He shook his head. "No, not dead."

Ian dropped against the wall and buried his face in his hands. "Oh my god," he croaked. "Oh my god."

"Get a grip," Ernest said. "We're not through." He removed the gag from Nolan's mouth, and a trace of spit and vomit trailed away with the cloth.

"Now what?" Ian asked, choking back tears, trying not to cry.

Ernest picked up the smelling salts. "We continue with the experiment. Should we remove the blindfold now?"

"But..." Ian scratched his head and stepped forward. "But then he could identify us."

The other two exchanged glances before turning back to Ian.

"What did you think was going to happen here?" Ernest asked. "He's got a metal block up his ass. Did you think he was going to just walk away?"

Ian swallowed and shrugged.

"I told you earlier this wasn't going to end well."

"Yeah, Ernest, but—"

"And you promised! You said you wanted to be a part of this, that you would always be one of us. You swore along with Caleb and me, fucking told us we were your brothers!"

"I didn't know you meant murder!"

Ernest looked at the floor before speaking, using a patronizing voice not unlike his father's. "I told you this would be difficult. I told you this would end badly. I told you we would be sharing secrets for life. What about all of that didn't you understand, you fucking idiot? What the fuck did you think I was referring to?"

"Come on, Ian," Caleb said. "You've got to see Nolan for what he is. A non-person, just an asshole getting a free ride. He's a leech, a guinea pig. He's a goddamned lab rat."

Ian looked from Ernest to Caleb and knew they planned to finish. Could he see Nolan as just a giant lab rat?

He tried to justify what they were doing to the slab of meat on the butcher block table, hidden away somewhere in a room that reeked of damp, dead wine, a room lit by a naked bulb dangling by a single thin wire. The expressions on the faces of his fellow scientists were feral, somehow evil. They were enjoying this too much and would never need to justify their actions. Ian tried to reason this was all for posterity, tried to forget this was how Nolan would spend the last minutes of his pathetic life.

"Okay," Ian whispered. "I'm with you." He didn't know whether or not he really meant it. For now, he did mean it. For now, he would stand with them.

Ernest handed him the notebook and pen. "Good. Let's get going then. First entry was, say, 6:00 PM. Let's see..." He played with the webbing between his thumb and index finger. "Level One. Subject gagged and blindfolded. Nipple clamps and insertion of rods and tubes. Slight bleeding. Subject.. uncomfortable.

"Level Two. Jot down, like 6:45. Level Two, melted metal enema injected Subject in extreme pain and passes out. I guess this is where we begin Level Three."

Glancing at his watch, he said, "Blindfold and gag removed. Subject will be revived and questioned for response. Start Level Three at 7:00 PM."

Ian wondered what sort of doctor Ernest would become and then remembered his particular fondness for forensic medicine.

Ernest continued his dictation. "About to revive subject." Then he grinned. "Level Three. Wake the fucker up."

Caleb waved the salts beneath Nolan's nose. There was no reaction. He waved them for another few seconds, then lifted the vial to his own face and sniffed. He jerked back his head and snorted. "Nothing wrong with these!"

"Oh, god," Ian moaned, peering into Nolan's face. "What's wrong with him?"

Ernest rolled his eyes. "Are you serious?" To Caleb he said, "Keep working those salts. See if you can revive him."

Caleb waved the salts and slapped Nolan's cheeks.

He continued the dictation. "Level Three. Subject so far unresponsive. Efforts to revive subject have been unsuccessful. Unsure at this point what—"

Nolan rocked his head away from the salts. His eyes rolled around in their sockets, trying to focus, unable. The whites of his eyes were tinged with pink, distorted Easter eggs.

Ernest leaned over, his mouth by Nolan's ear. "Can you hear me?"

Nolan moaned.

"Nolan? Come on, man, wake up. We need to know how you feel. For posterity." Ernest looked up at Ian. "Jot this down: Subject unwilling or unable to respond. In great deal of pain."

Nolan's eyes focused. He blinked and tried to press himself into the table. Opening his mouth, all that escaped was a belching groan.

"Next level before he passes out again," Ernest said, moving to the simmering pot.

"Burns..." groaned Nolan. "Help me..."

Ernest said, "This is going to be tricky. Ian, your turn. Grab his dick. Put on the gloves first."

Ian got into place and did what Ernest instructed.

"Hold it up, as straight as you can. Hold it steady." He turned back to the pot.

"Wha..." Breathing came as gaspinfg hitches, making speech impossible for Nolan. Tears streamed, dampening the hair along his temples. His eyes were glistening gems, brilliant and dying at the same time, a beautiful comet blazing to oblivion.

Ernest held up an oversized syringe. "Hold him steady. I'm going to inject this." The rod in the urethra was narrow, much thinner than the needle on the syringe. "Okay, hang on. He'll thrash around, so hold him. Steady now."

He stuck the syringe into the tip of the rod. Moments later, the liquid metal traveled the length and filled the inside of Nolan's penis.

His shrieks reverberated off the cellar walls. He strained against the ropes, as if in the throes of a seizure. A sudden snap followed Nolan's trailing screams before he passed out.

Ernest tossed the stethoscope to Caleb and traced his fingertips over the damaged flesh and bone of Nolan's broken leg. "Jesus christ, that was a hell of a reaction. He broke his own goddamned shinbone."

Ernest examined the rest of the body. The flesh on the other ankle was torn and bloody, but the rope had held. He secured the broken leg to the table with another length of rope before checking on Nolan's wrists.

Ian pulled the rod from Nolan's body. The liquid metal inside his penis had already begun to harden.

"Hold it up," Ernest said. "If you put it down the liquid will drip out."

Caleb held up the stethoscope. "He's still alive."

Ernest smiled and wiped his brow with his sleeve. "Level Three was a success, I would say."

"Look at this," Ian said, pointing to the underside of the penis. "The skin's burning away over here. But nothing's leaking out. I think it's already solid."

"I can't believe he's still alive," Caleb said, shaking his head. "If it was me, I'd sure want to be dead."

Ernest glanced at his watch. "Write this: Level Three achieved at 7:20 PM. Subject in agony, yet continues to live. Asked for help. Barely able to speak, yet screamed his head off a minute later. Level Three consisted of pouring liquid metal into his urethra, creating a permanent, solid block in his urinary passage."

He cleared his throat. "Now at… 7:35pm, we will attempt Level Four. Will see if administering liquid to victim while asleep revives him at all."

Ian raised his eyebrows. His hands trembled as he wrote the notes, jotting every word, wishing this ordeal were over. He leaned against a wall, exhausted from exertion and strain.

Caleb handed him a small bottle of water. "You okay?"

Ian nodded, chugging the water down his parched throat.

"Hey, look at this," Ernest said. Nolan's penis—ramrod straight and granite solid—jutted up and rested against his stomach. "Come on, break's over. Let's do Level Four."

He held up two small cylindrical tubes. "Ian, write down whatever I say. Try to capture whatever he says or does. If he wakes up."

"You have to hold his head back tight, Caleb. If he went nuts before… I don't have a clue what he might be capable of. These are going up his nose now. If he shakes his head, that shit's going everywhere. Hold him as tight as you can."

"Up his nose?" Ian said. "Won't that kill him? That'll like, fry his brains."

Ernest thought for a moment. "I'm not sure. I would guess it'll fry his brains, but in other tests I've run, it didn't kill the subjects right away. They kind of went nuts, but they didn't die right away."

He tilted back Nolan's head and inserted the small metal tubes into each nostril. Nolan's breathing became whistling gasps, and his mouth popped open to compensate.

"He's waking up," Caleb yelled, bending low and holding on tight to Nolan's head.

Dipping two metal basters into the pot, Ernest filled them with the liquid and rushed back.

Before Ernest even touched him Nolan responded, crying out and bucking on the table.

Ernest had to yell to be heard above Nolan's steady stream of guttural and hysterical cries. "Level Four! Pour liquid into nasal passages!"

Nolan fought, spit and sweat and blood flying everywhere, terrible grunts and animalistic growls erupting from his destroyed body. Placing the tips of the basters into the tubes, Ernest injected the liquid into Nolan's nasal cavities.

Inhuman screams poured out of him, seeming to come from some other level of existence. He strained against the ropes securing his body, fighting and stretching so spastically and furiously that sinewy cords snapped up and down the length of his body.

Blood gushed from deep ruts in his skin. Then he passed out.

Ernest collapsed. "Oh my god," he panted. "Level Four complete. Did you get all that, Ian?"

Ian's heart pounded and his head thudded. "I feel sick."

"We're almost done. Hang in there."

"Can't," Ian said. "Gonna be sick."

"We can't stop now and leave him hanging. We have to put him out of his misery. Take a deep breath. Get a fucking grip, man."

The three stood around Nolan. His once not-quite-handsome face was now a gnarled and hideous ruin, a distorted parody of his former self. Metal patches stuck to his skin and hair. His cheeks were open sores, oozing pustules of flesh and exposed bone where metal had leaked through. The lining of his nostrils were two solid metal caves. Bloody tears trickled out of the corners of his eyes.

Ian gently squeezed the nose and felt the soft metal shift beneath his fingers, felt the spongy mass of tissue give beneath his touch. His stomach flipped, and he wished he'd ignored that strange compulsion to touch Nolan.

"Level Five," Ernest said. "We end this. See what sort of resolve or strength this freak has left."

Caleb listened to Nolan's chest with the stethoscope. "His heart's strong, I guess," he said, licking his lips, stepping away from the body. "It's still beating, anyway."

"I thought he'd be dead by now," Ernest said, staring off at nothing. "Let's do this. Final level."

He grabbed a length of tubing from the tray. "This is flexible, like a garden hose, but it's metal. Coiling of some sort. I snagged it from the garage, when the mechanic wasn't looking. Open his mouth."

Caleb tipped Nolan's head back and pried open his mouth. Ernest fed the tube down his throat.

"Write this down: 8:00pm. About to attempt Level Five. Tubing has been fed into subject. The tube acts as a sort of trachea. Get ready, guys. This is it."

Ian nodded and licked his lips. His heart pounded so fiercely his temples ached.

"Hold him tight, Caleb!" Ernest placed a funnel at the end of the tubing in Nolan's throat. He turned back to the pot and filled a quart-sized metal measuring cup, then dumped the molten metal down the tube and into Nolan's throat. He pulled the tube out as the throat and mouth filled with the liquid the neck and throat bulging.

"Level Five!" Ernest cried, a look of triumph filling his eyes and spreading into an enormous grin. "Subject appears to be suffocating. His eyes are—"

Nolan's movements were lightning-fast and unexpected; in the throes of his mindless, adrenaline-powered paroxysm, he broke through the last of the thick cords and bolted upright, his head whipping. Blood poured from deep gashes across his body where moments before he'd been restrained. His arms and legs pinwheeled and struck out in every direction at once, searching for help, his brain now mush, his actions primal, mouth gasping for air.

Metal, blood, and vomit flew everywhere, coating the walls and the young men. Nolan's pupils disappeared and he searched and pawed blindly, trying to scream through the terrible obstruction in this throat, trying to pull it out gasping and retching, stuffing his fingers into his mouth and reaching down his throat, his body trying to vomit out the foreign objects.

Nolan was free from his restraints but his actions were primal and desperate. His bulging eyes had focused enough so they trained on a terrified Ernest, who was now trying in a blind panic to remember where he had left the exit.

Nolan grabbed Ernest from behind, searching for help, a desperate young man tortured beyond recognition, searching for someone to save him from his living hell. So it was his fortunate luck, and Ernest's piss-poor luck, that he was able to exact his revenge without even knowing it.

For in his final moments, Nolan—weighed down by the metal filling every major cavity in his body—gurgled and sputtered his final gasping breaths falling forward, impaling Ernest's tailbone, piercing major organs with what was possibly the world's hardest and sharpest dildo.

This contorted mess of twisted body parts fell forward into the table crashing to the floor. The metal-filled pot overturned, spilling its boiling contents on Ernest's head.

He screamed, arms flailing, the liquid hardening into a layer on his head and shoulders, the skin beneath bubbling and dissolving off his bones.

He died melting like a crayon in the sun, his colon impaled by his very own test subject.

Some time later, Ian pulled himself up off the floor. In a daze he extinguished the light and pulled the door closed, shutting the carnage in behind him. His mind was numb, his body trembling.

He remembered earlier walking through a series of doors and now just walked down the passageways shell-shocked, trying to recall the way they had come just a couple of hours before. It felt like he had been down there for days. He realized it would be years before the bodies would be found, if ever.

When he reached the third door, Caleb was sitting there on the floor. Ian shined the flashlight beam in his glazed eyes.

"I forgot about you, man," Ian said, sitting on the floor beside him. "When did you sneak out here?"

"Right after Nolan fell on Ernest. I got the fuck out of there. I thought you fainted or something."

"They're both dead. What are we going to do?"

Caleb exhaled, and ran his hands through his hair. "Do? We're royally fucked, Ian. Look." He shined the flashlight in the air and the beam fell on a combination lock, a keypad with the series of number 0-9.

Ian stared at it, remembering only that the combination was seven digits long.

"Oh, shit," he squeaked, quickly getting up and entering random patterns of numbers into the keypad. "We can figure this out. I mean, how many combinations can there be?"

Caleb raised his eyebrows. "Are you serious?"

Within an hour Ian was pounding away at the keypad. He wailed on the solid oak door as well but only succeeded in smashing his knuckles and cutting the fleshy pads on his hands.

"What are we gonna do?" he cried, kicking Caleb, who stared into the darkness.

Ian searched the basement for an exit, a window, a crawlspace. All he found was hallway after hallway of solid rock.

Two weeks later the food supply was rotten beyond their desperation. Every last drop of dead blood—their only source of liquid besides the small reserve of bottled water and their own urine—had been consumed.

Starving now, Ian, whose fingernails were bloody pulps from his efforts to tunnel through solid rock, his throat raw from screaming for help hour after hour, wondered how long he would be able to survive on Caleb's dead body. Or better yet, his live body… and wondered how quickly mangled, chewed body parts would heal, could provide him with an endless food supply. Wondered what warm blood tasted like.

And from the look in Caleb's eye—that leering, hungry look—Ian figured he was probably wondering the same damned thing.

ASHA

Eyes open, Asha thinks... feels her lids fluttering, the tips of her lashes brushing the tops of her cheeks. Utter darkness and unable to move; arms pinned to her sides. Like a coffin without the comfort of satin, without the room to move, to turn on her side, like sleeping in a dresser drawer. Tries to lift her head but even that is restricted, forbidden, forehead bumps into wood, that tiny gesture stirring the pins and needles in her dead legs and screams them awake. Panic now, deep breaths, clogged nose, mucus trickling and she can't even wipe it away.

By her feet a panel opens, or is removed, light falling into her black space, consuming it like a cancer. Grief replaced by hope and she gasps, tries to call for help but has no voice, just a harsh whisper in place of words.

The room begins to slide away, or rather her bed does, her platform, sliding toward the exit, toward that beam of harsh light, moving now like a package of meat on a conveyor belt. She wonders if she's been locked inside a morgue, a cadaver drawer, somehow mistaken for dead. This is what it feels like, the confined space a drawer in a series of drawers.

The drawer stops sliding, halts abruptly but she's only halfway out, her legs protruding into the light, her body from the stomach up still cloaked in darkness and stuffed in confinement.

Naked, she realizes, now that she has that bit of light. Cold and naked.

Hands on her thighs, spreading her pinging legs, fingers and things unseen probing and touching and then something inside, some*one*, fucking her, tearing at the dryness of her vagina, pounding, shredding her until she's wet with blood and his cum. She feels him ejaculate inside her and she wants to scream and thrash and kick, wants to kill him but has no voice and no energy and no room for movement.

When he's finished raping her, the pseudo-bed is pushed back into blackness, the door panel shut solidly below, and she passes out from the strain of her pretend screams, voice gone from days of unanswered crying.

*   *   *

Time has passed, surely, but no way of knowing. A sudden light above her head disturbs her, and water is pressed to her lips, and she greedily and eagerly swallows every drop. What feels and tastes like bread is fed to her and she devours it.

Then the light disappears.

Shortly after, unable to prevent it, she urinates, the warmth running behind her buttocks, down her thighs, stinging the tender flesh. She dreads having a bowel movement but that happens a short time later. The stench steals her air, makes her retch, and in her own filth she waits, until the panel by her feet finally opens again and she is wiped clean.

Clean for a moment. Soiled again by rape.

This ritual goes on for... days? hours? weeks? No way to know. Time is endless, as are her thoughts, her only companion her memories, and even those are disjointed and fleeting, flashes of faces and events she can't remember having been part of. Can't remember a time outside this box. Memories, trying to trick her, lull her into a sense of safety she never quite trusts. So she fights them and soon can't ascertain which are memories and which are hallucinations.

The next time the panel by her feet opens she hears a voice, a man's voice, and her heart pounds jackrabbit fast, painful thuds. The drawer slides out, and this time fully enters the light.

"This one," he says, barely able to see him, see what he looks like, barely able to see because her eyes *burn* and ache and try to fight the light that's trying to claw its way into her head.

Finally able to crack them open, just enough to see the man with the square-rimmed glasses and gray curly hair. He leans into her and she can smell corn chips, a smell like a dog's feet after a bath. Hands on her stomach, her ribcage, breasts, cold and strong hands poking rubbing squeezing.

The sound of doors, file cabinet doors sliding open and slamming shut, and she catches a glimpse to her side and realizes it's not a file cabinet but a row of doors, the same row she'd just come from, someone there opening and closing the drawers, reaching inside, pulling people out and pushing them back inside.

The man with the square rims stops poking her body and pushes her table against the wall.

"This one too," the other man says, scratching his scruffy beard with what seems to be a pencil but she's not sure, too hard to see from where she is and her eyes still burn and refuse to focus.

Another woman is pulled from the row of drawers and Asha can see now how they have this set up, how the removable beds are platforms on gurneys and move so easily because they're on castors.

Down a narrow hallway, unfinished rockface comprising the walls, dim lighting and smoky corridor like something out of a Hammer flick. Feeling has begun returning to Asha's limbs and she tries to flex her fingers, undetectable movements, to see if she can. Wriggles her toes and hopes the madmen haven't noticed.

Moments later they stop, inside another room, hot and humid like the tropics, unwashed sweat smell hanging in the air, a rancid perfume. She hears moaning, and the stench of something burning. Eyes dart to one section of the room, sees the source of the smell and again wishes she could scream.

"Put this one here," Square Rims says and his voice rushes into her and she suddenly remembers him. Remembers meeting him for coffee because her friend Melissa said he was a terrific guy, "works down on Wall Street, he's got money, don't you just love it?" and remembers wondering why Melissa would even say that, didn't she know Asha has her own money and doesn't need this guy, and remembers thinking he seemed like such a sweet guy, maybe just a bit older than she was used to dating but hell, what's a few extra years?

The coffee, rich and strong because this coffeehouse burns their beans, but also tasted odd, slightly bitter but unfamiliar, not the bitterness of overly-potent coffee but an acidy tang of something like aspirin. Remembers leaving with him, wanting a cab but climbing into his car instead, thinking at first it *was* a cab but her head was spinning or maybe the world was spinning and she stopped thinking clearly and went to sleep instead. When she woke she was surrounded by blackness, trapped in the coffin-like box, and even that now felt preferable to being in this room.

Now she wonders how she could have been so careless, so stupid, blaming herself even though she knows she was probably drugged.

Girl beside her, young girl maybe seventeen, eighteen, curly brown hair spread about her shoulders, hanging from the table she's tied to. Lying naked, hands restrained to her sides, arms and legs restrained as well. Legs spread wide, feet almost dangling off the outer edges.

Can see this clearly because Asha is able to move her head, able to see the room, the women occupying it. On her other side is another woman, short jetblack hair looking blue-tinted in the oppressive overhead fluorescence. Small John Lennon glasses half on half off her face, cracked lens, and both women are crying. The black-haired woman with the ruined glasses is quivering, her limbs twitching beneath her multiple restraints.

The two men come together near the curly-haired girl, carrying objects that look out of place here, common household items and Asha shakes her head as if trying to force the meaning into her mind.

The one with the scruffy beard takes the curling iron and pushes it inside the girl's vagina, the curling iron's cord dangling between her legs like an errant tail. The girl sobs harder, louder, chokes on mucous and tears, a soulful wail spilling out of her lungs and mouth. Begging *no*, shaking her head, and Asha is afraid of what the girl is so terrified of.

The men ignore the girl for a moment and approach the black-haired woman instead, and she starts to scream, throws herself into the restraints as if she really has a chance of escaping. Her movements are limited, miniscule almost nonexistent. A steam iron is laid flat on her stomach, the cord dangling to the floor.

Across the room, Asha notices several other women but can't see them clearly, hard to make out their condition through the blood and the smoke.

"This one?" the bearded man says, hand stretched toward Asha, and the one with the square rims shrugs.

"Didn't you have something in mind? Why'd you bring her in here?"

He shrugs again. "I did have a plan, but you brought curly instead and stuck her in the corner. Why don't you share your thoughts with me next time?" and the two men argue over who was right and what to do with the extra woman in the room.

"Put her back in the cabinet then," bearded guy says.

"Leave her here, Patrick."

"What for?"

"Cause I'm not going all the way back inside," Square Rims says, cocking his head, fingertips massaging the gray swirling through the hair above his temples, and he adds, "We can do her when we finish with these two."

The one called Patrick shakes his head and coughs into his palm, and Asha thinks he doesn't look anything like a Patrick, looks more like a Butch or a Joe with his wiry scruffy beard, and she can't understand why she's thinking this as if it matters at all.

And she knows this is wrong, knows she's not stupid and wonders how she could have ended up in this situation. And she wonders if she'll get out of here alive.

"Let's get this done," Patrick says, leaning over the black-haired woman grabbing the steam iron's cord and letting it slide through his hand until it reaches the end, the small black plug in his fingers.

The woman's eyes are huge now, and glassy, like the dead eyes of a mounted deerhead, almost too big for the rest of her face, and Patrick stoops to plug the steam iron into the outlet.

At first there's little movement from the woman, no place to go anyway no reason to panic because the iron isn't too hot yet, probably still lukewarm to the touch, but Asha trembles at the sight of it lying flat on the woman's stomach.

Square Rims stands with a video camera pointed toward her, its low hum indicating it's recording.

Screaming now, steam rising from the iron, only it's not steam Asha realizes, not steam at all but smoke, the woman's flesh sizzling and smoking the tiny crackles as fine hairs are singed into nothingness, cooked flesh smells coalescing with the smoke in the air and the woman thrashes, tries to throw the iron off her body. The iron jiggles and bounces and Asha sees the angry ed blistered and bubbled skin. The shrieks replace the cooking flesh sounds, ounds like ground beef sputtering in a skillet. Patrick holds the iron in place is the woman flails, muscles and tendons straining and overworked against he straps, bulging in desperate attempts to break free. Blood trickles down her stomach, over her hips, soaks the sheets beneath her. Intense scarlet emphasized against the ivory soap whiteness of the rest of her cadaverous body.

It seems like forever before the screams dissipate, before the only sounds eft are the slow endless sizzle of the iron and the metronome clicks of the video camera.

Patrick releases his grip on the iron but leaves it on her stomach, the wound worsening, flesh all but dissolved from her stomach, the skin on her arms and legs raw from the stressful pressure of her movements. He lays his forefinger and middle finger on her carotid artery just below the jawline.

"Dead?"

Patrick shakes his head. "Way too soon. Erratic pulse though."

The girl with the curly brown hair has fainted, and Square Rims slaps her cheeks but she doesn't wake up this way. The camcorder is in his other hand, dangling at his hip.

Patrick glances back at Asha with longing, as if staring at a long-lost friend. He turns quickly back to the girl on the table. He produces a small vial, waves it beneath the girl's nose. She sputters into consciousness, coughing and gagging.

"Welcome back, Katie," Patrick mutters sadly.

Katie begins to scream, and Square Rims clamps his hand over her mouth. "Save it," he says, only Katie is shaking her head.

"Why?" she cries after he removes his hand. "Why are you doing this?"

And Asha wants to know the same thing, why are they doing this, why her? and the room darkens for a moment and she fights the desire to black out.

Square Rims is exchanging the tapes in the camcorder now, and Patrick leans into her ear but speaks loudly. "Your daddy," he says, scratching his chin somewhere behind all that wiry hair, "he says he doesn't like you dating niggers. Says you won't stop, that you're ruining the family name."

Her mouth opens and closes and when it opens again says "what?" right before the sobs begin.

"Sorry, kid," Square Rims says, "nothing personal."

Katie looks lost, confused, her eyes wide and round like China plates. "But why? *Why?* Oh god, why?"

Patrick frowns, shakes his head.

"Don't do this," she pleads, frantic, her voice hoarse. "Please just kill me. Don't burn me up!" but Patrick steps away from her and Square Rims raises the camcorder and rests it against his neck.

"I'm sorry, kiddo," Patrick says, "but this is what your daddy paid for."

And Asha sees the empathy in him and wonders how he could do this. Wonders what made him this way. Sees the struggle within him and knows what struggle feels like.

"God no!" Katie howls, already bucking against the restraints, and Patrick reaches down and plugs the curling iron into the outlet.

Asha knows from painful experience how hot curling irons get, once burnt her neck using one after it touched her skin for barely a second, suffered through a blistering second-degree burn when she accidentally sat on it because she'd left it on the toilet lid to heat up.

Within seconds the smoke rises from Katie's crotch, her pubic hairs singed, the flesh inside her vagina popping and crackling, burnt flesh smells like pork swirling with the smoke.

Katie goes mad, kicking her legs wildly, busting through an ankle restraint but there is no need to secure it; she's unable to move anywhere at all.

Square Rims records while Patrick makes sure the curling iron stays imbedded in the girl's vagina. Katie's screams pierce Asha's eardrums, sends shivers dancing along her skin, tickles the fine hairs on her arms, heart pounding furiously now, her skin clammy and stomach lurching and flipping.

Katie stops moving. Her head drops to one side, tongue hanging like a panting dog on a hot summer day, the smell of her burnt body thick and sweet.

Patrick checks her pulse. "Not yet," and he wipes his hands on his pants. He also checks the black-haired woman's pulse and nods, and removes the iron from her stomach. "Dead," he says, and Asha sees a blackened red mass where there once was skin, the border raw and jagged and oozing pus, blisters forming a puckered kiss around the rim of the wound.

There are two other women in the room who haven't said a word, haven't made a sound at all, and Asha looks over, praying for hope. Wondering if this is a nightmare because it can't possibly be real, they can't possibly have been burnt to death, tortured that way. Hope maybe one of these women in the other side of the room will save Asha from the madmen. But as her eyesight strengthens, as she is able to focus more clearly, she realizes those other women are dead as well.

Numb head to foot, unable to imagine a more horrible way to die than what she's seen, movement no longer possible because she is terrified.

"What about her?" Patrick says, and Square Rims shakes his head and says "He didn't say." They approach Asha and she cowers, tries to melt into the table, wants blood and marrow to ooze into the sheet beneath her.

Patrick touches her arm and leans over her head. "There are some sick people in this world."

Asha cracks open her lips and licks them, forces her lungs to obey and squeezes out a word. "Who?"

"Derek, " he says. "He was angry you dumped him."

On some level she knew there could be no other possibility, had assumed this somewhere in the deep recess of her mind. Mean-spirited, callous he'd been, so this doesn't surprise her. But the realization rushes at her from its charred remains, choking her with the bitterness, and Asha is too stunned to weep.

"He wants it to be painful," Patrick says wearily, wipes his brow with the back of the hand not clutching her elbow, and Asha closes her eyes, tears rolling back into her ears, wanting a death that isn't painful but not really wanting to die at all. He removes his hand from her arm and her eyes pop open in panic, and she struggles into an upright position.

"Please," she says, throaty words mingling with tears and desperation. 'Don't."

Patrick shakes his head. "It's what we do. I'm sorry."

"It doesn't have to be this way," she pleads. "Save me from here," she whispers, "and we can be together." She wonders why she says this to him, and wonders if she means it.

Square Rims has disappeared and returns carrying a butcher knife, and pushes Asha back down on the table. She punches at him, tries to sit up again, tries to kick and claw and bite but Patrick secures her to the table, Velcro fasteners clenching her limbs. Naked body thrashing, squirming, futile attempts to slide away, and Square Rims leans into her torso for support, bringing the barracuda-teeth blade to the edge of the breast.

"Double mastectomy," Square Rims says to Patrick. "It'll take a while, but she can bleed to death. Grab the camera."

Patrick doesn't move though, stares into Asha's pleading, wild eyes instead.

"Did you hear me?"

Patrick nods. "Yeah, Mike, I heard you." But still he doesn't move, still stands beside Asha, and she stares back, painful breaths choking, chest heaving and body shaking, skin pale and clammy and goosebumpy, a juxtaposition of hot and cold everywhere at once.

At his feet is the camcorder, which Patrick lifts but doesn't turn on. Mike releases his vice-grip on Asha's breast, removes his elbow from her sternum. "What's wrong?"

"This doesn't feel right. I don't want to do this."

"We can't let her go. Not after this. Besides, we have a job to do. This is what we *do*, Patrick. Just like you said."

Patrick glances across the room as if seeing it for the first time, as if the scope of the horror is just dawning on him, and he says, "This feels wrong."

Mike crosses his arms, butcher knife protruding from beneath his elbow and cocks his head like a confused puppy, flash of white upper teeth as he chews on his lower lip.

"I'll pay you," Asha begs, last-ditch frantic attempt, "I have money and I can pay you."

"What are you doing?" Mike asks Patrick. "Why this one?"

Patrick's tea-colored eyes return to Asha's, and he looks confused, looks sad and confused and he sighs as if unable to find the words to answer the question.

Mike leans forward again, plants his elbow against her belly button and grabs her bruised breast, small pink nipple. Presses the knife against the flesh and says, "I'll videotape the corpse then; you're useless," and the knife slices away the edge, cleanly severs part of the breast from her chest before the pain registers, before she notices he's already begun the assault. Blood seeps from the wound, her life washing away in a warm bath, the shock catching her breath several moments before she begins to scream.

"Stop!" Patrick yells. He rushes Mike and grabs the knife. He wrestles Mike away from Asha's body.

"What the hell are you doing?" Mike says, shoving Patrick, almost knocking him off his feet. Patrick regains his footing and rushes Mike headfirst, knocks him to the floor, and the fight is over almost before it begins. Mike drops awkwardly, hands spread to prevent the fall and the knife is aimed toward the ceiling and Mike is impaled on it, the edge stabbing through his shoulder and coming through the back of his neck. Saint Vitas dance, Mike's body spasming and thumping, a landed fish, and half a minute later lays still, blood quickly puddling beneath him, flowing into the drain several feet away.

"Oh god," Patrick moans and drops to his knees, checks Mike's pulse. "It was an accident," he says to the corpse, square rimmed glasses shattered beside the dead man's head.

Somehow the pain has been forgotten, endorphins and adrenaline replacing the blood in her veins, severed tissue not on her mind for a moment. But when she glances down reality floods back, the gaping hole where the connective tissue should be now filling with air, searing heat marking the outline of the wound. Patrick presses a cloth against the damaged breast, pushes against the agonizing wound, and the cloth is saturated with blood.

"How much money?" he asks, almost whispers, and Asha understands his motivation now, knows this is the only reason Mike is dead and she is not.

"Grandfather... left me money," she says through gritted teeth, slow measured breaths against the pain. "Lots."

Patrick snatches a roll of duct tape from a table a few feet away, presses a clean cloth to her wound and secures it with the tape. Caresses her hair and stares longingly into her eyes.

Without another word he is gone, and Asha waits several minutes before realizing she doesn't hear any sounds; no footfalls, no breathing, alone with a roomful of corpses, tied useless to a table, slowly bleeding to death. She calls Patrick's name several times but the effort hurts too much, each echoing word bringing a fresh bout of searing pain, so she lays quietly and waits, not knowing how long to wait, or why he's left her like this. No clock to mark the passage of time, no windows to allow sunlight or moonlight to filter in, to indicate how long she lay shivering and bleeding and sobbing on the table.

Footsteps now, many footsteps, getting closer, either following a corridor or descending stairs; impossible to tell.

Breathless, face tinged pink and sweaty, Patrick returns to her side.

Bizarre relief to see this man, her torturer, her rapist, the memory of the rape having been forgotten until now, replaced by fresh torment. But she remembers fingers probing, stroking, remembers being fucked inside a coffin, inside a drawer but the conflict of emotions makes the acid in her stomach churn. Feeling compassion and gratitude for the man who saved her when it was probably the same man who had tortured and raped her.

Sweat-sheen face hovering above hers, slight smile through scruffy, wiry terrier beard, and he plants his hands on her shoulders and gently squeezes. "I'm back," he says. "We have to figure out what to do here."

She wants to respond, wants to say "how so?" but the words fail her, the blood that fled her body stole her words, stole her strength and ability to respond.

He peels back the tape and removes the cloth to examine the wound. "It's really not that bad," he lies, rifling through the contents of the first-aid kit he lays on her stomach, cold metal box sending shivers through her body. "You're mostly in shock I think. The cut's not that deep."

Hydrogen peroxide bubbles in the wound, sizzles and foams like an antacid tablet in a glass of water, and it stings but the pain is bearable. Iodine next, the brownish-red liquid tickling as he pours it. Out of her line of sight he's working on something, and she hears the slow rhythm of his concentrated breath. He turns back to her, snaps on a pair of rubber gloves, lights a match to sterilize the needle he's holding.

"Just a few stitches," he says gently, and she shakes her head, the relief she felt just moments before dissipating until the only feeling that remains is dread. "You have to stay still. I'll work fast."

Stabbing pain as needle penetrates skin, the creepy tickle of the thread feeling like spider legs, passing through the fresh puncture wounds, and it's repeated and repeated and she clamps her eyes shut against the pain, against the sickening feeling of being sewn.

"Okay, done." Muscles relaxing, relief from the strain, she feels him carefully bandaging the stitches, covering the wound with gauze and surgical tape. He covers her with a blanket and she whispers "untie me," but he shakes his head, loosens the Velcro bindings but leaves her restrained.

"Not yet," he says, stroking her hair, and pulls up a chair to sit beside her.

"Why are you doing this?" she asks weakly, finding her voice again. "Why heal me if you're only going to keep me a prisoner?"

Eyes lowered, he doesn't answer, strokes her forehead instead, gentle touches lulling her into calmness, enticing her into an exhausted sleep.

It seems like only minutes have passed when she opens her eyes again, but the room if different now, the bloody reeking corpses gone, charnel house now an almost-empty room of stone and concrete and glaring fluorescent light. Several feet away, the outline of a body beneath a sheet, lying on a gurney.

"Patrick?" she whispers, parched throat and parched lips, swallows and tries again. "Patrick?" louder this time.

Patrick returns carrying a tray, steaming mug of what smells like coffee or soup, maybe both. He lays the tray on an empty table by the door and gently lifts her head and neck, props pillows behind her. Retrieves the bowl of soup and blows on each spoonful before feeding it to her. Noodle soup tasting odd because of the metallic tang on her tongue, remnants of blood and sickness but she eats because her empty stomach hurts, feels queasy. He feeds her soup and coffee and wipes her mouth with a napkin.

The body across the room begins to stir, struggles unseen beneath the sheet, makes no sound other than a muffled, snorting grunt.

Patrick sets the dishes on the tray and sits beside Asha again. He pulls the blanket down and untapes the wound, replaces the gauze and tapes it closed again. Asha had forgotten about her nakedness and modesty blossoms pink on her cheeks.

"You said you have money," he says as he covers her again with the blanket.

She nods, weary, wonders when this will finally end, wonders why he's even bothered to treat her if he plans to kill her for her money.

Leaning forward he presses his face near hers. "You have a decision to make," and he's moved away, is now behind her head. Clinking sounds of metal, sharp scrapes of knives, metal against metal, and he returns to her side with a collection of knives.

"I don't want to hurt you," and he lays the knives beside her on the blanket and her eyes bulge in fresh terror, amazed she had become so complacent, had felt so safe somehow, had believed Patrick cared for her.

"I want to take you with me," he says, staring away at nothing, at a chunk of stone wall. "But I have to be sure. Do you want to come with me?"

Lids fluttering, mind racing and trying to understand what he's saying understand what his question means. "Yes," she whispers, and realizes she means it, realizes she wants to go with Patrick, to be with him. Doesn't know why and realizes the absurdity but believes she loves his compassion, his tenderness, her rapist-cum-rescuer, her Dark Knight in tarnished armor but she never was one to argue with the desire of the heart.

"I love you," he says, baby's breath wrapped around his words. "I know that's crazy, Asha, but I do."

She nods, slowly, unable to answer because she doesn't know if she loves him, does know there's no reason she should but also knows she wants to spend every waking moment with him.

"You know what I am. You know what I've done."

Again she nods, words failing her. She knows, and somehow it doesn't matter. Whether she'll still feel this way tomorrow, or months from now is a mystery, but for now this is enough.

"Then I need you to do something. For both of us."

Eyes questioning, hoping they speak for her, but he waits instead for an answer. "What is it, Patrick? What do I have to do?"

He walks over to the body beneath the sheet on the gurney; removes the sheet to reveal the restrained, gagged man naked on the table.

Asha gasps, almost chokes on the spit she's sucked into her throat. Stares in disbelief at the man on the table, his eyes huge, sclera tinged pink with broken blood vessels. Derek, hazel eyes pleading, some sense of relief apparent when he notices Asha. A look of dread replacing hope as he seems to remember why she is here in the first place.

Patrick returns to her side, all breathless and eager as he says, "I want us to be together, Asha, but there's only one way. Will you do this?" and after an eternity she nods, slowly, hungrily, hatred raging through her body like disease.

Patrick moves the knives to the chair and unfastens her restraints. Helps her sit up and hands her a shirt and pair of pants, helps her get dressed and is careful of her bandaged wound.

Asha slides her legs over the side of the table, pins and needles stabbing as the circulation returns. Stands on unsteady legs, blood and adrenaline rushing to her head.

He lifts the knives, an assortment of blades like a bouquet of stainless steel. This way I'll know. I'll know for sure. We'll leave here, Asha. Go to South America or somewhere like that. Leave this behind."

The idea makes her tingle, the plan exciting, her desire to be with Patrick all she can think about now. He takes her hand and leads her to Derek, and together they stare at him looking terrified and pale, sweat trickling down his face.

"Want to make this quick?" he asks, stroking her hair from behind, and she closes her eyes and leans back into him, presses against him, loving the tender feel of his hands, the hardness of his desire.

"Not really," she says, voice strong now, feeling the weight of the knife in her hands, light refracting off the blade. Lowers the tip to Derek's stomach and razes a light trail of blood from sternum to groin. Derek shudders, gasps, groans into his gag.

Asha lifts the knife, careful of her wound, and swings her arms behind her, blade facing out, and plunges it into Patrick's stomach. Snatches a second knife and whirls to face him, sees the stunned look on his face, his eyes and mouth the same perfect o-shape, and slashes the knife across his throat, crimson smile grinning blood. Patrick falls dead, impaling himself further on the knife protruding from his stomach.

She drops to her knees and clutches Patrick's head and whispers, "I've changed my mind. I want to keep my money," and stands again and hovers over Derek.

"You didn't tell them?" she asks the gagged man, and he shakes his head expelling the tears onto the sheet. "Ah. I see. So they didn't know. I was wondering about that. You should have warned them about me. Things might have turned out differently."

She pulls the gag out of his mouth and kisses him, tasting bile and salty tears, vomit trickling out of his mouth in a stream of spit.

"It was a good try, Derek. Very noble. But then, you always were a goody goody." The knife feels suddenly light in her hand, feels more like kindling than razor-sharp stainless steel blades. "My luck's improving, I see. I never expected Patrick to bring you here—that was a nice surprise. I thought I'd have to go hunting. Assuming I made it out of this mess... it was a close one, I'll give you that. You almost won this time."

"Please," he begs, "don't do this. I won't tell anyone about you. I'll leave you alone, I swear! I didn't mean for this to happen, Asha. Please!"

"Didn't mean for what to happen? For your little plan to backfire?" She laughs and shakes her head. "Silly boy."

Lips caress his forehead, and then she leans back and smiles. His noble attempts to rid the world of Asha have failed, and now he must pay the penalty as so many before him have. She couldn't help who she was. Didn't care to either.

She moves between his legs and begins to slice away parts of his body.

DESPAIR

He visits me sometimes, caressing my cheeks with soft, small hands, his touch like feathery strokes. Turning his head sideways, he smiles, as if this small movement is somehow amusing.

A gentle breeze blows through my hair like invisible fingers. I'm chilled, but only slightly. Crisp, dead leaves rustle, scattering across the brown lawn. They look black in the oncoming darkness. Black, like all things dead.

The child takes my hand in his and brings it to his chest, squeezing. I feel the warmth and wonder if it's him I'm feeling, or my own blood flowing. He looks at me, his sharp brown eyes a contrast, so unlike my own pale blue, and he forms a word on lips, over breath devoid of sound.

One word: Mommy. Mommy? I think of a book I read as a child, and I think of this lost child, searching for his mommy.

"I have no children," I whisper.

He stares for a moment, then walks away, disappearing into a dark blanket of trees, and I wonder where he goes. I wonder where his home is.

I wonder why I never try to stop him, or try to help. Somehow, he doesn't seem helpless, even though he's only a baby. A small child, perhaps four years old.

*   *   *

The dishes have piled up because I don't feel like washing them. I don't feel like washing myself either and have pulled my greasy blond hair into a ponytail to keep it out of my eyes. I've always been rather meticulous about my appearance, but lately I haven't cared too much.

Paul left me, and I just don't feel like doing much of anything. I feel like such a child, even though I'm twenty four.

I didn't think I knew despair. I was never the sort of person who cared all that much. Perhaps somewhere inside there's someone full of emotion, full of love and compassion, empathy, but she's alien to me. Sometimes it feels as though I'm watching another life unfold, as if I'm a voyeur rather than a participant.

Paul and I weren't very serious, but it still hurt like hell when he left me. I endured the slaps because I thought he and I had a future, isn't that silly? I heard he moved to California with a girlfriend, but since Paul never bothered actually telling me, I'm going by rumor. I wouldn't be surprised, him fleeing his life, thinking 3000 miles would somehow matter. But it doesn't matter, it didn't help, and now we're coasts apart. He left me with the ability to distance myself emotionally. I can go numb whenever I feel it's necessary. Neat trick.

*   *   *

I tire of staring at dirty dishes and wash them, dropping a glass in the nearly empty sink, tiny flying fragments scraping along the stainless steel. I pick up a large jagged chunk, feeling its weight in my hand. Drops of water pool along the fragment's base, plopping silently into the sink. I'm mesmerized. I can imagine using it, can see the sharp edge raking across the veins in my wrist. It would be warm, like last time. Last time it had hurt because I changed my mind, ran for a bath towel, wrapped my bloody arm and searched for help. I called my mother, but she didn't answer her phone. I don't even know if she was home. I called Joey, begging him to help, told him what I'd done. Joey… Joey was home. Chose to stay there. That was Joey.

Then I called an ambulance, and help was finally on the way.

So long ago, it seems, so many years now. Four, I think. I can measure the time because it was when I first felt anything like despair.

*   *   *

I drop the broken shard into the sink. I can't do it.

*   *   *

He's in the room with me again, the little boy. I didn't hear him come in. He never knocks. I ask him what's wrong, and he doesn't answer. I tell him to go home, even offer to take him. He leans against the doorway with his hands clasped in front of his body. His head is bowed, but I can still see the sad expression on his face. I ask his name and he shrugs slightly. He extends his hand, whispering. I reach out to take it but quickly change my mind. I don't want to touch him. He looks too much like Joey, and it makes me quite ill.

He leaves.

I watch him, leaning against the crabapple tree, arms folded across his thin chest, through the kitchen window. He seems to be waiting. He doesn't seem lost, seems too sure of himself. I wonder if he's waiting for me, but when our eyes meet, he looks away.

*   *   *

Joey didn't want children.

*   *   *

I go out to the yard, and even wrapped in mittens, my hands are cold.

He smiles at me, that little boy, beams as I approach, stands straight from his slump against the tree. Dead leaves torn from branches by the wind cover his dark hair like a cap.

I tell him he has to leave, he has to go home, and he nods, his smile quickly disappearing. He wipes at his nose. There are no tears. This is apparently not upsetting him. He's used to it.

I remember holding him in my arms. Wanting to, anyway. Wondering what it would feel like, to hold a tiny body, to press it against my chest. To hear a new heartbeat. To love someone unconditionally, to always have a person in your life who will love you forever, no matter what.

I never named the baby. Didn't even know if it would have been a boy.

*   *   *

Joey didn't stay long. Not long at all. He never wanted kids. I think he got scared at the possibility. Just the possibility. Coward. If I had known then Joey was going to leave, I think I would have handled things differently.

*   *   *

Paul and I never talked about kids. It was me he didn't want. I wonder if I'll ever be loved, if I am lovable. I think about that a lot, especially when I'm around knives, or broken glass. When I start to feel despair.

But the little boy gives me hope. I'm watching him grow up. He has Joey's eyes. He seems to have my mouth. I think I do know this little boy. Perhaps he's someone I was meant to love.

ONE BREATH

Their souls danced on febrile winds, twisting, contorting, flailing madly about as if enjoying their last moments of freedom. Racing in every direction at once, trying to escape, trying to avoid the inevitability of their return to corporeal form.

If they had known… if only they had known how wicked this curse would turn out to be, how painful, they would have settled for death.

The souls grudgingly returned to the trees, to spend the night once again in their human bodies. They waited yet again for the end of the night, waited for release.

The trees stood, untouched by fire, unharmed by wind or by man; this was part of the curse. A hodgepodge of greenery, the sawtooth oak and the pink dogwood rose amidst pines and firs. Their branches were thick with sap and aged with time. Limbs stretched, tried desperately to touch but never met. Unable to join, to hold one another, to feel anything but the dirt beneath their roots and soft rain on their branches. Occasionally, a gentle breeze brought leaves closer to leaves, the delicate touch of one another, but the touch would always be fleeting, maddening. Branches reached to the skies, contorted by rage and despair.

Now, the witching hour approached, and with its return, brought their freedom. A swirl of mist circled the trees, entangled itself in the thick foliage and caressed the bark, winding its way down the length of the trunks.

The trees were felled as if by ax, crashing to earth in a splintering roar. Again in human form, they moaned, thrashing and writhing on the ground, sweaty naked bodies rolling in dead leaves and a bed of pine needles.

*   *   *

They hid amongst the boxes of discarded paperbacks, rusty toys, and long-forgotten treasures buried beneath a veil of dust and cobwebs in the basement of the old house. It had once belonged to Jake, this house, had once hid the secrets of his youth beside the yearning of old age. Jake had been somewhere in-between, stopped short of achieving age by the curse.

Danielle had been his; he had been hers. They had shared the house in every way but name and they had planned to be together forever.

"We can't hide from her forever," Danielle whispered, her dusty fingers trailing his cheek.

"But you know we can't hide."

"Then why do we? Hide."

He sighed, turned away. "I wish I could protect you."

"If hiding is pointless, then why do we waste the time? It never changes. Why waste the time we have?"

He laughed in spite of himself. "Desperation?"

"Then let's go upstairs. Why do we always hide down here? Don't you want to look at them again?"

"You know we can't."

Danielle wrapped her arms across her naked breasts. "I'm cold."

Jake pulled her into his arms. "I know, I'm sorry."

"Don't be. It's not your fault."

But it is my fault, he thought.

"Maybe they're asleep. We can peek upstairs…"

He pulled her close, until his lips grazed hers. "Not much time left," he whispered. "I've waited so long to touch you." His head dipped until he found her breast and he gently sucked the nipple.

"I've longed for you too, Jake," she said, gasping slightly.

She reached down and touched his penis, tenderly at first, feeling it grow in her hand. Her back arched in response to his lips, her nipples hardening, the hunger and want growing rapidly inside her. Gently lifting his mouth from her breast, she shifted her legs on the cold dirt basement floor, bending over until her head reached his penis. It responded to her hot tongue, pulsing between her lips. His hands caressed her shoulders, squeezed the flesh, slid down her back.

She licked the shaft, her tongue deftly toying with him, seeking the sensitive spots she knew he loved so well. He swelled inside her mouth and she pulled it in deeper, until she felt it press against the back of her throat. She pulled away, moving now to his balls, tongue darting on the underside and sucking gently. His fingers dug deeply into her hair and he moaned, muscles tightening.

Gently he pushed her away, laying her down on the ground, her legs spread for him. He leaned into her and again found the breast, licking and nibbling the nipple. His fingers spread her lips and entered the slick, wet area between her legs.

She actually hadn't wanted this, hadn't wanted the feel of him, the closeness of sex. Wanted instead just to hold him, to caress him, let him know that no matter what, she would always be with him. She'd thought the sex was incidental. He felt wonderful to her, inside her, but that wasn't all she wanted

Their fleeting moments felt almost wasted this way.

But now, she couldn't stop. She wanted him inside her, cherished the feel of his fingers playing with her vaginal lips, rubbing her clit. She writhed against his hand, fucking his fingers, her juices dribbling out of her.

Then she felt his dick slip inside, rigid and powerful, quickly bringing her to climax. Her back rubbed against the floor, pebbles leaving tiny red patterns in her skin. She barely felt it. Legs wrapped tight around his waist, pulling him deeper. She wanted to feel him hard. Wanted to remember this. Wanted to forever remember the feel of him inside her.

They lay side by side, breathing hard, bodies slick with sweat despite the chill October night. The basement was poorly insulated and small drafts sneaked in through the mortar.

Danielle reached over in the darkness and clasped his hand in hers. "We need clothes. A blanket at least."

"I couldn't find anything."

"Of course not. Not in the basement. We need to go upstairs."

"But my kids—"

"Are old now," she snapped, exasperated. "They're no longer kids, remember?"

"Danielle…"

"I'm going," she said. "Stay here if you want."

She scurried away before he could stop her. From the bottom of the stairs, a sliver of light taunted from the kitchen above. She knew the hour was late, but it was Halloween and people tended to stay up late on this night. Trick or treaters, parties and who-knew-what else. Or maybe, they just left a kitchen light on at night as a beacon. She used to.

Jake came up behind her, wrapped his arm around her stomach. "Quietly," he said. "Just in case."

Together they crept up the stairs and Jake pressed his ear against the kitchen door. He found the doorknob and it twisted in his hand. He opened the door and peered into the kitchen.

He reached back and found her hand. They slipped inside, closing the door behind them. In the light, he could make out her features, frozen in eternal youth. He couldn't remember how many years they had been forced to endure this. He'd lost count ages ago.

"This way," he whispered, pulling her toward the living room, as if she didn't know the way. She knew the layout of the house as well as he did. Better maybe, since she had decorated so much of it.

They stopped at the threshold before stepping into the other room, shocked by the changes. Gone were the familiar furnishings, the dusty framed photos on the mantle. Instead, strangers peered out from grinning, posed shots. The grandfather clock in the corner had been replaced by a weightlifting machine.

"What the hell?" Jake tried to take it all in. "Did they move?" he asked Danielle, as if she had the answers. "Do you think that's it?"

She shook her head. "I don't know."

They walked through the living room and reached the flight of stairs that would bring them up to the bedrooms. Jake took Danielle's hand and they climbed up, careful of the creaking boards they knew all too well. The bedroom doors were closed.

"Great," he muttered, wondering which door might be safe. If his kids no longer lived here, there was no telling who did. He tried to figure out which room would at least contain clothing they could use.

"Wait here," he whispered, pushing her against the wall. Not that it offered her protection or would hide her should someone come along. "If someone comes... run."

She nodded, but in the darkness of the hall her movement went unseen.

Jake pressed his ear against the master bedroom door and listened for movement before entering.

Danielle waited for his return, her arms crossed over her chest, trying to hide her nudity, trying to keep warm. The house wasn't cold exactly, but against her naked skin, the temperature was uncomfortable. The wait in that dark corridor was interminable and Danielle shifted from foot to foot.

A few minutes later Jake returned. She hoped it was Jake. It was impossible to tell for sure. But, she felt sure that the owners of the house wouldn't have to creep around in it, especially if they were suddenly running away from an intruder.

"Danni?"

She rushed over to him, took his arm and discovered he was already dressed. They sneaked back downstairs until they were once again in the basement. He handed her a set of clothing: jeans, a sweater and a pair of tennis shoes.

"We can't come back here," he said. "This is no longer our house. I don't know who those people are... but..." He shook his head. "It's theirs now."

"We can come back, ring the bell? Ask what happened to William and Karen."

"No. I know what happened to them." She could hear the anguish in his voice.

She waited for him to continue and prompted him when he didn't. "What happened?"

His voice cracked. "I saw a newspaper..." He bowed his head and rested it against her neck. She held his hands in hers. "The year is 2004, Danni."

2004? She couldn't fathom how that had happened. She knew time held little meaning for them now, but she couldn't believe they had lost a decade. Jake's kids, twins, had been born in 1923 and their mother had died giving birth. Even if they were still alive, they would probably be in some rest home somewhere. If they were still alive, they would now be in their eighties.

"My whole life is gone," he said. "Everything I once knew, everyone I had once loved. Gone."

"I'm still here." She squeezed his hand. "You'll always have me."

He nodded and she could feel the movement on her shoulder. "You're everything to me. You're all I have left. But all I did was curse you."

Her fingers twined through the back of his hair as she caressed his head. "What do you want to do now? Should we go back?"

"Back? And make it easy on her? No!" He pulled out of Danielle's embrace. "Haven't we suffered enough? When will this end?"

"She said never."

"I know what she said. Doesn't mean I have to accept it."

*   *   *

They wandered along the streets as if they belonged there, holding hands, glancing in storefront glass, watching the remaining Halloween stragglers make their way home. Occasionally, a ghost or superhero ran past and a few hideous masks that neither Jake nor Danielle could identify, faces seeming to drip with dried blood, brains falling down the sides of their skulls.

"How could anyone wear such a thing?" Danielle asked and Jake shrugged.

Jake spied a clock in one of the stores. It was after four am. They didn't have much time left. Sunrise was just a few hours away. They had always been forced to return at sunrise.

"Let's not go back," Jake whispered.

Danielle stopped walking. "But that will mean our death."

"We're already dead. We just don't know it yet."

"We're not dead. She may lift the curse one day."

"After more than seventy years? She enjoys this too much, our pain. What do we have to look forward to every year? A few hours of joy? Then nothing. Do you retain your memories, Danni? Do you stand in the wind for hours and days on end wishing for my touch, wishing we could escape the curse? Because I do. Every single moment I spend wishing I could be with you. And now, she doesn't even give us a moment every year. More than a decade passed and I have lost everything I once held dear. I wanted one more glance at my children, to see who they had become. She stole that from me."

Now, he was crying and Danielle wanted to ease his pain. But, her pain was just as strong. She had loved those children as much as he did. They and Jake were her only family.

"Then we won't go back," she said, taking his hand and leading him down the street. "We won't go back."

Their words hung on the air, heavy and thick, and neither would say exactly what they were thinking. But, they both wondered how. How they would do this. How they would keep from going back. There was only one way.

They entered Tavern's Park and sat on the grass beside the lake. Moonlight illuminated the water, the reflection of the trees reflected on its surface. They held hands like teenagers and gazed at the houses lining the banks.

This had once been their life. They had once sat on this grass, had planned their future.

Late one night, driving home from a party, Jake having had perhaps one drink too many, their car struck a child on his way home from his own Halloween party. One careless act and their lives were over.

The child crumpled on the ground like a sack of wet leaves, chest barely rising and falling. One breath more, a cry for his mommy, and then he was dead. Jake and Danielle's lives would never be the same.

The child's mother had not taken the news well and had vowed her revenge. Jake and Danielle had feared for their own lives, and that of Jake's children. They thought she was perhaps a grieved mother gone mad. They had no idea who they were dealing with.

She appeared one night out of the mist, swirling before them as if part of it, intercepting them as they were about to enter their house. She raised her arms, her thorny robes flowing, snakes twisting and slithering about her shoulders and head, a crown of serpents.

Jake tripped over a porch step and landed on his butt, his teeth clamping down on his tongue. Danielle screamed and threw her arm over her head. At first Jake thought it was an elaborate Halloween costume, but there was something not quite human about her.

The witch walked up to them, her eyes slits, glowing red in the moonlight. "You murdered my child," she spat. "So you shall never know happiness. You shall never know your own children."

"Please!" Danielle cried. "Don't hurt the children. They didn't do anything wrong!"

"You will spend eternity watching the life you once had." She gestured to the small copse of trees across the road. "You will watch your life disappearing before you and you will always remember my child."

Jake climbed back to his feet and reached for Danielle, pulling her protectively toward him. "Get out of here!" he screamed. "I'll summon the police!"

The witch laughed and waved her hand at them.

"Why are you doing this?" Danielle said. "It was an accident!"

"There are no accidents! You are murderers."

"It wasn't her fault. I was driving."

"I don't care."

"Who are you?" Danielle whispered, wiping her damp face with the back of her hand.

"Go now," the witch snapped. "You get no chance to say goodbye. Just like I never got to say goodbye. Forever remain part of the trees, safe from man safe from fire."

"No!" Jake cried. "Please. Please! Don't do this." There was no doubt in his mind she was sincere or that she was capable of doing what she threatened. He didn't question how, just knew she could do it, somehow. Questioning his sanity wasn't an option; surviving this was. Or at the very least, even if she wasn't some supernatural creature, she scared the hell out of him. She might produce a weapon and kill them on the spot.

Jake fell to his knees and sobbed into his cupped palms. "Don't take them away from me. Don't make my babies grow up without me. Have pity! You're a mother."

"Was a mother," she snarled. Then added, "Your one chance at redemption is sacrifice. Make the ultimate sacrifice and you will be released from the curse."

"Sacrifice? What do you mean?" Jake asked, wiping away his tears.

But with that she returned to the mist, swirling in the maelstrom as if composed of wind and particles of sand and leaves, and not made of flesh and blood. The mist consumed Jake and Danielle, entered their bodies, and they screamed in anguish at the energy force that now controlled them.

Moments later, they had become the sawtooth oak and pink dogwood. They had stretched their limbs in a final attempt at freedom, had reached for one another, frozen in a desperate attempt to embrace.

"One final moment together," Jake said, Danielle seated in front of him on the grass. His legs were tangled in hers, his stomach pressed against her back. His chin rested on her neck and he nuzzled her jawline.

"I'm afraid," she whispered, leaning into him, reaching back to stroke his hair.

"So am I."

They didn't talk for several minutes, just stared at the water. Finally, Danielle broke the silence. "How?"

"How what?" he asked hesitantly.

"You know what."

He shrugged. "What's the most painless way?"

"Old age." She laughed.

Jake glanced at the sky. The sun struggled to break the horizon. "Come with me," he said quietly and pulled her to her feet.

They walked to the water's edge. He began to unbutton his shirt.

"What are you doing?" Danielle peered into the dark depths, barely able to see her own reflection. "The water must be freezing."

"I'll keep you warm."

"But Jake…" Danielle sighed and stepped away from the edge of the water. "It— it can't be this way. I can't do this."

He stopped undressing and took her hands. "What did she mean by 'sacrifice'? I think the only way to escape this is to sacrifice ourselves."

"Yes, but the water—"

"We'll be together. It will be over in a matter of minutes. One deep breath. and then it will be over."

Danielle shivered against his body. "I don't think I can," she whispered.

"Take my hand. Come with me."

They undressed, the starlight casting them in shadow, the brisk November dawn—the morning after Halloween—breathing its chill air on them. Holding hands, they stepped into the frigid water and he pulled her close against his body.

Danielle gasped, goose bumps breaking out on her skin. Jake entered her, knowing the freezing water would prevent him from staying hard unless he was already inside her. He led her deeper into the water.

He didn't let her dawdle, brought them quickly to the depths to more easily adapt to the temperature. Once they were up to their necks, he stopped and she wrapped her legs around his body, calves resting against his buttocks. His hands roamed, caressed, found her cold flesh eager for warmth. His mouth found her breasts and suckled one and then the other, the nipples already rigid from the freezing water.

His penis, hard despite the cold, moved slowly inside her. She squeezed her vaginal muscles in anticipation.

"So cold," she said, teeth chattering. "Make me warm. Please, make me warm."

His hands grabbed the back of her head and he pressed his lips into hers, tongue darting into her mouth. "I love you so much," he said. "This will be over soon."

"I know," she said, tears leaking down her face.

They submerged, keeping the pounding rhythm of his strokes, making love for the last time.

One deep breath, he'd said. But her lungs fought for life, refused to inhale water. Her lungs began to scream for air. She began to hate the feel of his lips on her mouth, the feel of him pounding inside her. She wanted him to stop. She wanted to breathe.

He moved away from her, but just his head. She watched as it broke the surface of the lake, and still he fucked her, moving rapidly now. She twisted and writhed beneath him, fought him, tried to escape his fucking.

Suddenly she hated making love to him, hated him touching her, hated being close to him. She would have killed him to escape now, if only she could.

The need to breathe became desperate. She thrashed wildly, moving impossibly slow in the water despite her efforts. She began to cum, her vagina spasming in orgasm, as she opened her mouth to draw a breath, no longer able to care about an orgasm, or about Jake. Wanting only to breathe. To live.

Jake watched her from the other side of the water, the safe side, the side with oxygen, tears dripping off his chin, sobs shredding his heart. She bucked beneath him, punched and clawed until finally she stopped moving. He watched her die. He watched her die and wondered if this sacrifice would finally set them free.

He pulled Danielle's lifeless body to the surface and sobbed against her chest, pulling her tight, unable to let go.

"You're free now," he said, choking on his words. "Free. Oh, Danni, I hope this sets you free."

He pulled her to the bank and carried her lifeless body beneath a tree, dressing her, wanting in some way to keep her warm, safe. The sun revealed itself, betraying Jake. But he was still alone. No sign of the witch, no return to the trees. He was free.

But now, he had no idea of what to do with the freedom. He had taken the cowardly way out; he had lived. But, he couldn't think to what end. This was not his world. These were no longer his people. He didn't know what was he going to do. He didn't know how he would survive without Danielle.

He wandered down the road to the familiar copse of trees that had once been his prison and sat cross-legged beneath a weeping willow. There was no good reason he could think of that he'd come back here, except perhaps because of the familiarity, no matter how awful the memories. He had spent decades beside Danielle here. And now, he had nothing.

"Was it worth it?" the witch asked, unseen, her voice part of the wind. As if she had sighed the question.

"Leave me alone," he muttered, eyes closed, remembering Danielle.

"Look at me," the witch said.

He looked. She stood before him, the wild, crazy look replaced by a calm demeanor and a modern façade. Gone was the hair of snakes and the flowing, thorned robes.

"What do you want from me? Have you come to gloat? Tell me I'm finally free?"

She laughed. "Oh, no. Nothing like that." She sat beside him beneath the tree.

"Then what do you want?"

"Did you think you'd get away so easily? That murdering the one thing that mattered to you would somehow appease me?"

He shook his head. "I have no idea."

"I don't forgive, Jake. And I don't forget."

"When you said I should make a sacrifice, what did you mean? What sacrifice? Didn't you mean me and Danni?"

"You'll never understand pure sacrifice. You're doomed to eternity as a tree, you fool."

"So what does that mean? I'm still stuck being a tree?" Somehow he wasn't surprised. Now, he wouldn't even have Danielle beside him to commiserate with. Now, he would be forced to endure this alone.

"Stuck being a tree. Is that the only thing you have learned from all of this? Is it still only about you, about your suffering? Have you still not learned why this has happened to you? You're a selfish, miserable creature!"

"Be done with it, witch! If you're going to do it, then do it! Spare me the lecture."

"Ohhh, you're even more stupid than I imagined," she crooned. "Still, I would hate for you to be alone. And you'll have another year to imagine what your reunion will be like. Enjoy!"

Jake looked up at her, confused. "What? What does that mean? What have you done?"

The witch cocked her head and sneered, one lip curling upward. She pointed at the figure walking toward them, a figure hidden by a whirling dervish of twigs and bark and leaves. The witch laughed, stuck her nose into the air and sniffed, like a dog on the hunt. She rubbed her hands together in pure delight, nearly hopping from foot to foot, and then disappeared in a flourish of wind.

In her place, Danielle appeared. Although what had once been Danielle was missing now. Standing before Jake was a pale, bloated lump of flesh, a wretched, leering thing that had once been his beloved. She reached toward him with nubby, pruned fingers, her lungs bubbling with water when she breathed.

"Oh my God!" Jake cried, scrambling away on his butt, trying to move away from the creature advancing toward him. "No!"

Her dead hand touched his face, bits of flesh sticking to his cheek, and he pushed her away. Still she kept coming, wanting to be reunited with her lover.

"No!" he wailed, squeezing his eyes shut tight. Her touch never came.

When he again opened his eyes, they had resumed their familiar forms. Only Danielle had now become a hackberry tree, devoid of greenery, riddled with lace bugs and aphids. Her knotty, twisted branches stretched across the air, trying to touch him. He tried to cower away from her but was unable to move. His full branches of leaves trembled in fear at the thought of her touch.

It was as if he could hear her talking to him, and her words were dowsed in water and dipped in poison.

He dreaded the thought of returning to human form.

SEARCHING

He's spent years searching for me. Traveling through deserts rife with expansive waves of heat, through rivers of sand that stretch into the sky, farther than the human eye can see. His thirst is great, yet he never stops, never gives up. Longing for shade doesn't slow him. Swimming vast oceans, enduring fierce waves and brutal winds, his face whipped by icy, salty water, his eyes stinging.

I thought I saw him the other day. I have his eyes: chocolate brown, with flecks of green. We have the same chin, the same mouth. I would easily recognize him. I know I would. It will be like looking at my own reflection.

Playing tea party will be his favorite game. He'll like chamomile. One spoon of sugar and no milk, just like how I drink mine, like I'm grown up.

He'll want to play dolls, but I don't care for dolls. They're silly. I like my stuffed bears and cats. They look like the real thing, and sometimes I imagine they really are real, and I talk to them and read Mercer Mayer books to them until they fall asleep. I'm too big for such books now, but I still read them out loud, because they enjoy it. Books left over from when I was a little girl, not big like I am now.

Years and years he's spent driving across the country searching for me. I can't remember how he lost track in the first place. Maybe I once knew and have forgotten. He drives and drives for hours and days at a time, calling out my name, stopping people in the street to show them my picture. He has my photo because he imagined what I would look like and he created it, because he can do anything he wants. He's like a magician, only better, because he's real.

I lie on my bed with my feet up on the wall and my head hanging off the edge. It makes the blood rush to my brain and makes my ears ring. Looking at my room upside down makes me giggle. My stuffed animals hang from shelves from the bottoms of their feet. My board games are suspended in mid-air, defying gravity. The tiny hotels and houses and Monopoly money never fall to the floor.

Mom yells at me. "Get your dirty socks off the wall." She picks up my underwear and throws it in the hamper. "Young lady, you can be such a slob

I'm not a slob. I'm just lazy. When I'm sure she isn't looking I stick m tongue out at her.

"I have to write a paper for science," I tell her as she flits around my room like a warm breeze. "Make a poster, too."

"Of what?"

"Our Solar System."

"That's nice," she says on her way out the door, but I don't think she reall thinks it's nice. I don't think she cares much about it at all.

He's still looking. I can tell. He's looked in every toy store because he thinks that's where all kids hang out. But I like books. And suddenly he think of that, because he likes books. He suddenly realizes we're so much alike hi search for me grows even stronger. In fact, he *vehemently* searches for me.

(*Vehemently*: eagerly, passionately. This is today's word in my Word-A Day Calendar.)

Mom calls me for dinner and I bring my science book with me.

"Look," I say, opening to page fifty-three. "This is our Solar System." hold up the book so she can see.

"Put that away during dinner." She scoops macaroni and cheese onto m plate.

I place the book on my lap. "Where's Dad?"

"He's coming." She calls his name again and I hear him getting up from the sofa, the fake leather making a noise like fingers rubbing a balloon. It also sounds like farting sometimes, and that cracks me up. In the summertime when it's hot and no one remembered to turn on the air, my legs stick to the sofa cushions and I have to peel them off.

Dad sits down and starts eating. We're having meatloaf, which I don't like.

When *he* finds me, we're going to have duck every night for dinner. I've never had duck before, and I don't even know if I'll like it, but it sounds ver elegant and it's the kind of food I'm sure he eats. Duck, and shrimp cocktai And oysters. Those are grown up foods and we'll eat them every night.

"I have to do a report, Dad."

He looks at Mom. "Gas prices are going up. Again."

"So?" She sits down and starts eating her dinner.

"What? *So?* So it's insane."

"We don't even have a car." She eats her green beans before anything else Mom always eats her vegetables first.

"Dad?"

He shoves food into his mouth and talks anyway. "That doesn't bother you?"

Mom shakes her head. "We've got our own problems. No need to worry about the cost of gas on top of everything else."

"Daa-aad, *look*. Lookit this. Da-ad!"

He glances over his shoulder, and even though he's looking at me, he's talking to her. "Cost of gas goes up, then taxes go up, it never ends."

Mom laughs and says, "Oh yeah?" and eats another forkful of green beans.

"Dad?" I say quietly, holding up my textbook, staring at the photographs of the galaxy.

After dinner Dad sits on the sofa and Mom washes dishes, so I sit on the sofa too. I don't want to have to dry but she'll probably yell for me to do it anyway.

I hold up my science book and open it to page fifty-three. "Lookit," I say, laying it across his lap, running my fingers over the glossy picture. "Daddy? See? I have to do a report."

He's staring ahead, at the television. The news is on. I hate the news.

"Dad?" I wait for an answer. "Dad?" I stare up at him. "Dad? Daddy?"

"Can't you see I'm busy?" he yells, knocking the book off his lap. It tumbles to the floor. He makes a sighing noise and goes back to staring at the television.

I pick up the book and bring it to my bedroom.

Later in my room, I start my assignment. "The Solar System, by Karen Brown. Our Solar System has eight planets. We used to have nine but now it's only eight. One planet that's not a planet no more is Pluto, and they named that one after a dog. The other eight planets are—" I copy the names of the planets. I copy some other stuff too. I draw a picture that looks like the one in the book.

Sometimes I pretend he stops watching the news and comes in to see me and throws his arms around me and tells me how much he loves me.

But that doesn't happen.

Sometimes I wonder if *he's* any closer. It's taking him so long to find me. My real father. The one who looks like me, talks like me, loves books the way I do. The father who would never ignore me to watch TV.

There must be a way for me to send him a signal, to let him know when he's close. One time I asked Mom who my real father is and she looked at me funny and asked me what I was talking about. So maybe she doesn't know. Maybe she thinks the man who lives with us is my real father. Maybe they switched places one night, and this stranger took my father's place.

Because he can't be. He can't be my real father.

He just can't.

My real father is searching for me. He walks or runs when he can't find a car or a plane. Sometimes he even hitchhikes, because he'll never give up. He knows he'll find me if he just keeps looking. I know my science projects will be fantastic when he helps, because he's really good at stuff like that. He's a scientist, and a doctor (brain surgeon), and even a lawyer. An actor too, I'll bet.

He searches, and I'm looking too. Like the other day, I saw a man who looked like me. That had been so close. I know it's going to happen. I just have to be patient.

And when my real dad finds me, it'll be great.

Everything will be perfect then.

LACHESIS

Across the street from the Freemont no-tell motel, Teresa spent the afternoon stealing glances out the window during a rather boring and impromptu meeting held in her client's office across town from her own office.

And along with the city's usual busyness, the hustle of suits rushing to meetings and power lunches, bike messengers playing chicken with cabs in midtown congestion, traffic cops trying to make sense of it all, she spotted Chris escorting the latest flavor of the week into the motel. Had seen him time and again with someone different, even though he always denied any adulterous behavior. She could never quite catch him—until now.

Not that Theresa was exactly shocked by Chris' transgressions, and it was hard not to wonder what he was doing at that moment.

An affair was an affair was an affair and smelled foul no matter who the cheater turned out to be. And how many times had she felt the outrage burning on her cheeks, had wondered why she was never enough for him? But then, she'd never confronted him with her accusations. And what did it matter, really, why he was doing it? The fact he was cheating was bad enough. She really didn't want to hear from him how miserable a wife or lover she was.

She glanced at her watch and concluded the meeting. A quick stop at the airport first, to pick up a special order for their small business, then home. Just recently she and Chris had added a Burmese python to their reptile family, one of the few non-poisonous snakes they bred.

"I saw you today," Teresa blurted while serving dinner.

Chris looked up from his plate and smiled. "You did? Why didn't you say hello?"

"Going into the Freemont."

He stopped chewing and looked up. "Freemont? I wasn't there today."

"Yes you were."

"No, T." A dimple formed in his left cheek when he smiled. That had once been enough to melt her heart. "I was in town to—"

"I saw you!" She regretted yelling—an impetuous move. She chewed on her bottom lip, hard enough to halt the tears that threatened to fall. "Who is she this time, Chris?"

He picked up his fork. Blinked repeatedly behind his smoky John Lennon glasses. "What makes you think I—"

"Please, Chris. Don't. I know about you and those women. I've seen you. I just didn't want to believe… never wanted to believe you could do this to me."

He stuffed food into his mouth and chewed slowly, enraptured by the bits of potato and meat floating in the stew.

"I just want to know why," she pleaded. "Why am I not good enough for you?"

"My god, T," he whispered, head drooping toward his plate. He pinched the bridge of his nose. "It's not like that. I love you, baby."

"It's not enough, Chris. I need to know this'll stop. Why can't I be enough?"

"You're all I want. I don't know what you think you saw—"

"At least have the balls to admit when you've been caught. Give me at least that much."

She watched him for a few seconds more, watched him study his food, poke his fork into the cubes of meat, pretending to have an appetite. Then she stormed out of the room, nothing left to say.

"I need help," he later called from the breeding cages. Thirty-six boxes of equal size, stacked one on top of the other, six across and six high. Glass encased. Each box opened individually, and beneath each, a drawer that housed the reptiles, easily accessible.

"Drop dead," she muttered from the living room, loud enough for him to hear.

"We still have a business to run," he said. They were partners in the snake breeding business, although she also preferred to work outside the home. It gave her freedom, time away from the house. Time to obsess about Chris' affairs.

Reluctantly she went to help, but only because she cared about the business, which generated a decent income, enabled them to enjoy a comfortable upper middle-class existence. Her knowledge of the care and handling of snakes nearly rivaled his.

"Look," he said, as he pulled out the drawer. "The copperhead had her babies."

Six small snakes squirmed in the sand-filled incubator tray, their mother coiled peacefully in the back.

He pushed the drawer back and began to count the snakes, taking inventory of the cobras, copperheads, bushmasters, rattlesnakes, and cottonmouths in he cages that mimicked the dense, swampy areas the snakes favored. The majority of the reptiles bred were *crotalidae*, the pit vipers, although they also kept the more dangerous *elapidae*, like the adders and mambas, the most deadly of toxic snakes. The more poisonous—the more dangerous—the better the profit.

"That makes forty-seven babies this month," he said, peering into the box over the top of his glasses.

She wiped dust off the cage with her sleeve. "Can't we talk about this?"

"There's nothing to talk about. You're convinced I've done something wrong. I'm sorry you feel that way, but there's nothing I can do."

His fingers stabbed the air as he began his count once more, poking each pane of glass, saying their names as if calling his children. "There's one missing."

"Don't bother," she muttered. Leaned against the glass, folded her arms.

His finger froze mid count. "What do you mean?"

"I mean you were right. One's missing. And you won't find him." The one thing she knew would get under his skin was the threat of harm to one of his reptiles. She enjoyed the business. He enjoyed the snakes.

He slowly turned toward her. "Which one?"

"Lachesis." So named after the Latin, *Lachesis Mutus*. The bushmaster.

His breath caught. The snake he loved most of all, she knew, the one he had raised from a snakelet, years ago now. The one that had fathered countless offspring and had generated a fortune in sales.

"Honey," he said slowly, through gritted teeth, in a dramatic style as if lecturing a child. "That's not funny. We promised to never do anything to jeopardize the business. Or my snakes. Right?" His lips pulled taut, stretched like canvas.

"And *you* agreed to stop screwing everyone in town. I guess we're a couple of filthy liars."

"Where is Lachesis?"

"Go to hell."

He slapped her across the face. She slapped back.

"This isn't funny, Theresa." He stepped toward her. "Where the hell is—"

"You ate him!"

Jaw muscles worked overtime. He scratched his head. "What?"

She approached until she was a few inches from his face. Breathed heavily through her nose, her cheeks flushed with the slap and the excitement. "You rotten cheater. You got what you deserve. Dinner this evening was bushmaster stew. I can't believe the poison hasn't killed you yet."

"You're lying. You'd never—"

"Wouldn't I?" Her eyes narrowed. "I'm sick of it, Chris. I'm sick of being a laughingstock. Sick of your little transgressions. Everyone knows what you've been up to, and they laugh at me. At *me*. Pointing their fingers, saying how incredibly stupid I am."

"You're insane," he whispered, blinking, blinking, eyelids fluttering behind too thick lenses. "You couldn't have done anything that stupid."

"You love a *snake* more than you love me. There's something wrong with you. Die now. Let the poison tear you apart. Should be interesting to see what it does from the inside out. This is what you've always wanted, isn't it? To be so close to your snakes. You get your wish."

He shook his head. "How could you?" His grief became anger and escalated to rage. His eyes bulged, tiny red lines forming across the retinas. The rage found its way to his fist, and he punched Teresa in the face, harder than she ever suspected he could.

"*Not Lachesis.*"

Blood tricked from her scalp as it connected with glass that shattered into a network of spider-web fissures.

Teresa opened her eyes and blinked back drops of dried blood from her lids. She wondered when he had become so violent. He'd never been dangerous before. And foolishly she never thought he loved that damned snake enough to actually harm her. Could he really value the life of a snake over hers?

Her head throbbed. She started to sit up, but Chris's voice suddenly filled the room via the loudspeaker.

"I wouldn't move if I were you."

The movement of her head was imperceptible; her eyes roamed the perimeter of the large room, which was filled with lush vegetation and was entirely encased in glass, like a giant greenhouse.

The controlled-environment room was filled with snakes.

She gasped, afraid to make even that much movement. Her frayed nerves felt electrified; sweat broke out everywhere on her body.

"Chris," she whispered, barely breathing the words. "This isn't funny. Help me."

"Help," he said. "You want help. Well let's see. We'll start with some advice. Don't move a muscle."

"Not funny," she wheezed, eyes roaming, searching for the more dangerous, more aggressive snakes. She knew the scent of her pheromones filled the air, stimulating certain snakes. Something she really didn't need right now.

The Green Mamba was coiled several feet away from her head. This was the snake to avoid, the most highly toxic snake they bred. This one, which Chris named Augustus after its Latin name *Dendraspis angusticeps*, was the male. The more aggressive of the pair of Mambas they owned. One little movement might upset it; any tiny vibration could cause it to attack. Its bite would mean death within minutes, even if they had the Antidendroaspis Antivenom available, which they didn't. Not all antivenoms were easy to come by.

The other snakes in the room explored, following the lead of their tongues, esting the air, determining how much of a danger Teresa was.

So far none saw her as a threat, which was the only reason Teresa was still live. Anything could upset them however—the slightest movement. Teresa knew this. But then, so did Chris.

But if she lay still as a corpse, and was patient, she might be able to wait hem out. The room would eventually cool, replicating nighttime, and the liurnal snakes would become lethargic. This would be her only chance.

Assuming Chris hadn't sabotaged the controls.

"This was supposed to be a surprise," he said into the mic. "I finished he room. Fixed the thermostat. Of course I normally wouldn't put all these snakes in here at the same time. Too many variations in type, desert versus swamp, things like that. But you should know that. For example, Augustus ikes the room cooler than, say, *Lachesis* would have…"

He sighed. "So what do you think? Looks good, right?"

She swallowed, trying to control her breathing, silently cursing him out and wishing for his death.

"No," he said sadly, "I guess you can't answer right now."

She'd never known him to be so cruel. They had their little games—the divorce game was one they normally played out within a few days. She'd never seen him so furious, but she'd never used a snake as leverage before. Knowing how much he loved his snakes, she realized what a stupid idea that had been. She'd needed her revenge—but where had it gotten her?

A Western Diamondback Rattlesnake he'd named Troy (*Crotalus Atrox*) slithered across from wrist to elbow until it settled in the crook of her arm, warming itself with the heat of her body.

She exhaled, unable to control the trembling in her arms and legs but knowing she had to. Huge eyes stared at the rattler that had nestled with her.

"Wondering if I screwed with the controls, aren't you?"

Her eyes widened.

"Let me put it this way: would I ever do anything to endanger my snakes?"

Was that a trick question? After what he'd done to her? If he were waiting for that inevitable death by snakebite, then wouldn't he do everything to ensure she got bitten? The snakes could always be replaced, even the ones he loved. So yeah, she supposed he'd do something to endanger a snake. Anything to get rid of her.

"No, sweetie. You have my word. I didn't touch the controls."

His word. That was rich! An exasperated cry slid out of her mouth, more movement than she'd intended.

The snakes didn't react. Troy was a perfect cylinder resting against her body.

The glass-encased room reflected the passage of the day. The sun was setting, the temperature in the room mimicking nightfall. The snakes would rest then, would curl up in some dark corner to rest.

She might be able to move. Troy would hopefully remain lethargic… she could only pray.

The lights in the room began to dim ever so slightly. They would never fully extinguish but would mimic a full moon. The temperature in the room dropped a few more degrees.

Teresa began to quiver, from relief and from the chill of sweat drying on her body.

The Gwardar slithered across her ankle, raising its olive head and tasting Teresa with its flickering forked tongue. She held her breath, mentally begging it to go on, not to stop.

Soon. Soon it would be time to try to get up.

The Gwardar decided not to stay and slithered away.

"Oh honey?" Chris's voice startled her. "Forgot to mention something."

She could see his shadowy reflection on the other side of the glass, staring in at her. "I made a new purchase. *Sweetie.*"

She couldn't image what kind of snake he'd bought. They already owned the most deadly snakes on the planet, and she knew how they behaved. She normally wouldn't have been concerned with such a new purchase. After all, a bite from a Cobra was almost as dangerous as a bite from a Mamba. The poison just took a little longer to paralyze and kill the victim. A new snake wasn't any more of a threat than the ones already in the room with her.

And as if reading her mind he added: "This something new isn't a snake."

She heard the clang of locks being thrown and doors banging open and shut.

Then he reappeared at the glass.

"You never should have killed Lachesis," he said. "I was willing to play along with your stupid divorce game, but you had to go and get nasty. I provided for you, gave you everything you wanted. The one thing I warned you never to do is harm one of the snakes. And that was exactly what you did."

She shook her head. Tears spilled into her hair. "I didn't," she whispered, afraid to raise her voice. "Listen to me. I didn't kill—"

But he wasn't listening, or just couldn't hear her.

Something was moving toward her. In the diminished light, she couldn't tell what it was, but it was scuttling across the sand.

As they got nearer, she could see them more clearly. Hundreds and hundreds of small black bugs.

"American Burying Beetles," he said. "Corpse eaters. But we have time, don't we? Eventually they'll get to eat. Should make for an interesting Eco test."

She sucked in her breath and moved a few inches, lifting her head, searching for the location of the snakes. Troy was still calm. Augustus the

Mamba—nasty, bad-tempered Augustus—was curled less than two feet away from her head, staring at her without blinking, in true snake fashion.

When she moved her arm the Rattler raised his head. The tail was still silent, a good sign. She moved another inch and then the rattles started... warily, the snake reared up, hissing at her, poising to strike.

She jumped up as quickly as she could and pressed herself against the glass, dodging the Rattler's striking head. It slithered away, choosing to retreat while it had that option.

There was nothing for Teresa to stand on to give herself height; the shrubs were flimsy and would sink to the ground, the Eyelash Pit Viper was draped in the branches of largest tree in the room. Its branches were probably too weak to support her weight anyway.

The few nocturnal snakes had become agitated by the movement of the bugs, and the sleepy snakes were incited into activity. The room became a death chamber of hissing and slithering cold-blooded bodies, striking at one another, fighting off the bugs that swarmed over them.

Teresa was frozen with fear, her vision clouded with tears and sweat, every nerve ending on her body electrified, every hair stiff.

Nowhere to go.

"Chris," she cried. "Do something. Please!"

She looked up and saw he had moved a bit closer and was studying the action in the room.

"Please," she shrieked, her face scarlet, her breathing ragged. He fingernails clawed at the glass wall behind her, seeking purchase of any kind, finding none, slippery, sweaty fingers streaking the glass.

"Lachesis is alive," she cried, words mixing with bubbling saliva. "Please, Chris, please! He's alive. I swear."

The bugs swarmed toward her. Snakes surrounded her.

"Snarky little bastards," he said. "Stay perfectly still, maybe the bugs won't bite. After all, they prefer carrion. So don't. Move. A muscle."

"Oh, *god*," she moaned, hyperventilating, frantically trying to keep track of the dizzying activity in the room.

"Then again... if you don't move, they might just think you're dead. Maybe you should jump around."

She could hear him laughing. *Laughing*!

The beetles reached her feet. She alternated lifting them, trying to keep her movements calm and steady, trying also to squash the orange-headed bugs. They swarmed around her, trying to find a way to climb onto her.

The rattlers had retreated into gopher holes, having become docile after the sun set and being the type of snake that preferred to avoid a fight. There were still two dozen other snakes to worry about, however, many breeds high strung and ready to attack even when unprovoked.

"Chris," she screamed. "The snakes! The bugs are killing the snakes!"

He cleared his throat. "No, honey. The snakes are fine. But thanks for your concern. The beetles won't harm them. It's you they want."

They poured out of the gopher holes and skittered across the snakes, oblivious to anything in their path.

Teresa ran to the thickest tree in the room, which was barely larger than a sapling, its trunk only about six inches in diameter, its thickest, strongest branch not even half that.

She shoved the Eyelash Pit Viper onto the ground before it could lift its head and react to her being in the tree with it. She clutched the swinging, swaying tree, hugging the small trunk with her thighs.

Chris's laughter echoed through the room, since he was considerate enough to have left the mic open.

The beetles followed her to the tree and circled the base, tumbling back onto themselves when they tried to follow her up.

The tree swayed left and Teresa used her thighs to steady it. Then it swayed to the right and she repeated the move, attempting to keep it upright. She did this dozens of times before her legs began to tremble and spasm… barely any strength left now.

"Please, Chris. Please. *Please*."

He sighed. "All right. Come on."

Moments later the door cracked open. *What?* She groaned in relief and searched the ground for a safe place to land.

The beetles were directly below, so she would have to jump over them. But jumping was certainly going to upset any number of the snakes.

"I need help. Can you get the snakes?"

"Uh, no hon, sorry. Can't. Too dangerous."

The ground to her right was where the Copperheads and Cottonmouths had chosen to rest. The area to her right contained only the Mamba, but he was the nasty one, apt to strike even when unprovoked.

Her thigh muscles cramped and she began to involuntarily slide down the trunk. She screamed and tried to find something to grab onto and caught a handful of leaves and buds. Using the trunk to kick off, she lunged from the tree and landed on her hands and knees, her face mere inches from the Cobra. It raised its formidable hood, hissing.

Using her left hand, she distracted the cobra, waving her fingers, taunting it. With a practiced movement she grabbed the base of its head from behind with her other hand.

The snake whipped in her grasp, and she threw it across the room.

The exit was three feet away now. *Three feet* to the door Chris had thrown open only minutes earlier. And she could see it was still open.

She struggled to her feet as quickly as she could—as she dared—her thighs still weak and trembling, not wanting to carry her away.

A Diamondback was asleep by the door, but she didn't expect him to be problem.

She ran the final three feet and reached the exit just as Chris slammed it shut.

"No!" she shrieked.

Lying several feet away, the nocturnal gray Jumping Viper with the black dorsal blotches raised its head and hissed, annoyed at the disturbance. It lashed up, striking her on her arm before dropping back to the ground.

She screamed and grabbed her arm. Her only hope was that the snake had been trying to warn her and not kill, that its bite had been *dry*. But she felt the arm already beginning to swell, the poison traveling through her bloodstream, causing excruciating pain.

She staggered away from the Jumping Viper, knowing it wouldn't hesitate to strike again. The beetles found her and began to follow her like trained puppies.

Chris stared at her. She felt his eyes, and when she looked at him, he shook his head sadly.

The poison was rapidly working its way through her body. Her fingers and toes were numb, and a wave of nausea made her double over. She dropped to her knees, upsetting the Green Mamba. Augustus struck her in the leg, his fangs sinking deeply in the flesh, milking his poison into her bloodstream.

Death was inevitable, but it wasn't immediate. Without treatment she wouldn't survive more than a few minutes. And she wasn't kidding herself about her chances. All Teresa could do was lie there and pray for a quick death. The poison worked quickly, paralyzing her, stealing her breath until it came in shallow gasps.

The beetles worked quickly, knowing her death was inevitable, not waiting for the near-corpse to grow cold. They tunneled quickly into the soil below her body, loosening the dirt until she sank into the freshly dug hole. They injected her flesh with secretions, preserving her, which would ultimately modify the decomposition of her body.

A mother beetle dug a chamber in Teresa's cheek and deposited her eggs. The father joined her and both beetles regurgitated partly digested food droplets into the hole in her cheek, storing up food for the larvae that would hatch in a few days.

All throughout her body, the beetles were preparing Teresa for the birth of the larvae and the ensuing feast.

The *neurotoxins* in the snake venom depressed the action of her heart and lungs; the *hemotoxin* damaged her blood vessels and other tissue. She felt her flesh dissolving, felt the hundreds of bugs boring holes in her. Her body began to spasm in a paralyzed agony, unable to fight them off, unable to protect her body from dissolution.

Within the next few minutes, she was dead.

Within hours she would be completely buried, her body serving as food and a birthing place for the hatching larvae.

Within days there would be nothing left of Teresa but bone, her flesh having been picked clean by the bugs.

Chris turned away from the glass after watching her spastic body make futile attempts to survive. The beetles were relentless, ruthless. When he'd purchased them, it was with the intention of conducting research. He never imagined the research would have taken such a bizarre turn.

He jotted his findings in his notebook, satisfied with the bugs' performance.

The glass room had been built on a steel and concrete foundation and was impenetrable. No creature could escape. Rounding up the bugs would be a daunting task, but he'd worry about that later.

He wandered into the kitchen and brewed coffee. The remains of the stew were congealing in a pot on the stove, and he disgustedly pushed it away.

If he'd had any doubts about her death, this squelched them. She was a lunatic, endangering (killing!) harmless snakes. And why? Revenge. Because he'd had an affair or two. Or three. That was why. But why punish the snake?

He puttered around the house for a while but was easily bored. He wondered how he would explain Teresa's death. Or her disappearance—he wasn't sure how he planned to handle this. The bugs would get rid of most of the evidence, but what to do with her bones?

And she'd claimed Lachesis was still alive—if so, where was he? He knew she'd lied to save her ass, and it hadn't worked.

In his bedroom he changed into his pajamas. The bed was lumpy, decorated with extra blankets and throw pillows. He pulled down the comforter and sheet.

Lachesis, coiled in a small, neat ball lifted his head, hissing, exposing his tremendously long fangs from the center of Chris's side of the bed.

"Well," he said, stepping back. He laughed. "You were telling the truth after all." But he was overjoyed at seeing his beautiful Lachesis. He ran into the lab and returned with a net and scooped Lachesis into it, carefully returning him to his tank.

He glanced into the glass-enclosed room and brightened the lights a bit. The majority of the snakes were sleeping now, and the beetles were still busy working on Teresa's body. Everything was perfect.

He returned to the bedroom, shaking his head when he thought about how stupid Teresa had been. Taunting him with Lachesis' death, and then trying to kill *him* using the snake. Lachesis would never harm him. Teresa should have known better.

He slid beneath the sheets, thinking of his latest lover, thinking about life without Teresa. He settled into his pillow and smiled, reaching over to click ff the lamp.

The sheet by his foot suddenly moved.

He threw back the covers and a snake he'd never seen before reared up, aising its dark brown head, wavering back and forth, suddenly striking so uickly that it bit Chris several times before he even realized it was attacking. his wasn't one of their snakes, but he knew it well.

Taipan. One of the deadliest snakes in the world.

He felt his lungs constrict as the poison quickly made its way through his ody.

"*Bitch,*" he slurred over his thickening tongue just seconds before he ied.

SOMEONE'S SISTER

It wasn't supposed to happen this way.

There was supposed to be some fighting, some bloodshed, yeah, right, probably. Expected that. Car boostin', knocking over a liquor store or one a them shitty bodegas, the ones run by the dotheads or spics.

No one said *nothing* about no kidnappin'.

Jimmy said I should shut my fuckin' mouth. Said I was gonna end up with my fuckin' throat slit if I didn't shut the fuck up.

Jimmy really likes the word fuck.

We grabbed her right after we boosted the car, see. It was Jimmy's idea and all, he like, master-planned the damn thing, but he made Big Joey and Mookie get outa the car and grab her.

You didn't say no to Jimmy, not if you were smart, not if you wanted to keep your guts where they belonged. And them guys didn't wanna look pussy.

She was a fighter, right from the beginning. Kicked an' screamed an' clawed at Joe an' Mook, but they dragged her sorry ass into the back seat of the car. She was cryin', too. Bawlin' her stupid eyes out. Joe had his knee planted in her chest. To hold her down and all. Mook held her hands over her head so's he could reach down easy and squeeze her tits. They let her scream. Wasn't no one around anyway.

Jimmy tossed back a roll of duct tape and told them to tape her hands and slap a piece over her fuckin' mouth.

They did what he said. You didn't say no to Jimmy.

We brought her back to the shed. It was just the place where we hung out and all, kinda like a headquarters or some lame shit like that. It was secluded anyway. That was the main reason we picked it. To get away when things got too hot. Just an old shack, nothin' great, but it kept us warm, and more important, it keep us hid.

Jimmy raped her first. Then Joe, then Mook.

Then me.

I din wanna look pussy. I ain't sure I wanted to rape her. I got sisters, you know? I got a Ma. I felt kinda bad about doin' it, an' I only did it that one time. Well, that night, anyways.

Her mouth was still taped and her eyes was squeezed closed real tight. Her hands were taped up too, and they were over her head, hangin' from the radiator. She wasn't wearing any shoes or pants or undies. She was still wearin' her shirt and socks though. That's cuz Jimmy said he wanted to fuck around with her tits, but he was savin' that for later. Right now, he just wanted to fuck her.

So I had another turn. Don't know how many times the other guys did it. I stopped watchin'.

She was screamin', too. As much as she could with her mouth taped up. The sound was kinda muffled, like yellin' underwater. Not real loud. Kinda annoyin'. Like a mosquito in your ear. I guess I can't really blame her. But Jimmy slapped her real hard a few times an' she finally shut up, thank fucking christ.

Later that first night, we was sittin' 'round, smokin' an' tokin', and Joey says to Jimmy, "What we gonna do with her?"

Do with her? Jimmy says. What that suppose to mean? He says he gonna keep her, like a mascot, or a pet. His own pet pussy. Then we fuck her anytime we felt like gettin' our rocks off. For Jimmy, that seemed to happen a lot.

Joe looked kinda surprised, but he didn't say nothin' else about it.

I didn't say nothin' at all. I mean, I was new here. But I knew what I was gettin' into when I hooked up with them. Sorta. The one thing I did know was when to keep my fucking mouth shut.

Jimmy moved over to the bed. "Hey," he said, shakin' the girl. "You up?" She opened her bloodshot, puffy eyes. "I'm gonna take the tape offa your mouth. You scream, and I'll beat the shit outa you, and it goes back on. Dig?"

She nodded. Joey and Mookie exchanged glances. Looked to me like they was as nervous as me, and they weren't gonna say nothin'.

Jimmy was crazier than a shit-house rat. I always thought that was a funny saying. I didn't know it could really be true.

He peeled the tape from her mouth and she yelled, not like yellin' for help, or nothin' like that, which I kinda expected from a girl. She yelled cause that tape gettin' ripped off her lips musta hurt like a sonofabitch. She ran her tongue over her lips, up and down, and in circles, and Jimmy starts grinnin' real wide. I think it was making him horny, cause a second later he's on top of her again.

"Shut your fuckin' hole. Don't scream," he says. Then he fucked her.

This went on for like three days. We fed her, brought her to the can. Jimmy kept her naked, said he liked her that way. She did have a great body, really perfect tits, you know? Even after Jimmy messed with 'em. Burned 'em, pulled on 'em, tied them up til they was blue.

I can't say I minded him keepin' her naked. Like a pet, he said. Cats don't wear no clothes, and neither did *his* pussy. Jimmy thought his little joke was very funny.

She never said a word, not even when she was gettin' fucked. She just kinda laid there, not cryin' no more. Her eyes were always fixed on the wall across from her, starin' at the clock. But I don't think she cared about the time. She looked like she was spacin'. It wasn't drugs, neither. I tried to pass her a joint once, but she just shook her head. Hell, I was *relieved* she did that, you know, shook her head at my question. Answered me. Like she would talk to me. Maybe had forgiven me. I figured she woulda been pissed at me.

*   *   *

Jimmy came in one day with a bag of food. It had been my turn to sit with her. One of us always had to be there. Always. Usually it was Jimmy. He stayed with her the most.

"She give you any trouble, Kevin?"

The question had been a joke. How could she have given me any trouble, lyin' on the bed, hands tied up? I shook my head anyway. Better to answer him. She was never any trouble, and that was kinda spooky. She just kinda laid there, lookin' sometimes like she was in a coma or somethin'.

Then Joey and Mookie showed up and we sat around playin' poker.

Joey said somethin' like, "We can't keep her here forever, man." He looked over at the bed, then lowered his voice. "I mean, my wife is starting to get pissed. I ain't home much, you know? She's getting suspicious that I'm up to somethin'. How much longer you—"

Jimmy leapt up from the table, grabbin' it, knocking it over, poker chips and half ate sandwiches flying through the air, cards scattered on the floor.

He snatched Joey by his collar with both fists and slammed him into the wall. Hard. Joe grunted, the wind knocked outa him.

"When I fucking say so," Jimmy said, his face so close to Joey's I thought they was gonna fucking kiss. "That's when. You keep your fuckin' mouth shut. You do what I say. Got that?"

Joey's head bobbed up and down till I thought it was gonna fall off. "Yeah, Jimmy. Yes."

He let go of Joey's collar. He turned around an' looked at the girl. As usual she was just lyin' on the bed, watchin' everything, probably prayin' someone would go up against him. She probably figured she'd have a much better chance with me or Joe or Mook. Maybe she figured one of us would let her go. I think she knew Jimmy had no intention of lettin' her go. Never.

Christ, we didn't even know her name.

*   *   *

Couple days later, I'm sitting with her again. My turn. She picks now to say her first words. Maybe she saw *asshole* written all over my dumb face.

I got no family. I got sisters and a mom, but I ain't seen them for a lor time. Years. It's not like we were close. We weren't the fuckin' Brady Bunc I got no real education, not past ninth grade, barely got a job, if pumpin' g for minimum wage twenty-eight hours a week counts as much of anything. know it's pathetic, this life of mine, and Jimmy is my family. My life. Not no fag way, man. It's like he's my brother or somethin'.

She said to me, "Please let me go. I won't turn you in, I swear. I know it not you. It's not your fault. It's *him*. It's not *you* I want to—"

She didn't finish what she was sayin'. I knew what she was gettin' at, kne what she was thinkin'. I knew what she'd meant. It really pissed me off, to Did she think I was gonna help her? Turn against *him*?

"I don't *want* to hurt him…" she said. "But if I have to…"

"Shut the fuck up." She didn't wanna hurt him? I knew the first thin she would do is run to the cops. First thing. Not hurt him. Yeah, right. didn't wanna hear any more. She was really pissing me off now. She was a re asshole.

She said, "Jimmy's your friend. But this is wrong and you know it."

"Shut up." I was gonna tape her mouth, and I'm sure she knew it, so sh finally shut up.

There was somethin' in her eyes. Somethin' that scared me. I couldn really tell you what it was, but it was weird. I remember the room seemed have gotten much colder, and the hairs were standin' up on my arms. I kno that sounds stupid, seein' she was all tied up and shit. But it's what happene

*   *   *

Weeks went by. I think we was all wondering what Jimmy was plannin He had to be thinkin' about doin' *somethin'*, right? Had to have some plan mind. This was just nuts. It had all started out bad, real bad, but what had th become? Insanity, that's what.

The girl was so goddamned well-behaved, too. That was the real bitch it. I don't think she ever tried to escape, not once. Didn't seem normal, not me anyway. If I was tied up like that, I would be actin' like a wild animal eve chance I got, tryin' to get away. She did at first, but that was before we broug her here. She stopped fighting right after that. Maybe we broke her spirit, lik a whipped dog, right from the start. I guess that's possible. Sad, too.

Jimmy's hand was down his pants, as usual. If that old wives' tale abou growin' palm hair from playin' with yourself was true, Jimmy would look lik the fuckin' Wolfman by now.

He looked up at me. "You haven't had her in a long time, man."

I shrugged. "You go ahead, Jimmy. I know you—"

"You giving me permission, fuck-face?"

"Naw, man, I didn't mean nothin'."

He grabbed hold of my neck with his huge free hand, pullin' me toward him. He was only a few years older than me—I think he was twenty-six—but he was so much bigger. He'd played football in high school. That was really the only reason he had managed to graduate. Played varsity. Linebacker, I think. He was still as big as a fuckin' tree.

"Fuck her. Do it now."

I nodded, but the truth was, I wasn't much in the mood, you know? It wasn't like that first night, with all the excitement, with my adrenaline flowin', her fightin' and screamin'.

It was a mess now. I didn't wanna rape her. I'd really had enough. I mean, I wasn't stupid about it. I figured when this was all over, I was gonna be spendin' some time back in prison. I hoped it was for kidnapping and rape though, and not as an accomplice to murder. I still couldn't do the right thing and help her escape, though. I guess I was more of a pussy than I had hoped.

Right now, the least of my problems was my limp dick. I felt like now *I* was gettin' fucked. By Jimmy.

I looked over at Joey and Mookie. They were lookin' the other way.

Jimmy stared me down. He crossed his arms over his massive chest. And he waited. And I could see the madness in his eyes.

I unzipped my fly and pulled out my dick. Lookin' at her lyin' there, spread-eagle, really helped of course. Hey, I was feelin' like shit, and I was scared, but I'm a *guy*, you know. I don't always control what my tool is gonna do. In fact, I think I *never* know what it's gonna do.

She smiled at me. That was the worst of it. Smiled like a goddamned lover, like this was consensual. It kinda pissed me off. She spread her legs for me. I was strokin' myself, feelin' it gettin' harder, and all that time I was gazing into those penetrating, forgiving eyes.

I leaned over and climbed on top of her; she moved around a bit, tryin' to position herself. She whispered in my ear, "I didn't want to hurt you. You must believe that. Remember it."

Hurt me? What the fuck—

I forced myself inside her, hard, and she cried out. I was angry, real angry, but I'm not even sure why. She just pissed me off. She was too compassionate. It wasn't normal, man. It was like... like she was raping *me*.

I fucked her hard, as hard as I could, smashin' her fuckin' head into the radiator. I *wanted* to hurt her, see? To wipe that damned forgiving smile off her face. Shit, I don't think *bleach* woulda taken that smile off her face.

"I'm sorry," she said. "I didn't want to hurt you. But this is your fault now. You had your chance to make it right."

I slapped her across her face right after I came. I was breathin' hard, and suddenly realized I was in pain. My dick hurt. Not real bad or nothin', cause I woulda noticed that. It just kinda... stung.

I pulled out and my dick was covered in blood. "Oh, Christ," I moaned.

"Oh, fuck," Jimmy said to me. "Got her period?"

I didn't say anything. I wasn't sure *what* just happened.

But I didn't think she had her period.

Jimmy, of course, was more aroused than ever. I think he's part rabbit, that asshole.

"Move," he said to me.

I moved.

Jimmy pulled his dick out of his pants and moved slowly toward the bed.

"Enough," she said. "I've had enough of your bullshit. When the hell do you plan on stopping this?"

He was genuinely surprised by her outburst. "When I'm good and goddamn ready," he said.

"I'm telling you right now, you motherfucker, don't touch me again. This is the only warning you get."

He laughed, laughed hard. Shook his head. "I'm gonna fuck you, then they're gonna fuck you. Then we'll all fuck you at once. Then I'll cut off your tits and fuck the hole."

She stared at him without saying another word.

And he raped her. Was on top of her in a flash, and what happened next happened so quickly, I thought I'd missed it. I wish I had. But I'd been watching, entranced by what was going on, absently wipin' blood off my dick with napkins. I was stunned by her sudden display of anger and aggression.

When he entered her, he thrust once, twice maybe, and when he tried to pull back again, she held him tight. Her hands were tied, of course. She was holding him with her cunt.

He started screaming. And I mean *screaming*, like a girl. He pushed against her, slapped at her, punched her face and neck. Blood was pouring down, soakin' into the bedsheets. It looked like it was pourin' from their bellies. There was just so much blood.

"It hurts," he yelled. "It's fucking biting me!"

Her face was stone, her body thrusting and spasming, and he was jerking and shrieking on top of her. Horrible sucking noises came from between them from their crotches rubbing together, like they were trying to pull each other down a drain. Slurping, grinding sounds coming from her pussy.

Then he was thrown from her, as if he'd fallen back from a gunshot recoil. He landed hard on his bare ass.

There was a jagged, bloody hole where his cock used to be.

It was still hanging out of her, pulsing and throbbing like it had a life of its own. It looked like a bloodstained vibrator. I couldn't tell if she'd been injured because she was completely red below her stomach, and she was coated in gore. I couldn't help but stare at her pussy, at the *thing* sticking out. Somehow it was still moving. A crunching, chewing noise was coming from her crotch. I swear I saw a flash of teeth down there.

Jimmy was lying on the floor just screamin' and cryin', blood gushing from his cleaved pelvis. His instant sex-change operation. His face had gone a shade of white I didn't know existed. Whiter than paper.

Then he goes quiet, just like that. Don't even know if he's dead. Haven't checked yet.

Joey and Mook never moved a muscle, not one fucking inch. Both of 'em just sat and stared, their mouths hinged open.

"Untie me," she said to me.

I didn't move at first. I looked around the room, taking it all in. I heard either Joe or Mook get sick, heard the retching, then smelled the vomit. Don't know who did it. Maybe both. I don't know why I didn't lose my lunch. I guess maybe it hadn't all sunk in yet.

"I said untie me."

This time I ran over and untied her. I don't know why—you'd think I'd have been better off leaving her tied up. But I think I expected things to be even worse if I didn't listen. Or maybe I was afraid of what she'd do when she did get untied. Or maybe I felt guilty—how the fuck should I know why I did it?

But she was loose, and that's all that mattered.

She pulled out Jimmy's dick with a slurping, oily sound, like a clogged drain after being rooted clear. She tossed it on the floor beside him.

She looked at me for a long time. I was terrified. Shit my pants. I don't remember doin' it, but it was there, sure enough.

She took her clothes from the shelf where they had sat for weeks and she got dressed. Blood still trickled down her legs, and she wiped at it with a small part of the sheet not covered with blood. A very small part of the sheet. It was pretty much saturated. Then she pulled on her pants.

"What happened?" I whispered. I looked at my own penis. I had wiped away most of the blood, and when I looked at it, I knew why it had stung. It was covered with tiny teeth marks.

Why had she waited 'til now to do this? Why didn't she escape right away? And how did she manage to—

But I didn't have a chance to ask her my questions. Maybe that was lucky. She didn't look like she was in the mood for twenty questions.

"This was bad, fellas. Real bad." She slipped into her Nikes. "I haven't decided yet what I'm going to do about it." She stepped over Jimmy's body, trying to avoid the billowing pools of blood. "Just remember what I said. This isn't over."

She smiled, and ran her filthy hand across my face.

Then she left. Just like that.

So here we are. Me and Joey and Mookie and Jimmy. We thought Jimmy was dead, but he's still squirmin'. His penis is still on the floor, right by his knee. You can't imagine how funny that looks. We can't even take him to the doctor. How the fuck would we explain it?

I wonder what she meant when she said this wasn't over.

I wonder what she meant.

I'm so scared I think I shit myself again.

DANCING INTO OCTOBER COUNTRY

He danced into town on scattered leaves, orange and red and yellow flourishes blowing a path along the streets and sidewalks. Dizzying swirls of crumbled and dried cut grass, the sweet-hay smell caressing the air like gentle finger strokes.

The children gleefully—innocently—chased after him and his colorful bag of magic tricks and candy. "Follow the Halloween man!" they cried, laughing and skipping and excited because Halloween was a time of candy and costumes and surprises and tricks, of no school and no homework. Halloween was freedom, and Halloween was youth.

Halloween Man transformed gaily colored balloons into poodles and parrots and twisted goblins, and when the children accepted the creations they were met with vile grins and outstretched claws that reached and grabbed and stole their pleasant dreams and ate them like candy.

He skipped down the street like an overgrown child, his pastel clothing shimmering and shining in the midday sun that heated the tar and warmed young skin. "Catch me, catch me, children!" Halloween Man cried, running fast, faster, too fast for the children to keep up, always just out of reach, always just that unbearable distance away.

The children fell to their knees and sobbed, wanting to catch the Halloween Man, the one who held the secrets, who understood the passage of things, who eagerly wanted to share his knowledge.

But he was just too fast.

Still, then children chased, as children always do, believing they would be the one to finally catch him and his passing fancy. A short-lived celebration only the very young can understand.

And for those rare few fortunate enough to finally catch the Halloween Man, those rare gems, ostracized by those who don't understand even though they pretend they do, they are the ones who will track the Halloween man into oblivion and beyond, following in his footsteps like lemmings out to sea.

FEEDING DESIRE
WITH JACK FISHER

In the Age of Rubens, Diana would have been considered a goddess.

Unfortunately, she was not alive in an era when fat was regarded as beautiful but during a time when *thin is in.*

For Diana, being thin was about as far away as Europe and not nearly as attainable. Folds of flesh covered a frame that, after worms and maggots someday feasted on her corpse, would prove to be of medium bone structure; meaning she would never be dainty or petite no matter what her weight; nor on the flip-side would she ever try out for women's rugby.

But rugby wasn't on Diana's mind. Food was. Though she had no desire to perpetuate the myth all grossly obese people got that way because they obsess about food, or that they're all lazy slobs without self control. Diana, being bed-ridden because of her rather rotund body had little else to do all day and night other than to watch television—and eat. Those were her two constants, and her two pleasures.

Diana lived in a studio and spent her life sprawled on a pullout sofa that hadn't been in its original position in half a decade. The sheet beneath her wet and stained flesh was filthy with crumbs and feces smears she couldn't quite reach to wipe away. The sheets hadn't been changed in months.

The task was certainly doable but required four people to help. They had to roll her over while the bedding was pulled out and the new sheet added, then rolled to the other side of the mattress on a frame that screamed at the shifting of her precariously balanced weight. Four people to have to ask for help, and then somehow not die of embarrassment when they arrived. Friends or relatives who would nod and smile kindly but secretly wondered—and Diana knew what they were thinking—how could she have gotten so *goddamned enormously fat? At her age yet. So young, so much to live for, has her whole life ahead—*

So the sheets rotted beneath her and the apartment rotted around her.

Mounds of garbage birthed new forms of life, moldering away for days at a time until Candida her housekeeper came in on Thursdays. Diana couldn't make it to the incinerator chute—hell, just getting to the bathroom ten feet away was a struggle. Most days she only managed a single trip.

Chinese food for dinner. The delivery boys knew the routine. The front door was never locked—an insanity in Manhattan, but she had little choice. Besides, what did she have that was worth stealing? TV, computer. They were replaceable. Diana came from a wealthy family and could afford to replace missing items. Could afford a life of doing nothing. Her family, frustrated at Diana's size and her indifference, wanted desperately to help and had sent her to specialist after specialist. Or had sent them to her. At first Diana tried dieting, then tried more extreme procedures like stomach stapling, but all ended in failure, and her family's insistence she seek professional mental help was ignored. Hiding behind her girth had become comfortable, and now she was content to live life as she was.

Breakfast was a quick call to the Stuyvesant Square Deli. Lunch, same. Dinner, whatever she was in the mood for. Life had become even better once McDonald's started delivering.

The young Asian delivery boy with the fine black hair knocked twice out of courtesy before entering. He stopped in the kitchenette off the front foyer. Diana's ears perked like Pavlov's mutts at the sound of the freezer door clicking shut.

She motioned for him to place everything on the end table.

He obliged, planting the bag and pulling out the menu. "Sixty three sixty." Lucky Dragon didn't run tabs, even for their best customer.

She handed him seventy dollars. "Keep it."

He smiled, nodded, and was gone.

Alone again. So much for social hour. She'd convinced herself sometime through the years she really didn't mind. That it was easier this way, easier than having to worry about relationships, jobs, friends. She considered herself retired now, at age thirty-four. Retired from work she'd never done, retired from a life she'd never lived.

She opened the shopping bag and assembled her dinner. Sweet and sour pork. Pepper steak. Chop Suey. Moo Shoo pork with extra pancakes. Spare ribs, double order, and a fried dumpling appetizer. Almond cookies. Fortune cookies. Two-liter bottle of Pepsi. A strange and eclectic mixture of smells and colors dripped from the small white containers, chicken and pork and peppers, sweet and vinegary, spicy and tangy. She wiped spittle from the corners of her mouth.

She ate while her mind and emotions remained numb, sedated and entertained by the massive quantities of food. Hours later she finished the last of it and drifted into an almost narcotic-like stupor.

The following morning, another call to the deli for breakfast. Half an hour later there was a knock at the door. Only this time, the delivery boy didn't enter.

She waited, confused, head craning back on her fat neck, trying to glance back toward the door. "Come in!" she yelled, irritated at this disruption in her routine. Anything that interfered with mealtime annoyed her. "Jesus."

She heard the door open, could hear his heavy breathing behind her. Staring, she was sure. Gawking. Having a good, long look. Staring and ogling and absorbing this sickening sight, like sneering at a geek in a sideshow display. She was the fat lady, only fat didn't quite do her justice. She was the Amazing, Colossal, Humongous Woman, Eighth Wonder of the World! A sight too unreal to imagine. Step right up, folks, and see Diana, the world's fattest—

"Come in," she snapped. "The eggs are getting cold."

"I'm new," he stammered.

"So I gathered." She was used to the stares, even while confined to her home. Used to stares from an endless parade of delivery boys, repairmen, doctors. It was Grand Fucking Central in her apartment.

"I—I'm sorry," he said, his mouth slightly ajar.

For some reason this one bothered her. Not exactly annoyed her, just made her... uncomfortable. She stared at him with the same vehemence he was showing her, and she realized the discomfort came from her attraction to the young man. This wasn't just some delivery boy. This was her Adonis, a decent cut of biceps just beginning to blossom. Legal, but barely. She guessed his age at twenty, twenty-two. Peach fuzz. Baby fat where a delineated jaw line might once appear. Mocha eyes, rich and warm and buttery. An Aryan prince. Probably named Fritz or Helmut.

This embarrassed her. Mortified her. For the first time in years, she wished she had covered her body.

He handed her the bill. "Thirty eight and—"

"I know." She handed him a fifty. "Keep it."

He stared at the money and then stuffed it into his pocket.

"Thanks," he said quietly, now staring into her eyes.

She nodded, feeling the heat spread on her cheeks. "You can leave."

"Can I—is it okay if I stay a few minutes?"

He caught her off guard. What could he possibly want, if not to stare at her, to think up horrible and cruel names, bring stories back to his friends about the inhumanly grotesque blob lounging on east Twelfth Street?

It was enough of a surprise that she didn't know how to respond.

"I've made you uncomfortable," he said, closing his eyes, his brow creasing. "I'm sorry. I just thought you might like some company, at least for a few minutes. I have to get back anyway."

He shifted uncomfortably on his feet. "They told me about you. How you... live alone. Kinda stuck in your bed. You know." He paled, believing probably he'd said something dreadfully hurtful to her. She didn't care. "I just thought you might be kind of lonely."

Her eyes moistened and she looked away. She believed she'd forgotten how to cry. It had been so many years. Even when her father died three years ago and she'd been too large to leave her apartment to attend his funeral, even then she hadn't cried.

"I'm Justin, by the way. I'd like to deliver your food, if that's okay with you. Be your delivery boy."

She let him leave. And never said a word.

*   *   *

Lunch was bacon cheeseburgers with french fries, a barbecued chicken, potato salad, cole slaw, and a bowl of tomato soup. Another two-liter Pepsi. A quart of Haagen Dazs Vanilla Swiss Almond with hot fudge.

His sitting with her didn't inhibit her appetite. What shame she'd felt earlier was now smothered by her hunger.

Legs crossed, hands on his ankle, Justin watched, not saying much. Sat with her while she ate, kept her company, faking aloofness in his fascination of her amazing art, her perfected craft of self-indulgence. She was amused—bemused, perhaps—at his rapt attention, and at his attempt at nonchalance.

Several weeks went by, and Justin had begun visiting Diana even when he wasn't working. He brought her cakes and cookies and Italian pastry from a bakery on Second Avenue. He brought her Thai food and Greek cuisine and Vietnamese take-out.

He stole into her apartment one evening and crept behind her. She knew he was there, had grown accustomed to his footsteps, and the light, fresh scent of his soap. The night seemed much more brilliant than ever—smelled crisper somehow, and even the days had a sharper edge when he was around.

This was happiness, she decided. This was ecstasy.

"I have to talk to you," he said, his voice raspy and thick, as if he'd been crying.

She tried to see him, but he was behind her, and she was unable to maneuver. He held her shoulders and wouldn't allow her to turn.

So this is where the happiness ends, she also decided. "You're scaring me."

"I don't want you to see me like this," he said.

"Like what?"

"I have to tell you something." He sat on the edge of the bed and smeared the tears across his face with the back of his hand. "I need to tell you something, but I'm afraid you'll be mad."

So this was it. The inevitable, the horrible revelation. Now would come the taunting and torturing, the part where Justin would reveal how this had all been a terrible joke, a dare from his friends, something... something unspeakable.

He whispered it, and she asked him to repeat it. "I said I'm in love with ou. From the first day we met. I knew—"

"Get the hell out! Rotten bastard." She sobbed, and threw an empty chow
ein container at him.

"Please listen. Please!"

"How could you?" she cried. "How can you be so mean?"

Then he was inches from her, pushing her back, pressing his chest into
ers. His hands on her shoulders, digging into the flesh. He arched his neck
ad mashed his lips against hers, rough and sweet. Then they softened, his lips
nd hers, and he kissed her gently, his tongue probing, darting into her mouth.
Ie nibbled on her full lips.

"I don't understand," she whispered, pulling away, catching her breath.

"I've loved you from the first time I walked in. When I'd heard about you,
had to see for myself. To know if you were real. And—you're magnificent!"

She pulled away from him, not even realizing she had. "What?"

"I'm attracted to larger women."

"What the hell for?"

He stroked her shoulder-length brown hair and pushed it away from her
ce. Pulled strands from between folds of chins. Bent over and sucked her
arlobes, hands roaming from her hair to her face until they finally began to
ove to the hotter, denser areas of her body.

"I just am. It's like a fetish of mine. Don't you have any fetishes?"

He kissed her again, more zealously than before, his breath hotter and
uicker. His hands slipped between the buttons of her housecoat and massaged
er fleshy abdomen and belly, stroking and rubbing, traveling over the lumps
nd folds of her torso. His hand reached her chalky breast and he rolled his
alm over the nipple.

He sat up, moved closer. "Is this okay?" he asked quietly, but didn't wait
or a response. Pulled open her dress. His tongue circled the areola and flicked
e nipple, biting and licking.

Diana was torn between feeling morbidly embarrassed and completely
roused and settled for a combination of both. She grabbed his head and ran
er fingers through his hair.

His hands massaged the length of her body, wandered over mounds of
tty flesh, cottage-cheese skin, over hills and valleys until he reached her
ubis. She rolled back, propping herself up. He spread her legs and found
er clit, teased it with his thumb. He lowered his head between her legs, and
he felt his hot breath... and then his tongue, flicking her clit, sucking it, his
ngers entering her cunt. Thrusting them in and out, probing deeper, faster.
Iis tongue worked her clit while he finger-fucked her, and an incredible
armth spread throughout her body. Her cunt tingled, felt thick and meaty,
nd her muscles tightened, waited for that powerful release. She gripped the
heets, her body screaming for liberation, shaking with ecstasy.

A part of her couldn't accept this, not completely. *This is the cruel joke.*

She waited for the inevitable humiliation. Still, it didn't come. Still he playe
with her massive body, seeming to enjoy himself, showing no revulsion, as od
as that seemed to Diana.

He stripped off his pants and underwear and tossed them on the floor. Pr
cum glistened on the glans, and he stroked himself stiff. He leaned forwar
and she took him in her mouth, tasting the salty droplets of cum, teasing th
tip of his cock with her tongue. She took him all the way in, felt him pulsin
in her throat. His cock slid out of her mouth and she tongued the shaft, han
working it, gently cupping his balls. Flicked the head and pulled it back int
her throat, bobbed up and down on it.

He pulled out of her mouth and climbed between her legs, pressed u
against her stomach. Plied through layers of flesh until he discovered her cur
and entered her, lay on top of her like a climber halfway toward peak. Groun
his angular hips into her.

She felt his cock inside her, but then he pulled out, massaged the ti
against her throbbing clit. She tried to grab his sack but was unable to reac
past her stomach. He entered her again and leaned up, sucked her breast lik
a baby feeding while he rammed himself to orgasm, waiting for her to cum.

Diana could remember the last time she'd fucked—twenty years ago no
when she was fourteen. Didn't want to remember... her only experience unt
now. Back then it had been traumatic, a mixture of pure shame and exquisit
desires that had been too much for her to handle at such a young age. It ha
begun her descent toward food and oblivion.

But now... now, being brought to orgasm by a man she loved... a ne
experience, a fusion of feelings and emotions she was unprepared to handl
The feeling of utmost satisfaction, an ecstasy so deep it made her shudde
made her flesh undulate, and she came again. Her body exploded, her cunt o
fire until she unclenched, every muscle exhausted, aching, every nerve endin
sizzling and shooting sparks.

He rolled off, spent and glistening, his thin chest rapidly rising and fallin;
He scaled the length of her body and lay beside her.

Diana leaned back, inhaled, felt her lungs pull in a full, healthy breath fo
the first time in years. She laughed—really laughed, and then wept deeply an
profoundly, like a mourner at a funeral.

That gnawing discomfort, having to pretend she didn't mind him lookin
at her body, pretend she wholly enjoyed his tender caress. Truth was, sh
would love to feel that way, but how could she trust? After a lifetime of abus
and hiding, trust wasn't something that came naturally. There was an elemen
of enjoyment there, and she couldn't deny she'd craved the intimacy that ha
been missing from her life for so many years now. Even when she was thi
as a child, safety and intimacy were foreign to her. It was this mixture o
embarrassment and enjoyment Diana couldn't reconcile. This bizarre yin an
yang that existed as polar opposites within her world.

He held her hands, kissed them, sucked her fingers. Wiped away her tears. He seemed to truly love being intimate with her; he was somehow her other half. She believed he enjoyed being lost in her folds, as if falling into piles of unkneaded dough, glutinous and sticky and absorbing.

When he returned the following afternoon, he carried a large shopping bag, and was sporting a grin. "I have a surprise." He dropped the bag at the foot of the couch.

She assumed they were sex toys of some kind because he'd mentioned wanting to try something a little offbeat. Slightly alarming for Diana. Not only was he seeing her naked on a regular basis, he now wanted to throw bizarre objects into the fray.

But instead, he pulled out a pastry box, and she realized the shopping bag wasn't from Purple Passion or Pink Pussycat but from Zabars.

After he cut the strings and opened the box, he lifted it and held it beneath her nose. "Mocha chocolate and raspberries."

She looked up at him.

Another box. Another cake. Decadent Chocolate Mousse. Then a bowl of English Trifle.

"You hungry or something?" She felt her cheeks flushing.

He stopped emptying the bag. "Oh. I'm sorry. I—I didn't mean—"

"What are you doing?"

"I want to feed you."

"Why?"

"It's—this is what I like to do. I'm a Feeder."

"A Feeder? This is your kinky surprise?"

"Well yeah… it gets really erotic." He looked down, away, anywhere but at her eyes.

"Does it?"

He looked up and smiled.

She realized she was clutching the sheet and had at some point pulled it up to her neck. Not that she was naked, but she still felt exposed.

"I don't understand," she said.

"I'll show you. Will you trust me?"

Good question. "But all that cake. I'll just get fatter."

"It'll be fine."

"Will it?"

That smile—the one that carved pits in his cheeks—disarmed her. He sat on the bed and trailed the tips of his fingers along her calf.

"I don't want you doing anything that makes you uncomfortable."

Hell, he'd seen her naked. And now he was talking about combining food and sex—her two favorite things.

"How does this work?" she said quietly.

He giggled, and jumped off the bed. Retrieved the cake boxes. No need to go to the kitchen for utensils. Diana kept a supply on the coffee table beside the couch.

"Close your eyes, Diana."

She closed them. The soft, elegant feel of silk draped around her head, over her eyes. Tied at the back of her head. Her heart pounded in excitement, anticipation. Then, the soft pop of a cardboard top being opened... A moment later, she felt a gentle poke at her bottom lip. Something sharp, yet not sharp enough to hurt. Her tongue probed and found tines. Not metallic but plastic.

He fed her. With her eyes closed, she couldn't tell which cake he had chosen. The tart tang of raspberries blossomed in her mouth, followed by the bittersweet richness of the dark chocolate.

Like a child at play he giggled, like a boy experiencing the pure delight of a first snowfall. "Do you like this?"

She nodded, and sighed, finally beginning to relax. "Is this it?"

"Unless there's something else you'd like to do."

She fingered the silk scarf. "Can I take this off?"

"Sure."

He was naked. His torso was smeared with dripping chocolate and outlined in whipped cream. His swollen, hot penis was inches from her hand. She reached over and grabbed the shaft.

She pulled the cake box across the sheets. Inside was half of what looked and smelled like the mocha cake. At her coaxing he leaned in, and she gently pushed his cock into the layers, covering it with the cake.

"Oh shit," he giggled, the sound of it adorable.

"Close your eyes," she said. "You're still the Feeder. You're still going to feed me."

He shut his eyes.

The box was pushed out of the way. Chunks of chocolate cake fell off his dick as she pulled him toward her mouth, licking away the pastry. It coated the length so she deep throated, pulled it in as far as she could, sucked away the food, licked him clean, slowly... gently... Pulled him out of her mouth and went for his balls, tongued them, held them inside her mouth, sucked them clean.

"Fuck," he gasped; his legs trembled, and he threw his head back.

The cake was gone. She sucked the tip of his rod like it was a lollipop, and her hand slid and squeezed.

She swallowed cake and chocolate and cum.

Every night he brought different kinds of food, pizza and Chinese and Greek and anything they might want to try.

Deliciously spent, he propped himself on his elbow, and gazed at her glorious rolls of fat. "I taste you," he said, "in everything you do. I smell your body's musky perfume. It stays with me all day. Keeps me alive."

"You're being silly," she said, but she loved his attempts at being poetic.

He craned his neck until he reached her ear, and sucked on the lobe. Bittersweet. Like chocolate."

The next night, he returned with another assortment of food. Cheeses. Several varieties of apples. Croissants and scones and muffins. Whipped cream and pudding.

The night after that, pizza and calzones, shells stuffed with manicotti, lasagna with bolognese sauce. Heavenly Hash ice cream. Food he brought from the restaurant where he worked, surprisingly well made.

Within a couple of weeks, Diana felt herself gaining even more weight.

Justin was in bed with her, feeding her rice pudding. His legs were crossed, and his naked torso rose and fell, his flat stomach rippling gooseflesh.

"I don't understand," he said, after she pushed him away. "What's wrong?"

"I'm getting even fatter, Justin."

He scratched his cheek. "So? This is what we wanted."

"No it's not. I never agreed to this."

"I don't understand." He looked close to tears. "Not to be mean or anything, but it's not much more food than you were eating before. And with all the fucking—it's all exercise, isn't it? How could you be gaining weight?"

The tears threatened to come. She thought he understood what she was feeling, but how could he? He'd never been fat, certainly not fat like she was. He couldn't understand her mix of emotions. "Justin, it's a lot more food than I was eating before. And you pumping away isn't exactly exercise for me."

He leaned forward, kissed her. "You don't enjoy this? Me feeding you?"

She blinked, thinking. "It was fun for a while… but I'm getting bored. And getting fatter."

He sat back on his heels. Palmed away tears.

She was suddenly aware of her nakedness. He was resting on the bed sheet so she couldn't pull it to cover herself.

"Bored? Even with the blindfolds?"

She nodded. "There's no challenge. My sense of smell is too strong. It was fun though. For awhile."

"But it's not about the food. It's about Feeding. About being fed."

"I'm sorry, " she whispered.

"Will we still… can we…"

"Fuck?"

"Make love, Diana. I want to make love to you." Weeping gently, he stretched toward her again, his slender body pressing against her fat, rubbing his cock into the folds of her legs, getting lost in the mounds of flesh.

You're breaking up with me, aren't you?

He didn't answer, and she realized she'd never asked him out loud.

His penis poked her stomach, her thigh, searched for her pussy. He squeezed her breasts, cupped their enormous weight in his palms, rubbed her nipples erect. She stroked him until he was even harder and spread her legs to receive him. Guided him inside her.

I love you, Justin. Can't live without you.

But she could never say that to him. She knew his reason for wanting to be with her was because he got off feeding her, and now she wasn't even giving him that.

He grunted, moaned, leaned into her. Pounded her cunt as if in anger, retribution for her decision to withhold his real pleasure. Rivulets of sweat ran down his face and dripped onto her tits.

She spread her legs wider. "Harder, Justin!"

He fucked harder, his face reddening, his shoulder and neck muscles cording.

"Harder!"

She wanted him to hurt her! Make her feel it! Feel *something*. Through layer upon layer of skin, reinforcement for the deadness inside her, a protective wall shielding her from heartache and loneliness. Wanted him to penetrate her defenses. He was so close... so close, but hadn't found the way. Not yet. It was much more than a physical feeling. She waited for that connection, the knowledge he felt the way she did. Hadn't quite convinced herself he truly could love her unconditionally, as she adored him. Hurting her would be a way through the layers. A way to make that final, irrevocable connection.

His back arched. His orgasm shattered, filled her with shards of crystal.

And now it would be too late, she'd pushed him away, and when he finished fucking her, it would be over. This was a pity fuck, a mercy fuck. One for the road.

"Please, Justin, harder. Hurt me!"

"Fuuuuuuck!" he cried, skin glistening, fingernails digging into her shoulders.

He hated her now, wanted to leave her, she was sure of it. It was inevitable, but she mourned its arrival. She could *feel* him, finally—could feel his cock in her, could feel his love for her deeply and profoundly, and she wanted to stay like this forever, wanted them to be one person. Wanted this to never end because once he was finished, she knew he would leave her forever.

He was slowing, tiring, grinding his groin into hers.

Then he was crying, lying on his back, his wet, flaccid penis draped over his thigh.

"I'm sorry," he wailed. "I couldn't cum. I'm sorry."

He was sorry... She'd crushed his manhood and he was the one apologizing.

She leaned back into the pillows. Her vaginal muscles twitched.

"I felt it," she whispered. *Don't leave me, Justin. Please don't leave me. I finally felt something...*

Using the sheet, he wiped his eyes. Leaned up, kissed her lips, nibbled on he bottom lip.

She took his penis, stroked it.

It wasn't responding.

This was how it would end. He would hate her forever for destroying him, or destroying his ability to fuck.

He buried his face between her pendulous breasts.

She wrapped her arms around him, pulled him into her. Lifted her legs nd bent her knees. He slid between them like a piece of puzzle fitting into a roove. She squeezed, wrapped him between her thighs. Her breasts moved nd he slid between them, his body filling in the furrows.

He found her pussy again, and semi-erect, slid inside.

They were one.

Diana held him, not noticing his struggles at first, not noticing the sort of novement coming from the young man she held in her arms.

His face was pressed into her chest, his neck and head covered by her reasts.

She could feel them join, feel the unity, the merging forms of grace and omfort.

Turned on her side, moved with him *as one*, arms entwined, crotches rinding and spasming. With just a bit more effort, Diana was on her stomach. he bucked her hips and felt him fucking her from beneath.

Couldn't pull away even as she felt his dick soften inside her, as she felt his ot breath on her breasts suddenly cease. Didn't want to pull away. Couldn't tand to watch him leave her.

Diana struggled to sit upright. She rocked herself back, climbed off him. Ie lay like a broken sparrow, outlined in the sheets, arms twisted. His head vas pressed into the sheets and his hair was spread out behind him, a fallen ird with shattered wings, its feathers splayed.

He stared up at her.

His blue lips were spread in mute protest, but there was a sense of calm n his face, a trace of a smile. He had been the ultimate Feeder; he had given imself to her as nourishment. His fondest dream had come true and she ealized she had been the one to give that to him.

But he'd left her. Just as she knew he would.

She held him in her arms, rocked his lifeless body, and sobbed over him.

She mourned the return of her loneliness.

NURTURING
TYPE

Daddy I'm tired, Daddy I'm cold. Daddy I'm hungry. Daddy do something.
)addy Daddy Daddy. I miss Mommy! Huuuuungry, Daddy!

They just never stop.

Hungry? We're all hungry, and complaining doesn't help.

How can they be cold? It's a hundred degrees on this blasted island. I
wear, there's always been something wrong with those kids.

So I was stuck with them. Stuck cleaning them and feeding them and
eeping them alive. Not that they appreciated it, cause they didn't.

My favorite: *Daddy I'm booooored.* What do I look like, the entertainment
ommittee? Go swimming, I'd tell them. *But there's sharks.* Go play in the
and. *But the sun burns us.*

What the hell did they want from me?

I'm sick of coconuts. When we get off this island, I'm never touching
coconut again. No coconut cream pie. No goddamned pina coladas. No
oconut nothing. Once in a while we find berries, and so far they haven't killed
s. Ever try to catch fish without tackle? And my hunting knife can sharpen
stick but can't actually do the hunting. There's nothing to hunt anyway. No
iatches to build a fire. And idiot son Burton, despite 150 years of cub scouts
nd half a dozen badges, couldn't manage it. He tried rubbing sticks together
nd all he came away with was blisters. Ten years old and good for nothing.

Barbara, their mother, got off easy—she drowned. Some days I wish I
ad too. But no, I survived, with Burton and the Princess in tow. Her name's
ctually Anastasia—their mother was warped when it came to those kids'
ames—but I call her Princess because she acts like a spoiled rotten brat.
lways wanting, wanting, asking for things. Eight years old. Where the hell
o kids get their ideas from anyway? But I'll tell you one thing, when we
nally get off this rotten island, *someone's* getting sued, and we'll be rich. The
liot who chartered the boat for us, the asshole who booked our vacation—
omeone.

When we first got stranded we tried to fish. No poles—they'd been left on the boat. So I sharpened some sticks and the three of us stood in knee deep water trying to spear the first thing that swam our way. One thing I learned fish are faster than they look. The only thing Burton had managed to spear was my foot. Thank god the kid is so damned bad at anything athletic, or it might have caused real damage. Then the sharks came and that ended that.

We spent all our time looking for food. There was nothing else to do anyway. Actually *doing* anything was a waste of energy, and when you're starving, you need all the energy you can get.

A dead fish had washed up on shore. The thing was bloated and reeked of sour ocean, but goddamned if I didn't drool. If we'd had a fire, I probably would've cooked it. And I still wish I'd eaten it raw, taken a chance that it hadn't been too rotten. But when I went back the next day, it was gone, washed back out to sea.

By then the hunger got to be too much. You know what I'm saying? We could fill up on coconuts and bananas and whatever wild plant looks somewhat edible but when it comes down to it, it's just not enough. Not when true hunger grabs you and gnaws at your stomach, making you lightheaded and dizzy. Real hunger makes you too weak to move. So yeah, I was weak, but so were the kids. Princess lay in the sand beneath the shade of a palm tree and just refused to move, acting dramatic, like she was waiting for someone to fan her and feed her peeled grapes.

She's a skinny kid. No meat on her bones. But Burton is beefy, big for his ten years. If he wasn't such an artsy fartsy fairy type he might actually play football or something. Stupid kid with his nose in a book all the time. No wonder he's fat. He hardly moves.

And just the thought of it… it wasn't an easy decision. But I had to look at the big picture. We were all starving and probably wouldn't last much longer anyway.

But then you think, what can you take? The part with the real meat—his stomach—well, obviously that's off limits. I mean, I didn't want to kill the boy. An arm maybe, but I would have had to take the whole thing from the shoulder down, cause there's not much meat on a wrist or even a forearm. That didn't seem fair, taking the entire limb. But part of one?

They do wonders with prosthetics these days.

It's a funny thing about kids. They don't disobey, not to your face, when they're standing in front of you and you're telling them what to do. Sure they run around behind your back because they never think they're gonna get caught, so I guess they decide the risk is worth it. I always did when I was a kid. But when they're standing in front of you they don't dare disobey. When I tell Burton to do something, he listens. He may whine and kick his feet, but he doesn't dare move. Doesn't dare disobey.

We sat huddled together in the sand, staring out at the ocean.

Then I told them what I had planned.

"What?" Burton said, his head cocked like a dog's, as if that helped him hear better. "But why me?"

"Well," I said patiently, "if not you, then who?"

He looked at his sister, then back to me. "No one."

"We have to eat, Burton."

His mouth hung open. Then he smiled. When I didn't smile back, his quickly faded.

"Daddy's joking," Princess said to him.

But Burton knew I wasn't joking. I could see it in his eyes.

"No, Daddy," he whined, the tears starting. "I don't wanna lose my leg!"

"It's not the whole leg, just part of it."

"It'll grow back, right Daddy?" Princess said, looking hopeful. I was hoping she was kidding. How could a kid be that stupid?

"They don't grow back!" Burton sobbed, clutching a handful of sand. For a second I thought he was going to throw it at me.

"If we don't eat we'll starve to death anyway. This is a better solution. It's the *only* solution."

"What about you?" Burton cried. "Why *my* leg?"

"How can I look after you and your sister if I'm missing a leg? Use your brain, Burton."

They cried and shook their heads, but neither of them ran. I dunno, maybe they figured I could catch them, but I don't think that was it. I think I have them very well trained, and I thought they wouldn't dare pull the crap I see so many kids get away with these days.

Burton had been filling up on bananas, so he wasn't starving like me and Princess, but even the fruit was running out. That kid'd eat dirt if I let him. So he wasn't listening to reason cause the hunger hadn't overtaken him yet.

Burton struggled, though he'd never tried to run, even when he slid right out of my hands and landed on the ground. He just lay there on his side, sobbing like a girl. And even when I tied his hands and arms to keep him from fighting, he never tried to escape. Part of me wish he had. At least that would have meant the kid's got a set of balls. Then maybe one day when some bitch tries to trap him into marriage, he'll be strong enough to get out of it.

I wish there'd been some way to knock him out—clubbing him over the head hadn't worked, just left nasty bumps. It hadn't been easy, either, sawing and sawing that limb, trying to keep him steady, ignoring his screams. Finally he passed out, and that made it a little easier. Even Princess tried to get me to stop. First the begging and screaming, then the crying, then hitting me in the back with a stick. A backhand across her face got her to leave me alone, finally.

I took his leg below the knee.

So much blood. The damned knife blade dulling, making me stop to sharpen it against a stone more times than I could count. Hacking through the calf bone. Bits of stringy flesh dangling below his knee after I'd taken the rest of the leg. Disgusting. I tied off the knee as tight as I could, using my belt as a tourniquet. If we'd been able to make a fire I would have cauterized it. The whole thing was extremely tiring.

Lots of meat on his calf. No muscle, not stringy or sinewy. Plain old juicy fat.

The kids refused to eat it so I took away the little remaining coconuts and bananas until they gave in. I even explained the Donner party to them, told them people did this sort of thing to survive. Princess threw up after I shoved a piece of meat in her mouth. I guess it couldn't have been easy to eat, being raw and all. But I'd managed, so why couldn't they? But by the time they decided they were hungry enough, it was too late. I'd eaten most of it and flies had hijacked the rest. Dumb kids never got any, except for the one bite Princess refused to keep down. I mean, it's protein. Surely they know they can't live without protein. You can live without lots of things, even fruits and vegetables, but you have to have meat.

So they went back to bananas and coconuts. Princess found a long stick and gave it to her brother to use as a crutch. Didn't take him very long to get the hang of it. Surprising. I didn't think he could do anything besides turn a page.

Their mother planned this trip and then got herself killed, fell overboard. Her fat ass fell into the Atlantic just as I was reaching for her stupid throat. Not that I really would have killed her. I was just trying to scare her, get her to shut her big mouth. All she did was yell at me. And always with the nagging. Not that I miss her, but having her around would be a shitload better then having to listen to these kids all day, having to take care of them, feed them, make sure they wipe their asses. I've become quite the goddamned nurturing type.

Yesterday they wanted to go swimming. So go, I tell them. Just don't bleed in the water, I tell Burton. You know—sharks. Then they decided not to go swimming. Tell us what to do, Princess said. Burton didn't say anything— Burton had stopped talking to me. Thank christ! He sounds like a girl with all the high pitched whining. Better he should keep his mouth shut.

Then they play Tag. Burton, hobbling around on a stick the size of a goddamned tree trunk. Moving goddamned well for a kid with one leg.

So I began to wonder if he could get around with no legs. I mean really, we have to eat. Burton seemed to be healing pretty well. Princess's legs are like pretzel sticks, though I guess we could eat them as a last resort. But I wanted Burton's other leg. I figured once we get rescued, I'd buy him a new set. He'd be fine.

"Aren't you hungry?" I asked them last night, after eyeing his leg.

I guess they noticed because they didn't answer.

"Aren't you sick of coconuts yet? Don't you want something more?"

"No, Daddy," Princess said. "I like coconuts."

"We're almost out of coconuts," I snapped. "Then what are we supposed to eat?"

I thought about what idiots they are, how they take after their mother. You can't let kids decide these things, because they always make the wrong decisions. *Leave him alone*, Barbara was always squawking. *Let him read. He'll come around.* Trying to bullshit me into believing the kid will become Joe fucking Namath if only I let him read his goddamned books. Well that didn't happen. All it did was turn him into a pansy, not a quarterback.

And Princess, who couldn't make up her mind to save her life. Cheerleading one week, violin the next, then ballet and fencing and karate. Figures the girl would be the one interested in sports. The problem was she never stuck with anything, and all the equipment and special shoes and outfits were costing a fortune. So I cut her off. Told her the next thing she picked, she'd have to stick with. So what the fuck does she pick? African dance. Jesus christ. By the time I found out it was too late to stop her without making me look like a racist at her school. Can't have people thinking that. If my idiot daughter wants to take up jigaboo dancing, then I guess I got no choice but to let her. Don't want people to think bad things about me.

"Tomorrow we eat," I muttered as I lay down. I thought they were already asleep.

So imagine my surprise this morning.

I open my eyes, and my head is throbbing like I'd drank a liter of Cuervo. Burton is standing over me, staring down, and it looks like the kid's shot up to six feet tall overnight. There's blood on the stick he's leaning on. I can only image that's why my head hurts so damned much. The little fucker must've clobbered me in my sleep.

He stares for another few seconds, watching me struggle against the restraints and I guess he decides I'm not going nowhere cause he moves away. It hurts to move my head but I manage. I got a strong will. So I look at what he's doing. Back to rubbing sticks together, working hard at it this time. I see blood on his hands and don't know if it's mine or his. If he's been working those sticks for any length of time, his hands are probably like hamburger.

Unlike his previous lame-ass efforts, this time there's smoke.

I have to admit, I didn't panic. Not at first. Maybe it was my woozy head, making my thoughts unclear. Not paying attention to the fact they had *tied me up*. Maybe part of me thought it was a joke. I don't know.

But neither of them said a word, not even to each other.

And Burton discovers fire.

Princess cheers.

They both stare at me.

I look a little further away and see they've fashioned some kind of spit between two trees.

And I start to panic.

As a cub scout, Burton had won a few badges. Knot tying. Fire startin
Probably fucking sewing, knowing Burton. But it's those other two badge
that have me worried.

"I saw a boat last night," I say. "Only we didn't have a signal fire so the
couldn't see us. But Burton, you did it! Now we can be rescued."

They're not paying attention. Burton is fanning the flames, and Princes
is gathering wood.

"Very funny, kids! Okay, joke's over. Untie me." They'll listen. They hav
to listen because that's what kids do. That's what *my* kids do.

"Untie me, goddammit!"

They keep ignoring me. Burton transfers the fire to a stack of woo
beneath their makeshift spit.

Where did I go wrong? I raised them better than this. I raised them t
obey me. They're no better than the welfare kids back home, running th
streets, disobeying their parents.

"Okay, listen to me," I plead. "I won't take any more limbs. We'll ea
coconuts and find a way to catch fish. You'll see. We'll figure it out!"

"Sorry, Daddy," Princess says as they start dragging me toward the fir
"We're hungry now."

When we get off this island, I swear to christ I'm giving them up fo
adoption.

SAVED

1

She slides across the bed, away from cooling sheets and drying body fluids.

He pulls her into his arms. "Gloo-reeee-uh," he sings, almost in tune, *a appella*, some golden oldie that's been stuck in his head. "It's not Ma-reee-hee-ne, it's Glo-ree-uhhh…"

She smiles in spite of herself. "That's really off key." Her head rests in the crook between his shoulder and neck.

This is wrong, he believes. This is not the way things should be. This is too perfect.

"Okay." There had been only one question, though he knows that *why* can mean so many things. He thinks about this, perhaps too long, traces his fingertips over the bridge of her nose, plays with the spatter of freckles she claims to hate. Why us? Why now?

Why not?

Didn't he deserve happiness?

He understands her. More than anyone does. More than anyone ever could.

"Stay," he says. "I'll scramble eggs."

"Your eggs suck," she says, but there is no way she could know that, he thinks. He's never cooked for her before.

"My eggs are fine." He pouts, some of it fake.

"No they're not." She pulls the sweater over her head and it falls against her naked breasts.

He prefers her better in bed, and not just because of the sex but because in bed she's sweet and sexy and charming. In bed they never argue over silly things.

"You've never had my eggs," he says, trying one last time to win this thing, stretching his arms out behind his back in a fake casualness. "You can't know if they suck."

For a moment she's taken off guard and he smirks, this tiny victory perhaps a little too satisfying.

But then she nods and says, "I can tell. You're the sucky-egg type."

He grunts and shakes his head and decides to let this go, realizes she shares his stubborn streak, his annoying penchant for always being right. Or always thinking he is.

"Then I'll make you pancakes," he says, forcing a smile, hoping to relieve the tension. Tension he feels guilty of for a second before deciding she's caused. Tension that feels so out of place in this room.

"Besides," she adds, "You'll just burn them."

You know you always do, every time, he thinks, knowing she's about to say that, exactly that, a peculiar déjà vu but not quite. More... a knowing. Being inside her head, knowing her thoughts before they have a chance to form. Worse than déjà vu. It's as though he shares a brain with her.

"You know you always do," she says. "Every time," and he bites his tongue to suppress a scream.

He repeats the question he asked earlier, asks her again to move in with him and she smiles that corny Mona Lisa smile, the smile that says nothing but speaks volumes.

"That's not an answer," he snaps. He's too old for this crap. But he also knows his request is ridiculous. There are so many things they haven't yet discussed, so many feelings, so many plans. He realizes he doesn't know anything about her. He only knows he loves her.

A soulmate was always something he'd read about, a fantasy, something to fill the pages of trashy romance novels, not something that truly exists.

Until now. Until Gloria.

She fulfills him. She exists in that narrow space between the soul and the heart.

"I can't," she says, pulling on her boots.

"Why? Are you married?"

She shakes her head for what seems like forever and mouths the word *no*.

"Then what?"

She slides across the bed and curls beside him. Gently strokes the small patch of hair on his chest. "It's only been a month. Too soon."

"I don't even know where you live."

"Does it matter?"

He smiles his own version of the Mona Lisa but knows without looking that it's more like a Cheshire Cat. "What are you afraid of?"

"It's not like that. I'm not afraid. I have no secrets."

She kisses him and then she's gone, and her absence provokes an unexplainable loss in him. She always comes back. But when she leaves he feels abandoned.

And he wonders about the secrets she claims not to have.

She'd come into his life only recently. After the vicious breakup with Cathy. After Cathy had told him she'd aborted their baby. Had made that decision without consulting with him.

Three months since Cathy had wrecked his life and Jake was still dealing with the despondency. Trying to understand how someone could be so selfish. So goddamned erratic.

He wandered past Fifth Avenue skyscrapers and wondered how high he'd have to climb for a fall to be effective, wondered how hard it would be to gain access to a roof. Maybe a building without a doorman. He began to compose a suicide note in his head:

Dear —

and realized the only person he cared enough about to leave a note for was Cathy. And now he hated her. Well, hated her with as much passion as he still loved her. How could he still love someone who had ruined his life?

The East River was too calm, he decided, staring at the gentle waves slapping against the stone barrier surrounding the water.

There had to be a way. It couldn't be this hard to kill himself.

Dear Cathy.

Nothing. He had nothing to say.

The Williamsburg Bridge beckoned, hinted that she offered solace. How many people had plunged to their deaths from this bridge? The Brooklyn Bridge was a hell of a lot more famous, but the Williamsburg was less secure; it was much easier to access the low railing. If he were lucky, he'd be squashed by a speeding car. Then again, he imagined jumping into that cold, filthy water, breaking his neck, and winding up a quadriplegic.

That'd show Cathy, he thought, then realized he was behaving like a child.

Despite the late hour traffic was still fairly steady. There was always traffic on this bridge, someone was always trying to get into or escape from Brooklyn.

He regretted not writing that suicide note. People would wonder. Or he hoped they would. He was terrified no one would wonder, no one would ask questions. No one would care.

Dear (fill in the blank): I'm not a weak man, I don't usually take the easy way out. And I thought this would be easy, but maybe I was wrong. Maybe this is incredibly difficult. Fuck, this is hard! I'm sorry I—

Sorry for what?

Screw the suicide note. Let them wonder.

He started up the road, keeping to the side. The shoulder was dangerously narrow, maybe half a foot from the bridge abutment. An occasional car whizzed by, horn blaring a warning as if Jake had no clue he was walking on a road in the middle of a bridge.

He peered over the edge, stared into the black water, the waves on the East River choppier than he remembered, or maybe the water was just rougher this far from the shoreline. He stretched one leg over the short wall. Just a few more quick movements and he'd be over the side and on his way to his death. He moved more slowly than he expected. But there was no reason *not* to do this. No reason at all.

Jake glanced at the approaching woman, not terribly surprised she was suddenly there. It didn't matter. He really didn't care. "Stay away from me."

"What are you doing?"

"What am I *doing*?" A hundred lame sarcastic replies lay dormant on his tongue. "Look, lady—"

"You don't want to do this. Trust me."

"Trust me. I *do*."

She stepped closer and he lifted his other leg over the wall.

"She's not worth it."

"She?" Of course the woman would imagine he was doing this because of some mysterious *she*. That made the most sense, he figured. Wasn't it always about some *she*? "What do you want?"

"To help you."

"You a cop?"

"No, I'm—" She stopped. "I'm not."

"Who are you?"

"Gloria."

"You know what I mean!"

"Please come with me. I promise it'll be worth it. I promise I can make you forget about her."

Jake smiled, appreciated her efforts. "Look—"

"I know she hurt you."

He groaned. "That all you got? Dimestore psychology?"

"I know you would have jumped by now if you really wanted to. You don't want to die."

Jake opened and quickly shut his mouth.

"Please," she said, reaching out to touch him. "Trust me."

*   *   *

He whispers the wrong name during sex, whispers *Cathy*, and he's never seen her this crazy, this upset.

She pounds on his chest with her fists. Tears drip off her chin. A trace of saliva dangles from her lip.

"How could you?" she sobs, collapsing into herself, thrusting her fists against her eyes. "I made you forget her! I made you forget…"

Jake was silent for a long time, afraid to touch her, not sure at all what to say.

"I made you forget…" she mutters, sniffing hard.

He says "I could never forget her" and realizes that that came out all wrong and wishes desperately he could redo the last fifteen seconds.

*   *   *

"I hate you," she says later, when she's calmed down. "You're a pig."

"You hate me?"

She doesn't respond, just sulks and turns away.

"Gloria?" He touches her arm and she flinches. "*Gloria*."

"Leave me alone."

"I said I'm sorry. I swear, I—"

"I've done everything to make you forget her."

"It's not your job to make me forget."

"What?" Her head snaps as if he's slapped her.

He groans, marveling at his constant ability to pick the wrong words. "I mean, you can't make someone forget someone. No matter what she was like, Cathy was part of my life. Even if I wanted. I couldn't forget her."

"Jesus Christ, you said her name when we were fucking!"

"It's just—you did something she used to do. That thing with your tongue."

After a time she says, "That's disgusting."

"No. Just… weird. You know."

She sighs. "Not good. This. All of this."

"All of?"

"No, not us. I don't mean us. Just the way things happen. How things can be so wrong."

"Are you breaking up with me?"

She slinks across the bed like a cat until she's curled beside him again. Her hands trace his inner thighs, caress the fine hairs, fingers climbing. "What thing with my tongue?"

He smiles because she's close to repeating it with her fingers. "Right here."

"Let's change the memory then."

She leans down and nips him, close to his groin, still on the leg, and he yelps in surprise.

"Will you forget her now?"

"If you stop bringing her up every goddamned second I might."

"Sorry." She concentrates her efforts on his crotch, licking, caressing, nipping. She swallows him, deep, pulls him into her throat.

She glances up at him, and he watches her play with his cock, licking the haft, sucking the head. Her fingers cradle his balls. When she pulls away, a trail of spit dangles between her mouth and his dick.

He believes she has the remarkable ability to make him forget. Still, this time he calls out no names.

*   *   *

"I want to tell you something," she says later, and he thinks *finally*, knowing in his heart she's been sitting on some secret, wondering what she is about to reveal.

They are wrapped together in a blanket of afterglow, arms and legs entangled, her head resting against his chest. He wants to stay this way forever but knows in his heart the next conversation will probably change everything.

He wonders if she's married. He wonders what she's done.

"Okay," she whispers, and takes his hands, drops them, sits up. "Okay," she repeats, and turns away from him.

"What is it?"

She turns back and says, "Give me your hands."

He offers them, but before she moves she says, "I think you're ready to know."

"Gloria—"

She flips them over, palms down, but instead of taking them grabs his wrists.

"I'm going to show you something. Close your eyes."

"Close my eyes?"

"Close them. It's hard enough without you interrupting."

Mona Lisa smile again, fading as he closes his eyes, wondering what she's planning. His quirky lover, all mystery and desire. He's never been with anyone like her and can't imagine her not in his life.

"Listen," she says. "Listen to the rhythm of my breathing. To the calmness in my voice."

And he listens, relaxing against the headboard, breathing slowly through his nose. In, out, in... following the pattern of her inhales and exhales. Relaxing, sure—he could easily fall asleep now, her quiet singsong voice almost a mantra.

The first image strikes his brain like lightning, so powerful it slams his head against the headboard. He tries to open his eyes, then tries to speak, finds he is unable to do either.

The images in his mind are not so much memories or scenes as they are snippets, a montage ripping through his brain. Not memories at all, though he recognizes the faces, or one of the faces, but in a place he's never been doing things he's never done.

Flash of Cathy, his ex, the woman he'd wanted to marry, the woman who'd ruined his life. Flash on the image of a man wearing a surgical mask, bloody hands held outward as if in supplication. Sounds now with this still-life imagery. Sounds of heaving breaths, of gasping almost sexual but not. Pain disguised as pleasure, carnal noises crossing the line into almost torture.

"Stop," he begs, still unable to open his eyes, unable to break Gloria's grip on his wrists.

Another image: Masked doctor reaching between Cathy's legs, legs suspended in stirrups, tray of steel beside those legs.

Final image: The bloody, pulpy blob of fetal tissue in the haz mat trash can beside the exam table. The fetus in pieces, its tiny malformed skull crushed by forceps.

Gloria lets him go.

His eyes pop open and he sucks in air, a drowning man who finally breaks the surface. "What the *fuck*?" he screams, scrambling away from her, clutching the sheet and pulling it toward his body like a shield, as if the sheet will protect him from what he's just seen.

"What was that?" he cries, tears on his cheeks, snot bubbling in his nose.

"I'm sorry," she whispers. "I thought you were ready."

"Ready for what?" he yells again, trying to make sense of it all. But none of this makes sense.

She slides across the bed, approaching him, not moving too quickly. He's startled anyway and wishes she would stop moving, would leave him alone.

"What the hell?"

She shakes her head.

"That's not an answer!" He swallows, stares at her and still doesn't know what else to say. Wants to ask questions but his brain isn't cooperating. "You're evil," he snaps, and her nervous laughter startles him.

"I would never hurt you."

"What did you—" he whispers. "Why would you do this to me?"

"You don't understand," she says, arms out. "This, this is so important, Jake. I, this is—" She falters, trips over the words. "Please," she cries. "I can explain. I can show you more."

"No!" He scrambles away again and this time falls off the side of the bed, the sheets twisted around his legs. "Just get out," he mutters from his spot on the floor.

2

Later, when he's alone with nothing but his thoughts, he makes an effort to *not* think about anything. To think about nothing at all. But that proves futile, the attempt to excise thought from his mind. Might as well ask him to not breathe. Images assault his mind even stronger than before, as if in an attempt to lend credence to their existence.

But they can't exist. They weren't his memories, not even snapshots. He hadn't been there for Cathy's abortion. He hadn't even learned about it until well after the fact. Until it had been too goddamned late for him to do anything about it. Had Gloria somehow been there? But even that didn't make sense because the visions he saw had never been his. She couldn't share her thoughts with him. Not that way. That was impossible.

But there she was, Cathy spread-eagle on the exam table, bloody instruments digging into her vagina until the fetus was torn away. The doctor discarding everything into a bucket like it had never existed at all. Wasn't a memory. What the hell was it then?

Now Gloria was gone, finally, had silently dressed and disappeared, and he'd never looked in her direction, only imagined her eyes on him. He didn't care. If he was being a prick, he didn't care.

Part of him wished she would never come back.

When Jake was six his cat Jasmine had delivered a litter of four kittens in his bedroom closet. Birth sounds woke him in the middle of the night, the cat panting and grunting and making noises he'd never heard before, and he switched on the night table lamp to see her ripping them out with her teeth. Three of the kittens squirmed and chirped like baby birds, writhed beneath their mother's warm fur.

Jasmine licked each kitten, cleaning away the strange, sticky looking substance Jake couldn't identify, a coating of what looked like gelatin. He moved closer to get a better look. When the cat reached the fourth kitten she nudged it with her nose and pawed at it like she was trying to wake it. When the kitten that was as tiny as a mouse and just as hairless refused to move, refused to respond, Jasmine picked it up in her jaws and chomped down, severing the kitten nearly in half.

The image Gloria had thrust on him, the image of that human baby, *Jake's* baby, the baby that was now destroyed had been like that stillborn kitten: red, mangled, and pulpy, its form almost discernable.

*   *   *

He mindlessly wanders the city streets as if Gloria has stolen the best part of him. As if her vision somehow sucked away part of his essence. He's confused, lost, feels horribly alone. His confusion is deep, and it reaches into his core and sucks the breath out of his lungs. He's unable to function, finds the simplest task impossible. Shaving has become so complicated he walks around with stubble, finding the effort too great, the result pathetic. Even worse, he doesn't recognize the face in the mirror. When he looks now, an old man stares back, a face scarred with experience he hasn't yet achieved. Wrinkles and lines that he hasn't earned pop out on his cheeks and brow. He forgets where he works and knows he probably doesn't have a job anymore anyway. He doesn't care.

He hates Gloria, however. Despises her with a passion he's never experienced before. Whatever she's done to him he wants her to undo.

*   *   *

She comes back to him one night, a night mired in filth and expectation, a night as black as the hole in his chest.

At first he doesn't let her into the apartment, leans against the door and slides down, as if his knees have disappeared. He hears her through the door and knows she can hear him too.

"Go away," he says not convincingly, hoping part of him means it.

"Please, Jake," is all she says. He hears her weeping.

The doorknob slips through his fingers and he think̲ opens the door anyway.

"You have to go," he says to the puddle on the hallway floor. leave."

Gloria stands, holds out her hands. "I have to—we, we need to ta̲

"You need to leave," he says, emphasizing every word, hoping this̲ they'll sink in. "Don't come back, Gloria. Don't ever come back."

She slips inside, softly, barely a shadow over the threshold. "I know you're upset. Angry. I know you're—"

"You don't know *fuck*!" he yells as the front door slams shut. He leans forward, leans into every syllable, veins standing out on his throat, on his temples. "You ruined my fucking *life*. Don't you get it? You killed me, Gloria."

"Please, Jake," she sobs. "I can explain. There's more to it. *Please*."

Jake throws his arms up in frustration and storms off. He goes nowhere in particular, as long as it's away from her.

She chases him, grabs his arm. "I love you," she says, pulling him toward her, or trying to, but he pulls away. "It can't end this way. Please. You have to let me explain. You owe me that." She touches his cheek with the back of her hand and he lets her.

"I owe you shit," he snaps, but his resolve is crumbling. Some masochistic part of him needs her to explain. Needs him to hear it.

They sit on opposite ends of the sofa and he cradles a throwpillow like a housecat.

"Do you remember the vision?"

"Like it was burned into my fucking cornea."

She licks her lips. "It—it was a trick. A fake. Not a real vision."

He waits for her to continue but she remains mute for an endless period.

"Are you waiting for me to say something? Because frankly, I don't care. About you or your visions or your fake visions or whatever it was you planted in my brain. I don't even care why you did it. Some kind of sickness in you or something, I don't know. But you are sick. There's something wrong with you. For doing this to me. For *wanting* to do this to me. You're disturbed, and I've known that from since we first met."

He knows she hadn't tricked him, showing him visions of Cathy, of the abortion, up close and personal. How she knew about it he couldn't imagine but he no longer cares. But why lie to him, call the vision fake? She couldn't possibly want to protect him. Not after everything she'd put him through.

"Jake—"

He holds up his hand, cutting her off. "The funny thing is, everything is different now. I can't remember a thing." He cocks his head and his lip curls up. "Just you. I only remember you. Like my mind's been wiped clean."

She swallows. "Jake, I—"

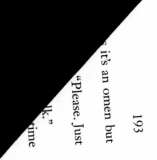

how weird is that? How, how odd?"

ers.

the question matters one damned bit, and
hen realizes he won't know the answer to
im.

tely, sarcastically, his face contorting into
d disdain, "I simply can't remember."

believes is around apology number forty-
t. But she surprises him when she whips
t been part of the previous apologies.

accepted," he mumbles, pushing his back against the edge of the sofa.

She wipes away tears with the back of her hand. Her face is damp, her eyes red and puffy.

"So, what? Now you kill me? Is that it?"

"You don't understand," she sobs. "I have to."

"Gloria—"

"Cathy was my mother."

Impossible. Gloria's in her thirties, and so is Cathy. Biologically it was impossible. But Gloria has the gun, so in Jake's mind, anything is possible. "Look, Gloria—"

"She was my mother, and..." She lowers her voice along with her eyes. "And she had an abortion."

"Just put the gun down. No need for the gun."

She swings it around in front of her, as if it had been forgotten and he reminded her it was in her hand. She can barely talk through her violent sobs, and he thinks about her trigger finger and her freaky state of mind and doesn't think this is going to end well for him at all.

"The only way... that, that, that we... the way we could..."

He wants to approach her, truly wants to comfort her, hold her in his arms but believes she'll just blow his head off.

"Tell me," he whispers, on the verge of repeating his words because he doubts she heard him through her hysterics.

She never stops crying, but the sobs subside, power down to hiccups.

But suddenly it doesn't matter. Suddenly he's aware of himself in the room, of the sheer and utter senselessness that is his life, and he doesn't care. He feels suddenly very old, ancient, that he should be dead and is somehow not, and that weariness takes control of his muscles. He really understands now that none of this has meaning, not his life, not hers, not any of it. Suddenly he's so tired he can barely find the strength to keep his eyelids propped open. He wants to sleep now, sleep forever, sleep away this mess. He needs to be away from here. Away from her.

He deftly turns, swivels on the sofa edge and plants his feet on the floor

He would prefer it if she shot him in the back though he doubts she will. She's no coward. Even so, if she shoots he hopes it will be instantaneous, his death, that it will be painless. His shoulders slump, head droops. What else is there now? His world has ended, more than once now. Why not get it over with, and he welcomes the thought of his death, of new bliss, of comfort, finally. Like the comfort he once thought he had with Gloria. He wants that again. Somehow, he wants happiness back. Just a taste, just a moment. Fleeting. That would be enough. But he wants it back again, wants to unhear things she's said. Wants to unfeel. Wants to die.

He hears the gun click—the hammer pulled back, not yet a shot—and doesn't look back.

"Wait," she whispers, but he doesn't. He starts to cry.

"You were my world," he whispers without turning. He doesn't know if she heard. He doesn't care. The words were for him.

He leaves his apartment because she won't. She can have it, he decides. She can have the memories and despair along with the coffee table and lamps and books.

He damns the day she came into his life. And praises the day as well.

He wanders the streets and knows he is a nonentity, a non person, a blur of skin cells in the crowd, bumping into no one and everyone, hearing nothing at all, his mind strangely blank, and has she taken that from him as well? His memories, his feelings, his pure thoughts? He realizes with some alarm that his mind really has been wiped clean. He remembers almost nothing, no matter how hard he struggles. Memories on the verge of being there, sitting on the very edge of his gray matter, falling into some void. His brain won't allow thought, won't seem to allow anything in or out.

But now what? he thinks, swallowing back tears, swallowing fear, choking on it, his eyes watering, heart pounding, palms clammy, chest tight, rubber band tight, squeezing, binding like s-clamps around his heart, and it hurts now, the pain getting worse, breathing becoming so difficult until he realizes he's lying on his back in the middle of the sidewalk with no recollection how he got there. A circle of faces peering down at him, concern twisting their eyebrows and scrunching their faces but stupidity creating supine forms.

He wants to cry because the pain is so awful and because they're standing around like a gawking bunch of assholes and why aren't they *doing* anything, why aren't they fucking helping? Are they just going to let him lie there in his own piss? He doesn't want to die, he discovers, not this way. Not here, not now. Not like this.

Help he tries to say and manages instead *hell* and realizes how goddamned appropriate that is.

3

It seems an entire minute has passed when he opens his eyes again an
this time some guy in a white coat is telling him how lucky he is to be aliv
Tubes snake out of Jake's nose and arms, and machines click away the second
in the background.

"You had a massive heart attack," this white coat man adds. Speakin
loudly, too loudly, and Jake winces, wants to say, *Don't yell at me you fool* bu
the tube down his throat prevents him from speaking.

"Your daughter is here to see you." White Coat moves away and Jak
realizes the idiot never introduced himself. The man's hospital ID is too smal
the print so tiny that Jake can't make out the doctor's name. And what was tha
about Jake's daughter? He has no children, none that he knows of. That's a
he needs, he thinks, rolling his eyes, someone else's kid clamoring all over hin
kicking his bed and unplugging his machines.

And then Gloria is beside him, just appears as if composed of clouds, as
she doesn't quite move through rooms but just appears in them.

He realizes how happy he is to see her.

"You had a heart attack," she whispers sadly, and he nods. He feels sorr
for himself. Was way too young to have had a heart attack. The thought of
at his age was almost ridiculous.

She grabs his hand, the hand free of tubes, and brings it to her mout
kisses the tip of each finger. "I'm so sorry," she whispers. "Not like this. I
wasn't supposed to be like this."

He nods because he doesn't know what else to do. Nodding has becom
his way of life where Gloria was concerned. There was no other form c
communication, and no better response. Better to just agree with everythin
for now and sort through the wreckage later.

No gun now, he notices, but that doesn't seem to matter anymore eithe

He pulls his hand away from hers and strangely doesn't recognize i
Doesn't recognize his own hand: the old, bony fingers, the thick ropey vein
the fat brown spots. This isn't his hand. This is the hand of someone ancien
This is the hand of his grandfather. Of his great grandfather.

"What's happening to me?" he manages to croak past the tube shredding hi
throat because he believes those words may be the most important of his life.

"It's complicated," she whispers, lowering her head in what he believes i
shame or embarrassment. Or worse, maybe pity.

He wonders if he's been in a coma, and for how long. But that doesn't fi
The coma would have been the first thing the doctor would have mentione
not the heart attack. So is this what happens after a heart attack? Your bod
ages? Your hands become gnarled and ugly?

"We have to get you out of here," Gloria says, and he thinks that's not suc
a good idea. "Sit up."

He tries but he's weak. As weak as a guy who's just had a goddamned hear
attack.

"Please try," she says with some urgency, and she pushes him into a seated position.

He grunts before he groans, expecting pain but still unprepared for it. His chest tightens again, breathing so difficult again, as if his lungs have been severed in half.

"Can't," he gasps. "Suh-top."

She ignores him, starts pulling tubes out of his hand, his arm. Pulls on the tube snaked down his throat, pulls fast and hard and yanks it out of his mouth.

"No," he says, fighting with her over the tubes she's pulled out of his body. "Why are you doing this?" he asks, not just about the pain, not just about the incisions but meaning everything, all of these nasty little surprises all rolled into one sticky sappy mess. *Why did you enter my life?* is what he means. What he really wants to ask. When did love become so painful? Not the usual pain, the heartache of longing or the melancholy of a stupid breakup but a deep agonizing meaningful shredding of every nerve ending in your body. When the hell had that managed to sneak up on him?

"Sit up," she says more urgently. "We have to go."

He shakes his head, tries to push her away. "Don't," he gasps, trying to catch his breath. "Can't."

She pulls his feet off the edge of the bed, pushes him into an upright position. "You can do this. Help me."

But he doesn't want to help. He believes this is wrong, knows he's too sick to do this, too sick to move, but the urgency in her voice, in her actions makes him do whatever she wants. He knows she tried to kill him before—or considered it anyway, waving that gun around in his face—he hasn't forgotten that, but she also saved his life on the bridge. The woman is nothing if not an enigma he decides and chooses to trust her. She wants him out of the hospital so for now he goes along with her desires.

She yanks a pair of jeans up his legs, jeans he knows he wore when they brought him here because he recognizes the bleach stain on the left thigh and the torn knee, the material shredded and looking a bit like a bird's nest, but somehow the jeans no longer fit. They hang off his hips as if they've grown a size or two, or as if he's shrunk a size or two. But nothing seems to surprise him anymore.

"*Please*," she says, the urgency again increasing, as if his ability to remain standing will solve all of life's riddles. "You can't—"

Her voice cuts off and he glances over his shoulder at her. She's staring at the floor.

"Can't what," he wheezes.

"Nothing," she whispers, and wraps her arms around his neck, clasps her hands together and rests them on his chest.

Can't die here, he imagines she was going to say.

He tries to support his weight and instead collapses to his knees, tips forward and catches himself on his palms, on his ancient, gnarled hands.

"No," he cries, realizes he's now begging. "Can't. I can't!" And even worse, he doesn't recognize his own voice. He wonders how badly that tube damaged his vocal cords, how shredded and raw his throat must be.

Gloria helps him up, helps him struggle back onto the bed. He stares at the small trickle of blood on his left knee.

She runs her palms through his hair, and then her fingertips caress his jawline. She leans in close and whispers in his ear. "Close your eyes."

He feels her hands move again, feels her fingers press gently against his eyelids.

"Breathe deeply. Listen to the rhythm of my breathing."

"No," he moans, panic setting in, unable again to open his eyes. Not this. Not another vision.

"It's okay," she says softly. "I need to explain. You need to understand."

He shakes his head, barely able to move, unable to open his eyes, his heart palpating wildly from the terror of anticipation. He's sure he's going to suffer another heart attack. Doesn't want to hear her. Doesn't need to. Doesn't care what she has to say.

"What's going on?" This one a strange voice, another woman's voice.

"Nothing," Gloria says. "It's okay."

Jake slowly opens his eyes. Too weak to move anything else.

"What's he—why's he sitting up?"

"He's okay." Gloria licks her lips, swallows a little too quickly.

"Mr.—?" The nurse glances at Jake's chart, apparently searching for his surname. Instead, she takes his hand, and he feels her fingers searching for his pulse. She peers closely into his eyes, leaning forward, and for just a second he believes she is going to kiss him. Instead, she steps back. Actually, he thinks with some dismay, she jerks back, as if she suddenly got a whiff of something awful.

"Oh my god," Nurse mutters, and Jake is too weak and too damned tired to get terribly excited over her little outbreak, to express true wonder at her remark although he wants to, really really wants to, wants to know what the hell she is looking at. When you sputter *oh my god* to a heart attack patient, you'd better be prepared to back it up.

Old Nurse, despite her alleged years of schooling, despite what is very likely an advanced number of years working as a nurse, Jake would guess since he also summed up *her* advanced years and figured her to be in her 60s, perhaps even 70s, is clearly unprepared for whatever she's now seeing when she looks at Jake. The stupid woman nearly trips over her own feet trying to back away from him. Jake wonders how he could have been ignored for so long, how a patient in Intensive Care wasn't given better... intensive care.

"He's fine," Gloria says, apparently judging her the same way Jake is, eyeing the nurse's incompetence, her decidedly stupid approach at surprise. Gloria seems annoyed now. Jake can tell, and some part of him roots for her despite his near hatred of her, roots for her fierce stubbornness, and her seeming need to protect him.

Nurse trips her way out of the room, walking backwards, never taking her eyes off of Jake.

He still doesn't have much of a voice but can at least handle a handful of words now. "Hah-app'ning. T'me."

Gloria caresses his cheek, presses her chin to his forehead. "Not here. There's still time. I can still get you out."

Jake still doesn't know what she's thinking, of course, but he imagines that his days—his minutes—are numbered. That her anxious desire to get him out of the hospital is so he doesn't die here. Though where better to die than in a hospital? Still, he's anxious to leave, too. Anxious to get away from the antiseptic smell and inane droning and clicking machines. Everything around him means death. Sounds of death. Smells and tastes of death. He needs air, and realizes it might be his dying wish. Still, there's a small park across the street, a small gated park with fresh flowers and a small fountain surrounded by a wrought iron gate. An oasis in the middle of Manhattan. He could think of worse places to die.

Gloria wraps an arm around his waist, lifts him easily to his feet. Most of his weight now rests on her, on her hip, and in her arm. He has become impossibly light, like a bag of groceries she can handle in one hand while she fumbles with her housekeys in the other.

When he glances down at himself he sees that he's so much smaller now, that his body is withering, his skin like moth's wings, like papyrus. He imagines he would easily tear now and somehow that doesn't frighten him.

He wraps his arms around her neck and allows her to fully support his weight.

"Love you," he whispers, and realizes he means it, and he leans into her neck, inhales the non-scent of her body, the stark, lack of scent that is somehow her. His chin rests in the soft spot above her collarbone, now damp with his tears. He doesn't remember when he started crying but finds he can't stop. This feels so comfortable to him, so familiar, so right.

"I love you too," she says, holding him tight, lifting him from the hospital bed.

She carries him out of the room, down the corridor, down two flights of stairs, choosing to bypass the elevator, past the registration desk and people waiting patiently and impatiently to be seen, past visitors always standing in the way in the lobby, past the janitor pretending to mop and security pretending to care. And every single person lets them pass, no one at all tries to stop them, and no one tries to hide the shock and revulsion when they get a good look at Jake. No one seems to find it strange that a young woman is easily carrying a man in her arms, and Jake wonders just how small he's become. He wonders if he has some strangely advanced form of cancer that is somehow eating him alive over the course of a handful of days.

As if she's read his mind—again—she carries him into the park and brings him behind a bench and lays him in the grass.

"There's not much time," she says, leaning over him. "You don't have much time left."

He nods, surprised that he isn't more afraid. He'd always feared death, even when contemplating suicide. He doesn't know that he would have gone through with it, jumping off the bridge, because dying had always terrified him. The finality of it. The not knowing. The lack of control. At least that was how he'd always imagined it. But now, somehow now it didn't feel so horrible. Maybe because Gloria had brought him happiness, if only for a short while. But that happiness had been profound. And it made up for what had only been a passing life, a fleeting, boring day to day existence. Until he'd finally met her. Until she'd finally found him.

She lays beside him in the nearly empty park. No one has followed them, and no one inside the park seems to care that they're there, two strange looking people lying in the grass. Jake figures they fit in well with the other indigents. The grass smells sweet, and it's slightly damp and tickles his neck and cheek. He's not surprised to find he still can't move. Whatever is eating his body cell by cell has also eaten his strength.

"You don't understand," she whispers, smiling at him.

He tries to smile back but doesn't have the strength. Besides, he finds it somewhat insensitive that she should be smiling at him at a time like this. Apparently she doesn't consider his impending death to be that serious a matter.

"Are you ready to know the truth now?"

If he had the strength he would roll his eyes. Instead he exhales, and blinks, because even nodding is impossible.

"You're leaving me, but you're coming back. This was the only way I could bring you back. Do you understand?"

Understand what? She hadn't said a word yet that made sense. Being unable to communicate frustrates him. Can't move his head, can barely blink. It's maddening. A fat tear rolls out of the corner of his eye and lands in his ear.

"I'm going to have to show you," she says. "Please don't be afraid."

He has no choice. He's a captive audience.

She takes his hands and kisses them, then brings them to her chest and presses them to her heart. "Close your eyes."

Eyes closed, he sees her again, holding hands, walking down the street as they did when they first met, window shopping, or sitting on the steps of St. Patrick's Cathedral so they could people watch. Gloria kisses him in this dream, this vision, this memory, whatever it is she's showing him now. She kisses him and laughs, throws back her head. *Don't be afraid* she says but he can't hear her, can only see her mouth move, can only imagine the sound of her voice as it matches the movement of her lips.

But she tears him away again, back to that abortion, back to that doctor soaked in red, back to Cathy lying spread eagle on the exam table. Back to the haz mat container and the assorted pieces of what had once been Jake's baby.

But Gloria is in the room this time, in the room and crying, reaching into the haz mat bag, retrieving the destroyed fetus.

Bringing the fetus to her chest. Hugging it as if it were her newborn. She holds it up, then out, as if offering it to Jake, offering it to the voyeur who is only a guest in this scene, as unreal as any spirit, unable to touch or feel or taste anything here.

But she hands it to him in this vision and he feels it in his hands, this tiny form, hairless and slick with blood.

He wants to take it and wants to hand it back. Wants to open his eyes to see more clearly what he is holding.

She says, "I've brought you back to me."

He knows this is impossible but decides it doesn't matter. Because she keeps showing him the impossible. Shows him that anything at all is possible.

"But Cathy—" he says in this vision, discovering his voice again, if only in his mind.

Gloria responds. "Cathy did this to you."

"No. Cathy was..." But he's dazed. Doesn't know what he's thinking. He thinks he remembers touching Cathy. Holding her. Making love to her.

Gloria says, "You had to know. I only hope you can forgive me."

Forgive her? Is this something even remotely forgivable? He strains to open his eyes but still can't.

"If you open your eyes, this will end."

"Then let it end," he says in his vision.

"Do you mean that?"

He thinks. "No."

"Do you love me?"

He thinks again. "I love you so much, I hate you."

"When you open your eyes, you won't remember anymore. Do you understand?"

"Yes."

"When you're ready." She digs her fingers into his hair and pulls him close, rubs her lips over his and kisses him gently. "When you're ready, open your eyes."

He nods, tears falling from his eyes onto her nose, over the spatter of freckles she seems to hate. His fingers caress her ears.

"I love you, Jake."

"Thank you. For my life." He knows it hasn't really been his, this life. He chooses to believe they were real, he and Gloria, though he isn't sure. He opens his eyes and the memories fade. Until he remembers nothing more.

ABOUT THE AUTHOI

Monica J. O'Rourke lives in New York City with three rescue kittie
She's had two novels published (SUFFER THE FLESH, and POISONIN(
EROS, co-written with Wrath James White). Her short fiction can be foun
in such magazines and anthologies as Nasty Piece of Work, Fangoria, Fles
& Blood, Nemonymous, Doorways, Brutarian, Darkness Rising, Red Screar
and Cthulhu Sex. Stories are forthcoming in Inhuman and Red Screar
magazines. Visit her online at myspace.com/deadlymojo

Also from

Two Backed Books

Anthologies:

Flesh and Iron
208 pages — $12.95

Four stories where the tooth hits the bone. Hard boiled law enforcement squares off against hard fanged blood suckers. When every breath could be their last, the only things that matter are the heat of their flesh and the mettle of their iron. Works by C. J. Henderson, John L. French, John Sunseri and Diane Raetz & Patrick Thomas.

Horror Between The Sheets
164 pages — $12.95

23 mind-rending pieces ripped from the pages of Cthulhu Sex Magazine's early black and white issues. Includes works by Jeremy Russell, Mark McLaughlin, Lynne den Hartog, Brian Knight, Christine Morgan, David Annadale and many more.

Collections:

The Book of a Thousand Sins — Wrath James White
192 pages — $14.95

Delve into the tantalizing works of master erotic horror writer Wrath James White, author of *Succulent Prey*, in this thrilling romp through 15 of his most cruel and enlightening stories.

> "If Wrath doesn't make you cringe, then you must be riding in the wrong end of a Hearse."
>
> — **Jack Ketchum**, Author of *The Girl Next Door* and *Red*

Apple of My Eye — Amy Grech
134 pages — $11.95

This tasty collection brings together 13 disturbing stories of horror and erotica from the notable author Amy Grech.

> "Amy Grech has a cinematographer's eye and a surgeon's hand — at once brutal and tender, unsettling yet humane. These stories linger like traces of an acid trip. Highly recommended!"
>
> — **Jay Bonansinga**, National Best-selling Author of *Twisted*, *Frozen*, and *The Sinking of the Eastland*

www.TwoBackedBooks.com

Printed in the United States
126776LV00002B/141/A

9 781933 293455